SATURN CONUNDRUM

Book One of The Saturn Accords

SATURN CONUNDRUM

Book One of The Saturn Accords

D. Bishop
Miritish Publishing

Published by Miritish Publishing

This book is a work of fiction. All names, characters, and references to places and events, other than 'Oumuamua' and planetary alignments in 2037, are fictional constructs of the author's imagination and are not to be taken literally. Any resemblance to actual persons, places or events is entirely coincidental.

Dedication

This book is dedicated to my wife
and long-time supporter, Ann.
Thank you for your patience
and understanding.

Acknowledgements

I would like to thank my fellow members of the Chaffee County Writers Exchange for their many constructive suggestions and careful editing of this manuscript. A special thank you to my beta readers, Cam Torrens and Tom Dury. All of you fine folks have helped me become a better writer than I ever thought I could be.

Credits

Planetary alignments 2037 through 2043:
https://theskylive.com/3dsolarsystem
Cover Design: bravoboy with 99designs.com.
Cover Fonts: Ethnocentric Typodermic
Lato Łukasz Dziedzi
This book was written and formatted using Microsoft Word on Windows 11.
Interior Fonts by Microsoft:
Garamond, Arial, Arial Italic, and Courier New

Part One

Chapter 1

October 3, 2037: Earth Orbit

First Lieutenant Wei Li dimmed the control room lighting to better make out details on his monitor. 18,000 kilometers from his post in the Chinese space station, a small drone under his guidance fired its thrusters. His monitor displayed the image of an American communication satellite, its larger antenna directed toward Mars. Wei Li deftly manipulated his joystick, orienting the drone's thrusters and nudging the drone forward until it made physical contact with the American satellite.

A more forceful nudge from the drone forced the satellite receiver to deviate from its programmed orientation. Thrusters aboard the comsat immediately fired in sequence to realign the antenna with the distant signal from the American Mars-II crewed spaceship, *Aurora*. The drone thrusters fired again. The American satellite wobbled off course, no longer able to maintain orbit. A third and final nudge sent the satellite into a spinning plunge toward Earth's atmosphere and a fiery re-entry.

The lieutenant exhaled deeply and smiled. His task completed, he rotated the drone and directed it toward the glistening blue planet below. He then activated its main engine to expend what fuel it had left and send it, too, to a fiery death.

A job worthy of a fine bonus. And all evidence of the orbital encounter eliminated.

Aboard *Aurora*, enroute to Mars

Rae Anne Chavez looked up from the telescope monitor on *Aurora's* flight deck. Over the last hour, the faint blip she was following had grown noticeably brighter than the myriad stars in the background.

"The *Minh Xi* is coming straight at us. We can only hope they plan to fly right by," she said to her two colleagues. Her tone betrayed a level of pessimism, unusual for her.

"I still think their course change three days ago was simply to reach Mars before us. It's only a coincidence that they now cross our path so close to us." It was clear to Rae Anne that Rob Harris, *Aurora's* pilot, was trying to ease the tension all three astronauts felt.

"But they would have beat us by a week even without the course change. That's why they strapped two extra boosters to their ship before launch."

"It's all speculation at this point," said Mindy Jackson, Mission Commander. We've done all we can to prepare for an attack. We can only wait and see what happens." Her no-nonsense, take command voice sounded forced, perhaps to quell her dread at the looming encounter.

As Communications and IT Officer, Rae Anne was in constant contact with Mission Control, though the one-way communication delay at their distance from Earth was now over three minutes. Strategists at the US Interplanetary Exploration Agency (USIEA, or the 'Agency') had warned of the possibility of a hostile attack on *Aurora*. British intelligence had obtained evidence that *Ming-Xi* was equipped with fragmentation missiles just prior to launch.

As a precaution, the three astronauts were fully clad in their EVA suits should an attack result in a hull breach. Raw anxiety electrified the cabin.

"*Ming-Xi* is now 5000 kilometers out." Mission Control's announcement echoed through the cabin. "It is closing at 750 meters per sec…"

The transmission abruptly went dead.

"What happened, Rae Anne?" Mindy looked over to her communications officer.

"No signal. We've lost contact with Mission Control."

"Well, forget Mission Control. They can't help us anyway. That last report was over three minutes old. We've got more important things to deal with now."

Her resolute determination propped Rae Anne's spirits. She glanced again at the telescope monitor. The bright dot had morphed into a distinct shape, growing larger with each passing minute.

They would have passed us and beaten us to Mars even without the course change. Now they're headed directly at us. We're only four months into our mission and just half-way to Mars and we're faced with this. I certainly don't buy into the 'coincidence' theory!

Mission Control, USIEA
Peterson Space Force Base, Colorado Springs

"Communication with *Aurora* is down," Penny Stevens reported on the emergency line to Ian Bentley's office on the third floor of the USIEA Administration Building. Ian had been assigned Director of Communications for the Mars II mission when he returned from a three-year stint as commander of LOTS-I (Lunar Orbit Transfer Station-One).

"Any indication why?"

"The only thing showing on the comm panel is 'Earth-Aurora Comsat-C link is down' and 'Aurora Signal Lost'."

"Run a full diagnostic on Earthside uplink. We need to re-establish contact with *Aurora* as quickly as possible. *Ming-Xi* will be crossing *Aurora's* flight path in less than two hours."

"Diagnostics already begun."

"Good. Let me know what you find. Can we re-orient Comsat-D to pick up *Aurora* ahead of its scheduled slot?"

"That's a negative. D won't clear the horizon for another 93 minutes."

"How about our land-based backups? Who's currently linked to *Aurora?*"

"That's what's odd. Australia was receiving fine until a few minutes ago. Now all we're getting is heavy static. Some sort of interference is washing out the signal. It's as though they're being jammed."

The frown lines etched on Ian's forehead deepened. A lurch of bile surged in his throat. Intelligence reports had suggested that the Chinese might be planning to sabotage the American mission to Mars, and losing contact with *Aurora* at this critical time didn't bode well.

"If you find that the uplink isn't the problem, get D online as soon as possible."

"Roger that."

Damn! I can't believe losing both C and Australia is just a coincidence. Especially now when we urgently need clean communication with Aurora.

Chapter 2

October 3, 2037: Aboard Aurora

All three astronauts clutched spray canisters of dye, although their EVA-suit gloves made handling them awkward. The plan was to spray dye into the air should the hull be punctured in an attack. They could follow the course of the dye to locate any holes. They placed buckets of emergency patching fabric and resin on each of *Aurora's* five decks. Jason, *Aurora's* computer AI, was monitoring all sensors. The entire ship was on red alert.

"They'd better damn well not fire on us." Mindy's face was flushed red with anger.

"We're as ready as we can be. If only we had some way to protect ourselves." Rae Anne sighed, wishing she could exhibit Mindy's confidence and bravado

"There's nothing more we can do, Mindy." Rob's voice remained calm, though Rae Anne was sure he didn't feel that way. "If this were a fighter, I'd eject a cloud of flares or release a decoy to divert an attacking missile. As it is, we're just sitting ducks."

Flares and decoys. Exactly what an experienced fighter pilot like Rob would do. Flares and decoys…and ducks.

Ray Anne's thoughts flickered with a memory of hunting with her uncle near Elephant Butte Reservoir in New Mexico when she was a teenager. Sitting in a duck blind, watching the decoys bob up and down in the glistening water, awaiting the arrival of some live ducks.

"Dios mio! Eject a decoy. That's it!"

Rob and Mindy's helmets both turned in Rae Anne's direction. "What?" they asked in unison.

"A decoy. When you said 'eject' it brought to mind the fuel tanks we ejected during launch as they emptied. But we still have four empty fuel tanks. The ones slated for Mars orbit that the Agency plans to build a Mars station with. We could use those for decoys. We could eject one of them toward *Ming-Xi* if we detect a missile launch. That might deflect their missile or at least work as a shield."

"Holy Moly!" Rob exclaimed. "Why didn't I think of that? If a missile detonated against the empty fuel tank instead of us, any shrapnel hitting *Aurora* would be low velocity stuff from the fuel tank. Not nearly so dangerous. We might even come out of this unscathed."

"Jason!" Mindy commanded. "Rotate *Aurora* so an empty fuel tank is positioned directly between *Aurora* and *Ming-Xi*."

Rae Anne felt *Aurora*'s gentle roll as the ship's attitudinal thrusters adjusted its position.

"*Aurora* is situated as directed," Jason reported.

"Now, Jason, the instant Rob ejects the fuel tank, rotate *Aurora* as quickly as possible to bring another empty fuel tank into the same position."

"That will create a centripetal force that may damage anything not securely fastened down," Jason warned.

"Understood," Mindy replied. "But do it anyway. OK, everyone, brace yourselves and hang on."

Too bad our suits are too bulky for us to strap into our couches. This is really awkward.

Rae Anne struggled to pull herself closer and more firmly to the back of her chair.

Good thing I cradled the telescope. I hope it survives.

They anxiously watched the monitors as *Ming-Xi's* radar blip became ever larger. Tension on the flight deck was palpable.

Will the Chinese really attempt to destroy us?

The answer came when a second smaller blip appeared on the radar screen, moving rapidly away from *Ming-Xi* and directly toward *Aurora*.

Oh my god. There it is!

"Incoming!" Rob called out, almost too calmly. "Hold tight, everyone."

Rae Anne held her breath, sure her heart had stopped. Each astronaut firmly grasped the backs of their acceleration couches. Rob took charge with an air of calm command, as though he were in his fighter cockpit preparing for a dogfight.

Press the button, Rob. Now. Press the button.

Every muscle in her body tensed. Time seemed to have stopped.

A muted 'thud' shuddered through the ship's structure as Rob activated the explosive clamps holding the first tank in place. The ejected tank headed directly toward *Ming-Xi* and the approaching missile.

At that instant, Rae Anne found her feet flying up level with her head. She gripped the back of her couch with all her might. *Aurora's* abrupt spin jerked to a halt as thrusters activated on the other side of the ship.

"Empty fuel tank two is now in position," Jason reported.

The three astronauts nervously waited and watched in silence.

A new radar blip appeared on the screen just before a cacophony of metallic clangs reverberated through the ship. Alarms burst to life on all five decks. The flight deck went pitch-black except for console LEDs, many of which were flashing red alerts.

HULL BREACH…HULL BREACH…

Dull red emergency lighting flickered on, giving the deck a surreal aura. Rae Anne glanced at her crewmates. The lighting accentuated shadows, transforming them into alien caricatures.

"Losing pressure on all decks," Jason declared.

"We've been hit with tank shrapnel from the first explosion," Rob announced as he released the second fuel tank. *Aurora* spun again bringing a third tank into position. Rae Anne nearly lost her grip on the couch.

The second inbound missile was closing fast. A flash burst behind the expelled fuel tank. A second round of metal clattered against the hull.

Ming-Xi's radar blip rapidly receded into the void.

"Jason, status!" Mindy shouted as she scanned the life support console. It was covered with flashing red LEDs. Rae Anne could see their angry reflection off Mindy's face shield.

"Minor breaches on all five levels," Jason reported. "Pressure is dropping fastest on Levels 2 and 3."

"Rob, you take Level 3," Mindy commanded. "We'll tackle the galley." Rob disappeared headfirst through the hatch in the flight deck floor. Rae Anne and Mindy followed and Rae Anne sealed the hatch behind her just as Rob was closing the hatch between Levels 2 and 3.

On Level 2, Mindy and Rae Anne sprayed whiffs of dye into the air and watched the brightly colored spray veer directly toward the leaks. After dislodging jagged pieces of metal sticking through the hull, they began patching the holes. Prior to the attack, they had practiced doing quick, temporary repairs to stop the leaks. A permanent fix would be applied over each temporary patch later once the ship was secured.

"I've taken care of three holes, including this one," Rae Anne announced as she crawled out from under the table. "EVA suits were definitely not designed for work in tight places!"

"I've patched five. I think that's all on this deck." Mindy sprayed some dye into the air. The droplets spread out but showed no discernable direction.

"Pressure is stable on Level 2," Jason reported.

"I'll take Level 1," Mindy announced as she opened the ceiling hatch to the Level 1 flight deck. "You head down to Level 3 and see if Rob needs help. If not, take Level 4."

Rae Anne opened the Level 2 floor hatch and propelled herself through it, closing it behind her. Rob had moved the lounge couches from the walls to access the damage. The exercise area and hygiene cubicle were on the opposite side of the deck and undamaged. An odd mist of water droplets permeated the air.

"What can I do here?"

"I think I'm OK," Rob said. "The problem is these damned water-curtain radiation shields. Shrapnel has punctured the fabric on some of the curtains and they're leaking. As soon as we've got the hull patched, we'll have the devil of a time vacuuming up the water. That's one good thing about the EVA suits. We're protected from the toxic heavy metal salts in the water."

"Glad to see the wall monitor survived. This would be one long trip without our movie theater. I'm off to Level 4. I'll face the same water curtain problem down there. At least these are the only decks with the curtains," Rae Anne said as she slid through the floor hatch and closed it behind her.

"Damn." Disgust permeated Mindy's voice through their intercoms. "One of the shrapnel pieces destroyed my mass spectrometer."

"Are any of the other science lockers damaged?" asked Rob.

"No, the rest of the science lab area up here seems intact," Mindy announced. "But I was so looking forward to analyzing Mars samples with that mass spec."

"I sure hope my telescope's all right." Rae Anne shivered at the thought of losing the one instrument she used every day, both for research and for relaxation. The telescope was mounted on a platform atop the communication housing, a large fin-like structure attached to *Aurora's* hull.

On Level 4, Rae Anne pushed the three netted sleep pods to one side and began searching through the water curtains for hull breach holes hiding behind them. After moving several aside and spraying dye behind them, she ran into a curtain that seemed stuck to the wall. Tugging it free and spraying dye, she noted the dye stream to a small hole. A quick patch there and she stepped back, letting the curtain fall back loosely in place.

Interesting. Maybe I can speed this up by swishing the curtains and locating the ones stuck to the wall. The vacuum outside sucks the curtain fabric against the hole.

Her new strategy helped her quickly locate several other small holes, and she was soon finished with Level 4. Dye from a test spray hung listlessly in the air.

"Level 4 is secure. The good news is none of the water curtains down here have been punctured. I'm headed down to Level 5."

She swung down through the hatch. Her heart sank in dismay when she glanced around the storage deck.

"Hey team, we've got a problem on Level 5. All our supplies and the life support equipment are in the way of hull repairs."

Mindy's voice came over the EVA comm-link. "We'll lose too much pressure if we take time to move things first. Seal Level 5 off and we'll see if we can do repairs from outside. Dents and discoloration in the hull should identify where repairs are needed."

"That's a good plan, Mindy," Rob agreed. "A good excuse for an EVA," he added.

Back on Level 4, Rae Anne slid the floor hatch leading to Level 5 closed and sealed it. She then checked again to be sure the water curtains were intact and circled the room, jostling each one to verify none were sucked against a hole she might have missed.

"How does Level 4 look now, Jason?"

"Levels-1 through 4 are now secure. Level 5 is sealed from the rest of the ship and is still losing pressure."

Lighting on the four decks returned to normal and the alarms shut down. For a moment, Rae Anne thought she had gone deaf, but Mindy's voice soon echoed in her helmet

"Jason, evacuate Level 5 into holding tanks," Mindy commanded. "No need to lose yet more precious oxygen to space. If we repair Level 5 from the outside, it will have to be evacuated before we can work on it anyway."

After a few minutes, Jason reported that Level 5 was evacuated.

Mindy and Rob did a high-five as Rae Anne floated into Level 2 from below.

"Against all odds, we have survived an outright attack on our ship," Rob announced in triumph as he assembled equipment from the tool chest in the airlock to vacuum up the water droplets floating around Level 3. Water-vac in hand, Rob slid through the floor hatch and slid it closed to keep the droplets from contaminating the rest of the ship while he cleaned up the mess.

"I can't believe the Chinese bringing military hostilities to Mars!" Rae Anne felt the heat of anger and disgust coursing through her body. She began helping Mindy remove her life-support pack.

"Evil and arrogance often go together. The bloody bastards tried to kill us! And for what?"

"They apparently want to claim the planet for themselves."

"That violates every international space treaty ever signed," said Mindy, shaking her head in disgust.

"Maybe so. But look at the constant problems they're causing on the moon. We've had to arm our bases with weapons for defense to keep them at bay."

"Well, see if you can get through to Mission Control. We need to report this incident ASAP."

"If we hadn't lost contact before the attack, they'd have a full video of this atrocity. All we can do now is send them our own recordings and sensor readouts. They won't hold near as much weight as evidence." Rae Anne hung her suit inside the airlock and shut her gloves and helmet in her locker. Then she headed for the hatch leading up to the flight deck.

"Those recordings may be the only direct evidence the Chinese were anywhere near here," said Mindy as the floor hatch rotated open and Rob appeared from below.

Chapter 3

October 3, 2037: Aboard *Aurora*

A row of angry red lights atop the communication console grabbed Rae Anne's attention when she arrived on the flight deck.

That's odd. These would indicate the problem is with Aurora. But we lost signal before the attack.

"I'm rebooting," she called down to the others.

When she flicked the switch, a deep grating buzz reverberated through the cabin. She stopped the reboot and the noise ceased. Trying the reboot again produced the same result.

Mierda! We've got a problem.

She turned to the others who joined her on the flight deck. "I think the antenna's been damaged."

"I can check when I'm outside making hull repairs," Rob said. "If it's not too serious, I may be able to fix it."

"We should run some tests first," Mindy suggested. "We might be able to solve the problem from here. If not, we can at least get an idea of what to look for when you're out there."

Rae Anne concurred, not willing to take unnecessary risks during an EVA. Rob agreed, although he was clearly anxious to get outside and perform the hull repairs.

Once Jason presented the schematics, Rae Anne scanned through the trouble-shooting list. She quickly eliminated all the remedies that could be taken inside the ship and still had no clue as to what had gone wrong. Only an EVA would reveal the extent of the damage to their communication setup.

"Too bad we don't have a larger crew," Mindy said as she helped Rob suit up for his EVA.

"How so?" asked Rob.

"Standard procedures would have two of us working together on EVAs. But with Rae Anne focused on the comm console for the repairs, I need to remain inside to keep tabs on everything else. So, you have to go it alone."

"Not to worry. I'll be careful. Any suggestions on what I should take with me?" Rob asked as he lifted his helmet from the locker.

Mindy shook her head. "Since we don't know exactly what needs to be fixed, we'll need a second EVA to deal with the problem. Your job this time out is to survey the damage and take pictures. Then we'll make a list of what needs to be done."

"Will do." Rob placed the helmet over his head and secured it while Mindy checked and rechecked the fittings.

"Don't forget your SAFER, Rob," Mindy reminded him as she clipped the hand controlled 'Simplified for EVA Rescue' jetpack unit to his suit. "No one's ever needed to use one, but you never know."

"Thanks, Mindy. I sure don't intend to be the first!"

Rob stepped into the airlock and pulled the hatch shut behind him.

"How's it look?" he inquired through his intercom after sealing the hatch and evacuating the chamber. Everyone was being particularly cautious. This was the first time they had used the airlock for an EVA, and they didn't want to screw anything up.

Mindy surveyed the readouts. "You're good for EVA, Rob."

Rob locked his tether to a hull bracket inside the door and opened the outer hatch. He worked his way slowly around the ship towards the communication housing. The large satchel he carried contained patching compound and fabric. He had two additional self-retracting tether cable boxes attached to his suit's tool belt.

"God," he exclaimed. "It's beautiful out here, so much more than I ever imagined. It's…It's overwhelming! I've never seen so many stars. None of them twinkling like you see on Earth. No air thermals. All just steady pinpoints of light. And the depth. I feel like the universe trying to suck me into its bosom."

"Enough sight-seeing, Rob. We've got work to do," Mindy gently scolded.

"All right. I'm on my way."

After a few minutes he reported in. "I've locked my second tether to the hull ring below the side thruster at nine o'clock. I'm now removing the first tether from my belt and locking it into the same ring so it'll be here when I come back."

The video feed from his helmet showed the bracket with the two locking carabiners firmly in place.

Rob continued his methodical crawl around *Aurora's* hull. When he reached the antenna housing, he repeated the tether exchange at the bracket at its base and fastened the satchel to it as well. Then he began to mount the fin-shaped structure to reach the platform at the top.

"Whoever designed this series of handholds didn't have EVA-suit gloves in mind. This is a real pain in the butt."

"Take your time, Rob," Mindy admonished. "No need to hurry."

A long six minutes passed while Rob mounted the structure containing *Aurora's* communication equipment. Rob's steady breathing was the only indication everything was OK. Nevertheless, Rae Anne and Mindy awaited each of Rob's reports with anxious anticipation.

"I've reached the platform with the antennae and telescope. The telescope looks fine, Rae Anne. But the communication set-up took several direct hits." The camera feed relayed much of the damage Rob reported.

"It looks like some debris knocked a basketball-sized chunk from the top section of our main receiver dish."

"Damn," Mindy exclaimed. "We're lucky that one didn't hit the hull. It could have caused some serious damage."

"No way we can repair that," Rae Anne noted. "Even if we manage to get the system working again, our incoming communication from Mission Control will be pretty ugly."

"Too bad we don't have a backup dish," Mindy sighed.

"Shouldn't the antenna be aligned with the length of the ship, facing back toward Earth?" Rob asked.

"Crap. As if we didn't have enough problems already. We'll need to get the antenna re-oriented or there's no hope for communication, tenuous or otherwise." Rae Anne shook her head in resignation.

Rob's camera scanned up and down the length of the antenna boom. Some scarring, but no real damage to speak of. Rob poked around at the antenna's base.

"Damage on the motor housing. The cover is badly dented and there's a piece of shrapnel poking through it. That's clearly part of the problem. It explains why the motors aren't working."

"Rob, can you get more light on that area? It's hard for us to make out the details." Rae Anne adjusted some settings on the monitor.

The light intensity increased. It revealed much more damage than Rob had initially reported. It was obvious why the antenna positioning mechanism had failed.

"We'll need to replicate several parts on the 3-D printer," Mindy observed. "Jason can help us locate the printer instructions for parts we need in the ship's digital library."

"Anything else you want to see?" Rob asked.

"Let's take another look at the opposite side of the antenna base," Rae Anne replied. "We need to make as thorough a photographic survey as we can."

Rob crawled around the antenna and highlighted the requested area. When Rae Anne was satisfied, he slowly climbed down the housing, rearranged tethers, unhooked the satchel with the patching compound, and backtracked across the hull to the thruster.

"I'm attaching the first tether to my belt. It's locked. Unlocking the second tether." Again, they had a clear view of the carabiners as Rob manipulated them and checked that he had properly locked them onto his belt. He then worked his way to the damaged hull outside Level 5.

"I only see five holes," he reported after inspecting the area. "They're all pretty obvious from out here. I'll have these patched in a jiffy and head back inside. Good thing the lander was on the opposite side of the ship. I wouldn't want to trust a patched-up lander to take us down to Mars' surface."

Rob spread repair compound over four of the five holes, covering each area with a piece of Kevlar[T] and covering that with another swath of compound to protect it from sunlight.

"Jeez, look at that!" he exclaimed when he turned his attention to the fifth hole. A large triangular shard from the fuel tank was tightly wedged into the hull. Rob tried pulling the piece out, without success.

"Be careful not to puncture your EVA suit, Rob. Those edges look pretty sharp," Mindy cautioned.

"Thanks, Mindy. I can't seem to get the leverage I need to pull the sucker out."

"Can you tie one of your cables around the base of the piece and use that to extract it?" Rae Anne offered.

"I'll try that." Rob replied as he removed one of the two unused tether boxes from his tool belt and looped one cable end around the shard and fastened it to itself. He uncoiled the line over a nearby thruster and down through a hull bracket, giving him the leverage he needed in the zero-G environment.

Tugging upward on the rope planted his feet firmly against the hull, allowing him to put his full strength into the effort. The shard suddenly pulled free and shot away from the ship.

"Shit!" Rob, too, was forcefully propelled from the hull into space.

When the shard reached the end of its length of cable, it sprung back, narrowly missing Rob, and slammed into the hull, then rebounded. At the same time, Rob's tether became taut, yanking him back toward the ship as well. He did a jarring body slam against the hull but grabbed a hull bracket before rebounding. He held on tightly as his legs flailed outward. Eventually, he stabilized himself and gained a sitting position beside the thruster.

"Rob, are you OK?" Mindy's anxious voice echoed in his helmet. "What was all that banging?"

Rob was panting heavily. "Once the shard broke free, the force my legs exerted against the hull was suddenly directed outward. I should have anchored myself first. EVA Lesson One. Think twice before you act. Lesson Two. Beware of unintended consequences."

After a few minutes, Rob had the last hole patched and called for Jason to pressurize Level 5 to 20%.

"How's the pressure holding, Jason?" he asked after about five minutes.

"The pressure on Level 5 is steady, Rob."

With the patches secure, Rob made his way back to the airlock.

Once safely inside, he stripped out of the EVA suit and let out a deep breath. "That was the most awesome experience I have ever had."

"Bouncing around on a tether in free fall doesn't sound so awesome to me," Rae Anne observed.

"No, no. I mean being outside. I was this insignificant speck, millions of kilometers from Earth, surrounded by the black emptiness of space. Yet it was like the stars were embracing me as a parent might reach out to their child. I was overwhelmed. I was aware of being part of something far bigger than anything I could ever fathom."

Rae Anne spent the next several hours scrutinizing the videos Rob took of the antenna and the schematics of the motor mechanism. She identified twelve parts that needed to be replaced. Once Jason had brought up their printer instructions, she and Mindy retired to Level 5 and began the lengthy process of printing replacement parts on the 3-D printer while making step-by-step repair instructions they hoped would be sufficient to return the comm-link to operation.

Chapter 4

After three days of continuous printing, Rae Anne and Mindy had the newly fabricated parts they needed to begin repairs on the antenna drive mechanism. They laid the parts out on the galley table and inspected them carefully, comparing them to the specifications Jason had retrieved from the archives. Satisfied that they matched, Rae Anne bundled them into the EVA satchel and sealed it closed.

She and Mindy assumed Rob would do the EVA again, but as they gathered the appropriate wrenches and drivers for the job, Rob spoke up.

"You remember my comments about how overwhelmed I was when I went outside on my EVA? That experience was so profound it has altered my perspective forever. You both should have the opportunity to experience it for yourselves before we get back home, and this would be a perfect time for one of you to go out."

Mindy and Rae Anne looked at each other, surprised Rob had made an offer of such generosity. They were both anxious for the opportunity to do an EVA, so the question was which of them would go.

"It will have to be you, Mindy," Rae Anne said reluctantly. "My time will come, I'm sure. We'll be on this trip for a long time. But I need to stay at the communication console while you do the repairs so we can test them with you standing by outside to make adjustments. I might also have to tweak the program from in here to get things to work right."

The satchel containing replacement parts and tools was bulkier than they would like, but Mindy reminded them that it should be no problem in zero-G. She stepped into the airlock and began to put on her EVA suit. Rae Anne checked and double checked the fittings and attached the SAFER unit to her tool belt. She stepped back into the galley and sealed the hatch.

"Break a leg, partner," Rob called through the intercom as Mindy signaled a thumbs-up through the window and pulled the lever to evacuate the airlock.

"We OK?" she asked after the chamber was evacuated.

Rae Anne checked the readouts. "You're good for EVA, Mindy. Good luck. Stay safe."

Mindy locked her tether to the door bracket as Rod had done and opened the outer hatch. As she stepped through the hatch, she looked like a Sherpa on a Mount Everest climbing trek. The duffle bag of parts hung from the neck of her EVA suit and every loop and pocket on her tool belt was packed.

She slowly pulled herself along the hull. Although the baggage she carried was weightless, it was bulky and possessed considerable mass, forcing Mindy to stop frequently to keep it from swinging to the side and throwing her off balance with its inertia.

Rob and Rae Anne watched as Mindy swapped tethers midway to the antenna. Slowly, she inched her way to the damaged structure. After fastening her third tether to the bracket beneath the antenna housing and removing and securing the second tether to the same anchor, she cautiously propelled herself up the scaffold and onto the antenna itself where she began to straighten bent struts and flatten sections of the damaged dish.

"It'll be amazing if we receive anything with this antenna. I'll try to trim some of the jagged edges that might cause interference. That should help." Mindy pulled out a set of shears and began trimming the edges around the hole. When she finished, she worked her way down to the antenna's base.

Mindy scraped away the chunks of debris penetrating the controlling mechanism and removed the motor housing faceplate. Her heavy breathing filled the comm-link. Rob furrowed his brow and shook his head in concern.

"Mindy, take five. Your EVA suit needs to take a rest. It can't keep up with all your activity."

Rae Anne smiled.

That was quite diplomatic, Rob. Good job. I sure wish we could have had someone out there with her.

After a few minutes, Mindy began to work again, removing and replacing parts one piece at a time. They couldn't replace the drive motor, so they could only hope it was still intact. They wouldn't know until Mindy finished the repairs.

After nearly three hours and several short rest periods, Mindy slid away from the antenna mount and anchored herself against the telescope housing.

"I'm through here," she announced. "I'm clear of the machinery. Take her for a test drive, Rae Anne."

This had better work! If it doesn't, I don't know what more we can do.

Rae Anne powered up the antenna's directional unit and waited a few moments. "Mindy, power is on. How do things look?"

"Everything's OK here. No sparks."

"I'll rotate the antenna clockwise. Stop me if you see any sign of a problem." Rae Anne slowly rotated the locator knob ten degrees clockwise. A reassuring hum vibrated through the ship's hull.

"The antenna moved, Rae Anne, but it just stopped."

"No problem, Mindy. I only rotated it ten degrees. I'll give it another 80 degrees. It should stop at right angles from its initial position."

Again, everything worked as intended. Rae Anne rotated it an additional 270 degrees to take it to its starting position and Mindy reported everything appeared to be functioning perfectly.

"OK, Mindy. I'm setting it to auto-seek to locate our signal from Mission Control. Tell me what you see." She pressed the SEEK button and watched the blinking amber light on the console.

For about a minute, it blinked yellow. Mindy reported the antenna to be rotating slowly back and forth in ever widening arcs.

"The antenna has stopped moving," Mindy reported. "What's up?"

"The SEEK light just switched to green."

Rae Anne nearly jumped when a faint, crackly voice filled the cabin. "…is Mission Control. Do you read? *Aurora,* this is Mission Control. Do you read?" The message kept repeating but with heavy static.

Rae Anne and Rob exchanged high fives.

"Hooray! We did it. We're half-way there," Rob exclaimed. "Now if they can hear us too, we're home free."

"Everything's fine, Mindy," Rae Anne said. "We're picking up a transmission from Mission Control. It's only audio, though, and pretty sketchy. Pack up your tools and enjoy the view while we find out if they can hear us too."

Rae Anne clicked the transmit switch and announced *Aurora* was transmitting again, repeating the message twice. She drummed her fingers on the console, waiting for a reply, knowing it would take 7 1/2 minutes before hearing back from Earth.

When the reply finally arrived, they could hear cheering in the background.

"Sounds like they were as anxious as we were," Rob observed. "Are they sending video?"

"*Aurora* to Mission Control," Rae Anne transmitted. "Our receiver has been damaged. Lots of break-up and noise in the audio. We are receiving no video. Are you sending video? What is the quality of our transmissions?"

After another communication delay, they received assurances that Mission Control was transmitting both audio and video and they were receiving *Aurora's* communications perfectly. Rob and Rae Anne gave each other a big hug, smiles all around.

"What a relief! Looks like we'll have to live with no video and crappy audio for the rest of the mission," said Rae Anne as she turned to make additional adjustments on the console.

"At least our mission reports back to Earth won't be affected," Rob said. "As far as the mission goes, that's what is truly important."

"What happened to you guys?" It was Ian on the comm-link.

"Our worst nightmare, Ian. The Chinese hit us with two fucking missiles, that's what. We're damned lucky to be alive. They took a big chunk out of our receiving antenna, and we've been doing repairs ever since. I'll start sending the sensor logs and video of the attack now."

During the pause in communication with Earth, Rae Anne took a deep breath and turned to the EVA comm unit. "Mindy, we've got two-way comm to Mission Control. Your repairs are working! Get your bod back in here. It's party time!"

Mindy began to pull herself along the tether leading down the communication housing.

THUNK! Metal striking metal reverberated through the ship.

"Damn! The shears slipped from my tool belt and bounced off the antenna housing." Her helmet monitor swung upward and caught the tool floating away into the void. "I hope we won't need them for anything else. No damage to the hull that I can see."

Mindy's labored breathing registered heavily over the cabin speakers. She slowly descended the edge of the fin, exchanged tethers at its base, then began crawling along the hull. She seemed to have trouble keeping purchase on the hull, but she finally made it to the bracket beside the thruster. The monitor showed her helmet swinging back and forth, an obvious sign of fatigue.

"Take your time, Mindy. Catch your breath. You have plenty of oxygen. There's no need to hurry," Rob instructed.

"I'm OK. I'm OK," Mindy muttered without conviction. "I'm unlocking the first tether to fasten to my belt now." The monitor showed the bracket with the two locking carabiners in place. A gloved hand moved into view and unsnapped one of the carabiners. Both the hand and the carabiner floated out of the picture.

"Oh!" Mindy's exclamation filled the room and trailed off.

"No, Mindy!" Rob yelled. "That's the wrong one. Grab the tether. Grab the thruster. Grab anything…" Rae Anne's heart stopped cold and her whole body tensed. She glanced at Rob. His face was ashen.

"Mindy, the SAFER! Position the SAFER to propel yourself back toward the ship."

There was a long pause before Mindy answered.

"Sorry, guys. I left it in the airlock. Too much stuff to carry. No one's ever needed one… Till now. I'm so sorry…"

Rob buried his face in his hands. "No, no, no…"

"Rob!" Rae Anne screamed, grabbing and shaking his shoulder. "We've got to save her. Fire the thrusters! Chase her down."

Rob shook his head. "Won't work, Rae Anne. Huge ship. We don't have the fine control to do that."

"But we've got to do something! I'll take all three SAFER's out with me and bring her back," Rae Anne shouted as she headed for the floor hatch and the airlock. Rob caught her arm and they tumbled into the wall. They rebounded back into the room, Rae Anne beating on Rob's chest with both fists.

"Let me go! Let me go!" she screamed between sobs.

"Rae Anne, there's nothing we can do. By the time you suited up, she'd be too far away for you to reach her. Her oxygen would have run out even if you could get to her."

They returned to the monitor and Rae Anne slumped into his chest, sobbing. The monitor relayed the view from Mindy's helmet. In full view was *Aurora,* slowly diminishing into the blackness of space.

"Oh, Mindy…" She grabbed Rob's arm, her shoulders heaving.

Faintly, Mindy's voice came over the EVA comm. Her voice was calm, void of any fear or terror. She seemed to have come to grips with her fate. "You were right, Rob. I have never been so at peace. The entire universe is wrapping itself around me and taking me back to its womb. The stars…so many stars… They are telling me we are all family. We're all in this together. All of humanity.

"Take that message back with you. Let that be my legacy. A message from the cosmos to the whole human race.

"Don't be sad for me, Rae Anne, Rob. Think well of me, my friends. Visit my family when you return. I love you both. Farewell."

Rae Anne gasped when Mindy turned off her intercom. The sharp click knifed into her very soul. Rob reached over and drew her to him and they embraced, both sobbing.

How could this have happened. I feel so utterly, completely drained.

"Oh, Mindy…Mindy," she quietly sobbed.

Good-bye my dearest friend.

Chapter 5

October 11, 2037: Aboard *Aurora*

"I should have been doing the repairs. If I'd been out there, this wouldn't have happened. Mindy would still be alive," Rob muttered, staring at his uneaten dinner.

Rae Anne understood Rob's feelings. But after four days of listening to his self-recriminations, she was becoming irritated. She too was devastated, but where Rob was becoming more subdued and morose, she confronted her grief by focusing on a strict daily routine and her astronomy projects.

It didn't help that the Agency decided to treat the Chinese attack on *Aurora* as though it never happened, despite the evidence Rae Anne had uploaded from *Aurora*'s memory archives once communication with Mission Control was re-established. Ian explained that tensions between China and the West over Taiwan were near the breaking point (again) and a Chinese invasion might be imminent. The U.S. administration did not want the *Aurora* incident to fuel a fire nearly out of control already. Mindy was, apparently, collateral damage.

Those bastards. What about justice, anyway. Who's worse, the Chinese with their outright aggression or the politicians with their diplomatic agendas?

Realizing there was nothing she could do, she tried to put these thoughts to rest. But Rob couldn't let go. He slipped into a deep depression.

As he became less communicative, Rae Anne stepped in to fill Mindy's role as commander of Mars-II. It fell to her to convince the

Agency not to cancel the mission. Since the Agency already planned on leaving *Aurora* in Mars orbit void of crew, she knew she had a strong argument.

"Our primary goals are to take data and make personal observations on the surface, construct science stations, and collect samples for analysis on *Aurora* during our return to Earth," Rae Anne stated as forcefully as she could, trying to make her case as defensible as possible. She knew her arguments with the Agency had to elicit their full support for the mission to survive.

She waited impatiently during the eight-minute communication delay, nervously trying to think of anything else she might add to support her position. She was pleased when Jeremy, the mission director who rarely communicated directly with *Aurora*, came on line.

"You have a point, Rae Anne," came the crackly, broken response. "But we do have loads of surface data from decades of observations from landers and rovers. Actual physical samples will have to wait for Mars-III.

"Many of us had long and heated discussions before deciding to reduce the crew from seven to three in order to get to Mars faster. Several people at the very top weren't happy about leaving *Aurora* abandoned in orbit while all three of you were on the surface."

"But tell me how it is different now? *Aurora* won't care whether it's been abandoned by two or by three astronauts. That decision has already been made. And all NASA's Apollo moon landings were successfully accomplished with only two astronauts. They were flying far less sophisticated equipment than what's aboard our lander, and they didn't have anywhere near the computer capabilities we have. Jason has already proven many times over how his contributions are equivalent to our having another full-fledged member of the crew."

Rae Anne believed this last point to be her key argument. Everything aboard *Aurora* was far more capable and reliable than anything NASA engineers could have even imagined. She was confident she and Rob could carry out the original agenda with considerable assistance from Jason.

October 12, 2037: USIEA Headquarters

"The mission has lost 1/3 of its crew. In any military endeavor, that would spell disaster and warrant a withdrawal. Although this is a scientific mission, I can't see that my analogy is in any way misplaced."

Ian listened to General McGuffey's comment with disdain.

What the hell does he know about scientific missions, anyway. There's no comparison with a military operation. What bullshit.

The meeting had been called to include the department heads within USIEA in deciding what to do with the Mars-II mission. The room was about equally divided between military brass and the civilian management who dealt with the day-to-day operations of the Agency. This wasn't the first time the two groups had come to loggerheads.

The lone political figure in the room from congressional appropriations spoke up.

"We have over fifteen billion dollars riding on this mission, not counting hardware which, presumably, will be recovered in any case. That's fifteen billion dollars down the drain if we abort this mission. Do any of you appreciate how difficult it is to get that much money appropriated to any agency, let alone to a specific project? If there is any feasibility that Mars-II can be continued successfully and safely, I urge you to continue the mission."

Ian felt a stirring in the room, the rustling of papers, the slight scraping of chairs. These subtle clues suggested a softening of antagonism and signaled his moment had come to express his opinion. He stood and waited to be acknowledged.

"Ian Bentley from Astronautics Communications. You may not realize this, but we have two of the strongest, most capable, astronauts ever selected for a space mission on board the *Aurora*. And they are accompanied by the most sophisticated artificial intelligence our agency has ever produced. *Aurora* and *Eagle*, the lander, represent the very cutting edge in spaceship design. If ever there was a mission that could succeed with just two astronauts, this would be it.

"Astronaut Chavez has pointed out repeatedly that this mission exceeds anything NASA had in the 1970's by a thousand percent. I would put that at ten thousand percent. And NASA landed 12 astronauts on the moon, two at a time, without losing a single lunar mission. Even Apollo 13, despite the dangerous glitch in its life-support system, ended with successful recovery of the crew, thanks to the ingenuity and resourcefulness of both crew and ground support engineers. Our people today are every bit as resourceful and have technological resources miles beyond what NASA had. Should any problem develop, I assure you, the Agency will be able to handle it. I see very little added risk in pursuing Mars-II with Astronauts Harris and Chavez in charge."

Ian sat down, hoping his comments would make a difference. In the hours that followed, he noted that the few skeptics within the Agency had rallied behind him and were now forcefully arguing that the mission continue.

One by one, the military brass began to reluctantly fall in line, but with reservations and conditions that the Agency personnel could live with. Thus, a compromise of sorts was reached by the end of the afternoon. Ian went home with a load off his chest.

October 13, 2037: Aboard Aurora

On Tuesday, Ian delivered their decision.

"Rae Anne, Space Force Command and top Agency management have discussed the merits of your proposal at great length, and though some have come along reluctantly, they have decided to continue on-course with Mars-II. Depending on how the Mars landings go, they may decide to limit the number of sites you and Rob visit. They'll make that determination after you return to *Aurora* following your first landing."

"Hallelujah! We did it!" She leaped into the air and would have bumped her head on the bulkhead had her right hand not instinctively shot upward to stop her momentum.

She wanted to high-five someone, but Rob was not yet into high-fives. Nevertheless, she floated down to Level 3 where Rob was watching an episode of Bonanza from the ship's entertainment archives. When she excitedly told him the news, he looked up and complimented her on her success before returning his attention to the movie.

Did I see a hint of interest in his eyes, a twitch at the corner of his mouth? C'mon, Rob, I need you now more than ever.

She surprised herself with the realization that her feelings for Rob ran deeper than she had imagined.

Her next task was to draw Rob back into play. They both needed to be at the top of their game to pull off a successful mission. Fortunately, they were still three months away from Mars orbit, so time was on her side.

The day after Mission Control had given their approval, Rae Anne came up with a plan for reviving Rob's interest in their mission.

"Rob, we're equipped to explore three, maybe four, sites on Mars. The Agency's research has identified a dozen possibilities. Since you'll be piloting *Eagle* to the surface, you have the best insight into suitable landing sites. Would you evaluate each one and narrow the list to the best four? And rank them as well. We might only be able to visit two, and we want to hit the best locations first."

To her relief, Rob looked up from his tablet. "Let me see what I can do."

Once he began studying the data NASA and the Agency had accumulated over more than sixty years from various orbiters and landers, his interest in the mission returned and he plunged into the studies. Rae Anne felt no end of relief to see Rob's mental health return to normal.

October 15, 2037: Aboard Aurora

"I'm not sure which of these two sites to designate as number three and number four," Rob commented as he was finishing his report. "Both are strong contenders for the number three slot. What do you think?"

Rae Anne leaned over Rob's shoulder and looked at the advantages each site offered.

"It would be a shame if we have to discard either of them. Maybe we should toss a coin," she suggested.

Rob laughed for the first time since Mindy's accident. Tossing a coin in microgravity was ridiculous. Rae Anne laughed too, not so much at her own joke, but at her tremendous relief at hearing Rob's laughter. She leaned over and kissed him on the cheek.

Rob rose from his seat and reached around her, pulling her close. They hugged tightly and kissed, floating in microgravity. Rae Anne could hear her heart thumping and felt her face flush.

"Oh my gosh, Rae Anne. I'm not sure what came over me," Rob said without a note of apology.

"Hmm… Whatever it was, I would certainly welcome more of it," she responded, brushing her cheek against his.

She found it difficult to explain to herself how she felt about Rob following this spontaneous moment. Ever since the untimely death of her 'first and forever' true love, Carson Weaver, a year before, she had neither intended nor wanted to become romantically involved again, focusing instead on her job with the Agency.

Like Rob, Carson was an air force fighter pilot before being selected to pilot the Mars-II mission. This was when the Agency had still been planning on sending seven astronauts to Mars. But Carson had been killed in a freak training maneuver in his F-38 Talon. His death plummeted Rae

Anne into despair and serious depression. Had it not been for Rob and the other astronauts in her class, she would have left the program.

Carson's accident happened at the same time the Agency decided to reduce the Mars-II crew to three. The resulting reduction in weight for crew, provisions and equipment would give *Aurora* a velocity boost, hopefully enabling it to reach Mars before the Chinese who were planning to use the same launch window for their Mars ship *Ming-Xi*. It was this change, along with Carson's death, that placed Rae Anne's name on *Aurora's* roster. Both she and Carson were skilled computer scientists, and Rae Anne had enhanced her skill set with navigation and communications. She was an obvious 'shoo in'.

But now she began to feel her devotion to Carson's memory beginning to fade. Time, distance and isolation were taking their toll.

Rob is one attractive and desirable man. And he's obviously attracted to me. Not to mention we'll be spending the next year and a half alone together on this mission. It's time to face facts. Carson is gone.

Over dinner that evening, Rob reached over and placed his hand on Rae Anne's wrist.

"You know, Rae Anne, I've had this attraction for you since way back when we started our training. I couldn't believe my luck when you were selected to be part of this mission, and not because of romantic opportunities, either. I was really looking forward to just being with you."

"I guess I was so focused on Carson, I never noticed, Rob. But I could never forget the care and attention you gave me in the terrible week after his accident. If it hadn't been for you, I might have left the program, I was so distraught."

And now we're together and on the same page. I wonder where this relationship will go. Could I be falling in love again?

Unexpectedly, she discovered herself warming to a romantic relationship with Rob to help fill her life. Rob was warm and kind, sensitive to her needs. Hours that before were filled with silence were now full of conversation, two people catching up on each other's personal lives and innermost thoughts. Two people reaching out to each other with emotional support and care.

Their relationship continued to deepen and become more intimate. Although they hadn't yet had a sexual encounter, Rae Anne could see it coming and was looking forward to it. She checked the med cabinet and discovered a box containing condoms and birth control pills and began taking the pills 'just in case'.

I'm not sure how you manage sex in microgravity, but I'm sure we'll figure it out. I haven't felt this alive since Carson and I were first dating.

She felt her face flush at the thought.

Chapter 6

November 3 , 2037: Aboard *Aurora*

After Mindy's death, Rae Anne decided to devote time to Jason's programming. She had earned her BS and MS degrees in math and computer science at Stanford. Before being admitted to the astronaut program, she was working in the Agency's AI division. She figured her knowledge and experience were perfectly aligned with revising *Aurora's* AI. She planned to incorporate machine learning algorithms into Jason's programming to help him 'learn' from his interactions with the crew. Her goal was to develop a sensitive, empathetic, and understanding AI beyond anything yet devised.

"Yeah, sure, Congress will be glad to provide funding for a permanent base on Mars and an annual ferry service to support it," Rae Anne said with an exaggerated sneer on her face.

"What good news, Rae Anne. I'm glad to hear it," Jason responded with a happy quality to his voice.

"No, Jason, wrong response. That was an example of sarcasm. It's a prediction implying an action or outcome exactly opposite to what was said."

"That is not logical. How can someone know what you mean when you say the opposite?"

"Look at my face, my body language, and listen to the tone of my voice. Compare these two statements where I say the same words. In the first, the words say what they mean. In the second, the words are being used with sarcasm."

She repeated the earlier statement, first with a smile and happy gestures, then with the sneer and cynical tone in her voice.

"Interesting. I recognize the difference, but I see no logical use for sarcasm. Why would you bother to say something opposite to what you mean?"

Rae Anne sighed and wondered if a round-trip to Mars would give her anywhere near enough time to achieve her goals.

November 8, 2037: Aboard Aurora

"You know what they say about 'All work and no play'?" Rob asked one evening as they were cleaning up after dinner.

"Something about 'making Jack a dull boy', as I recall. Why?"

"Well, it seems to me that you spend almost all your time either with your telescope and your astronomy research or with your AI programming projects. I propose you add a little fun in your life to spice things up."

The tone in Rob's voice immediately caught her attention. A shiver ran up her spine and a tingling sensation of arousal surged in her groin. She flushed as she felt her heart quicken.

"I can't imagine what you might be suggesting," she responded coyly.

"Only that we've just had a fine dinner and there are several hours before we turn in. We could think about doing something together to fill the time."

"You mean a rousing game of chess or Monopoly?"

"I was thinking of something a bit more intimate." Rob floated over beside Rae Anne and put his hands on her waist. His face was inches from hers and he gazed into her eyes.

"May I?" he asked softly.

Rae Anne smiled warmly.

"Be my guest, you gorgeous hunk."

Rob pulled Rae Anne against him, wrapped his arms tightly around her and pressed his lips against hers in a long and sensuous kiss. Without realizing it, they floated off the deck and bumped into the ceiling.

"You really know how to sweep a girl off her feet!"

They both burst out laughing.

"You know, a lounge might be a safer place to pursue this further," she added when they recovered. "Assuming you're interested, of course."

"That, my lovely Rae Anne, is a most welcome suggestion. Come."

Rob caught the edge of the table with his foot and propelled them toward the floor hatch. Rae Anne slipped through the hatch while pulling apart the fasteners on her jumpsuit and leaving it to float to the ceiling. Clad only in her blouse and underwear, she settled into the lounge and beckoned Rob over. His jumpsuit joined hers and he slipped into the lounge beside her.

They embraced and fondled and kissed as though there would be no tomorrow. Other pieces of clothing soon found themselves randomly floating about the room. At some point Rae Anne loosely strapped their bodies into the lounge so they could concentrate more fully on their lovemaking. She was pleasantly surprised that making love in microgravity wasn't as difficult as she had imagined. In fact, she found the freedom of movement in zero-G made sex even more enjoyable.

Sometime later, Rae Anne awoke in Rob's arms. Rob seemed to be asleep. She gently moved his arms aside and unclasped the restraining strap, then floated up to the galley without bothering to retrieve her clothes. She was in the midst of making hot chocolate when Rob's head poked through the hatch.

"Did I happen to mention that I love you, Rae Anne?"

"Only a couple dozen times. But tell me again."

He floated over and embraced her, pulling her tightly against his body, and whispered into her ear.

Another long kiss and neck nuzzles followed.

"I'm making myself some hot chocolate. Would you like some?"

"That would be a perfect appetizer."

"Appetizer? For what?"

"For more of your delicious body, you scrumptious morsel, you."

Rae Anne smiled alluringly and pecked him on the cheek.

"You say the nicest things. Are you sure you can take time out for the hot chocolate?"

November 26, 2037: Aboard Aurora

Rae Anne looked up from her tablet and the telescope image of Saturn she had been studying. Rob was deep into a game of Go with Jason.

"Who's winning?"

"Is that a rhetorical question? When has either of us come close to beating Jason at anything?"

"Sad, but true. A thought occurred to me. Today is Thanksgiving. We should see if we can rustle some sort of meal worthy of a Thanksgiving dinner from our larder. With a little imagination, we might come up with something to create a memorable feast."

"I'll go along with that." Rob rose from the lounge and stretched.

"Shall I save this game for later, Rob?" Jason asked.

"No. I resign. Again."

"Very well. Thank you for the game. Your skill at GO is improving."

"Stuff it. Let's see what we can put together, Rae Anne."

Rae Anne led the way into the galley and slid the door to the larder open. She began rummaging through the supplies.

"I don't see anything that looks like cranberry sauce, but here's a packet of chunky apple sauce."

"We could mix in some cherry juice for coloring and maybe add lime juice for tartness."

"I'll see if I can find the cherries. There's still some lime juice in the fridge. Ahh. A packet of sliced ham. And here's one with turkey. Which should we have?"

"Why not both? Find some roasted chicken breast and we'll stack all three together for a turporken dinner."

"I've heard of turducken, but never turporken. Worth a try. The turkey packet contains gravy. I think I saw some mashed potatoes in here someplace."

Rae Anne handed the turkey and ham packets to Rob and continued to search through the hermetically sealed packages.

"Stuffing and apple pie would be perfect to round out the meal."

"Forget the pie. But here's some apple cobbler."

"That will do."

"And here's the mashed potatoes. We may have to do without stuffing unless we make our own using some English muffins."

"See if you can find some cornbread in there. We had some a while back. It wasn't very good. But if we crumble it with some breakfast sausage and onion and just enough of the turkey gravy to moisten it, we'd have a suitable stuffing."

After a bit more searching, Rae Anne located the remaining ingredients.

"One Space Thanksgiving dinner coming up!" she announced triumphantly."

Rob worked on the turporken and stuffing while Rae Anne prepared the mashed potatoes and faux cranberry sauce. She tasted the sauce. Her whole face wrinkled.

"Eww. The sauce tastes like limed apples Maybe some sugar will help. If it's at all salvageable, we'll have to use our imaginations on this one."

After a more-or-less enjoyable dinner, Rob excused himself to retrieve something from the flight deck. Rae Anne furrowed her brow, wondering what he might be up to. He soon returned, carrying a pint flexipak of clear liquid.

"A holiday feast would not be complete without an after-dinner toast with a suitable libation."

He retrieved two capped mugs from the cabinet and carefully squeezed half the contents into each mug.

"So that's what you've been doing at the chemistry lab these past weeks," Rae Anne said, nodding her head knowingly. "I thought you were up to something."

"The Agency can't enforce their prohibition on alcohol out here. A little yeast, water and sugar, and nature does its own thing. It's not my fault they included a fully functional distillation apparatus at the chemistry bench."

He handed a mug to Rae Anne and lifted his.

"To us and to a successful mission."

Rae Anne repeated his toast. They clicked mugs and sipped Rob's heady concoction.

Later that evening, snuggling in exhausted bliss together in their 'love lounge', Rob commented, "This turned out to be a great Thanksgiving. Christmas is just around the corner. Let's plan on doing this again."

Rae Anne chuckled. "That sounds good to me, so long as you're talking about the dinner and not the post-dinner activities. I have no intention of putting those off until Christmas!"

Chapter 7

December 17, 2037: Aboard Aurora

"Rae Anne, we have a problem," Rob announced, moaning, as his half-eaten energy bar floated toward the ceiling. Rae Anne glanced over her shoulder just as Rob doubled over and buried his head in his arms.

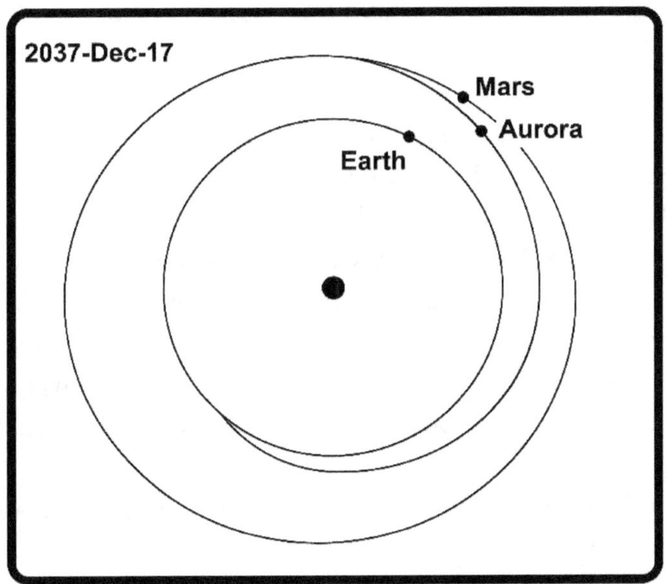

"Rob, what's wrong?" She spun from the prep counter to face him. He looked up, his face ashen. His forehead glistened with beads of sweat. Rae Anne lurched to his side.

She gripped his forearm with one hand for support and placed the palm of her other hand on his forehead.

Dios mio! He has a raging fever. And we're only weeks away from Mars orbit.

"Rob? Talk to me. Whatever it is, we can handle it."

Rob shook his head. He grimaced as he tried to take a deep breath.

"I have this sharp pain… lower abdomen… several days now. Suddenly unbearable. Antibiotics haven't helped. Pain relievers aren't cutting it. It's my appendix."

Rae Anne gasped. Her grip on Rob's arm tightened.

Oh, no, surely not. It's got to be something else. Anything else. Rob is the only one even remotely qualified to perform surgery. Could he do his own appendectomy?

She immediately realized how ridiculous the thought was. Any required surgery would fall on her shoulders.

And I have no surgical training or experience whatsoever.

"Could it be anything else? What tests can we run?"

"Pain location and severity. And the fever… checked my white blood cell count this morning… way over 10,000."

"Good god, Rob. What can we do?"

"You've got to operate. We have no other option."

"Rob! All I've had is the Agency's EMT training. You know what that covered. I know nothing about surgical procedures, let alone an appendectomy."

"Can't operate on myself. Maybe help…help get things set up. Get you started… If I'm conscious. You're the designated…designated hitter for this inning."

"Rob, your life would depend on my not screwing this up. I could end up killing you."

"Don't even think that way. You can do it. And you'll do it perfectly. I know you will."

"But are we even equipped to handle this?"

"I made up the list of medical supplies…for this mission. Trust me, we have everything we need.

"We'll operate here…on this table. I'll get things together. You go down and watch every video Jason can find in the medical archives. At least six. Imagine…imagine your own hands in each video, performing the surgery. Make a start-to-finish checklist with Jason. He'll be your virtual assistant.

"First call Mission Control. No need…no need to wait for a response. They have no other choice."

"Rob, you'll need an anesthetic and constant monitoring. How can I do surgery and monitor your anesthetic at the same time? And how do we get a drip going in zero-G?"

"Our battery-operated drip system… It doesn't need gravity. It rolls up a long tube containing the solution… forcing fluid out the end. We'll use it with saline. I'll prep myself with a local and…and inject a general just before you start."

"Can we really do this, Rob?"

"We have no choice, Rae Anne. I won't last a week otherwise."

Alright, Rae Anne. Rob needs you now in the worst possible way. Time to grit your teeth and do what has to be done!

"You do what you can up here, Rob. Dr. Chavez, surgeon extraordinaire, is on the way." She turned and floated up to the flight deck to let Mission Control know their situation, wishing she felt as confident as she tried to sound.

Then she hustled down to Level 3 and tried to clear her mind.

"Jason, bring up the ten best-rated videos showing step-by-step details on appendectomies. As I watch each one, you are to correlate the information and put together a single checklist I can follow to perform the operation."

Once Jason had set up the play-list, she slavishly watched every detail.

From the first video, she learned how little she knew about anatomy.

This is much more complicated than I thought. Much more than a simple cut through the abdomen, remove the appendix, and sew everything up. At least my EMT training gave me some experience with forceps, retractors, and scalpels. But this goes far beyond treating a superficial wound!

"Jason, there's a lot here to remember. All the layers of tissue to cut through. One is an oblique something, while another is an anterior whatsit. How am I going to learn it all in only a few hours?"

"The names aren't important. Concentrate on procedure. For example, just remember the sequence of layers, such as 'top muscle', 'middle muscle' and 'bottom muscle'. The same for the fascia lining each layer."

That response was incredibly cogent for computer AI.

"You're right, Jason. I'll ignore irrelevant details on the next video."

She followed Jason's advice and was surprised how things began to make sense. With the third and subsequent videos, she concentrated solely on procedure.

Maybe, just maybe, I can pull this off after all. If nothing unexpected crops up.

When she floated back up to the galley at noon, Rob had transformed the dining table into a surgical theater. He sat at the table with his head resting in his folded arms, panting. Rae Anne could see he was in a great deal of pain. He was naked except for a disposable blanket draped over his shoulders.

He had spread a large plastic sheet across the table and placed a collapsible surgical tent at one end with a tray of various surgical instruments set next to it, along with gauze, towels, sponges, and antiseptic wipes.

Rob raised his head and looked unsteadily at Rae Anne with unfocused eyes. "We're in luck. Mission Control has authorized the surgery."

Rae Anne shook her head.

Amazing. Even in pain, his humor comes through.

"They said they'd have a surgeon… online if you need one. With the ten-minute delay, that won't be much help. You ready?"

Rae Anne nodded. "As ready as I'll ever be, Rob," she said with more enthusiasm than she felt.

"All right, then, let's do it!" His positive tone, despite his condition, lifted Rae Anne's spirits.

He shed the blanket and climbed atop the table, groaning with each stabbing pain. He had already shaved his abdomen, including a large swath of pubic hair. Before lying down, he scrubbed his abdomen with alcohol wipes, grimacing with each swipe, and drew a three-inch diagonal line between his navel and his hip with a marker. After inserting the drip needle into his right arm and taping it in place, he pricked the area along the incision line several times with a syringe containing local anesthetic and gave himself an injection of general anesthetic.

Once the local took effect, he shakily draped the blanket over his lower body and lay down. Droplets of sweat drifted into the air above his forehead. His ragged breathing broke the silence as they waited for the general to take effect.

For a moment, a twinge of panic surged through Rae Anne as she realized she was now on her own.

Breathe deeply, Rae Anne. Calm yourself. You are a world-class surgeon specializing in appendectomies. This is just another routine operation.

"Jason, are you standing by?"

"I'm ready when you are, Rae Anne. Don't forget to scrub."

"Thanks Jason. I was so focused on the task ahead I'd forgotten that crucial point." She immediately lathered soap foam from the dispenser Rob had placed on the counter, then 'rinsed' with sanitizer wipes.

After donning a surgical gown, cap, and mask, she ran a strap across Rob's chest and another across his thighs to hold him in place for the surgery. She unfolded the operating tent, positioned it over Rob's torso, secured it with straps beneath the table, and turned on a small exhaust fan attached to the tent, verifying the filter was in place. She pulled on a pair of latex gloves and strapped her waist to the table to give her the leverage she would need.

"This is the first ever… first ever surgery under microgravity," Rob muttered, his voice shaky and barely audible. "It's going to be pretty messy."

Rae Anne placed the surgical tools under the tent next to his right side.

"I've got plenty of tissues and sponges. I'll sop everything up before it gets away."

She took another deep breath, pleased to see her hands were steady. "OK, Rob. Crunch time…" Rob moaned in response.

"Jason, I'll narrate everything I do for the record. If you detect anything that departs from your list, immediately bring it to my attention."

"I have you covered, Rae Anne," Jason said in his standard computer voice. Rae Anne wished he could sound a bit more sympathetic as she initiated her first (and she hoped her last) surgical procedure.

Chapter 8

December 17, 2037: Aboard *Aurora*

"OK. Jason. The patient is on the operating table and the abdomen has been shaved, sterilized and marked for incision. What are the next three things I need to do?"

Of course, Rae Anne knew what needed to be done, but checklists are made to be used, not ignored. More accidents have resulted from ignored checklists than anyone would care to admit.

Jason rattled off the first three items from his list of instructions.

After selecting a Number 10 scalpel, Rae Anne carefully incised the outer layers of Rob's flesh following the line he had drawn. Rob didn't flinch but his eyes were still open, unfocused.

At least the local is working. Breathe deeply. It's only blood.

She dabbed a damp sponge along the incision and used an electrocauterizing device along either side of the cut to reduce bleeding. She positioned a self-retaining retractor into the incision and spread its jaws to pull the skin tissue out of the way.

One more swipe with the scalpel and she had cut through the fascia overlaying the top muscle layer, the first of three she would have to cut through. Rae Anne marveled at the clean and precise cuts her razor-sharp scalpel allowed her to make.

"God that hurts," Rob moaned. "Even with the local. I should feel some benefit from the general any time now. The sooner the b…" His eyelids drooped and closed.

Rae Anne exhaled a deep sigh.

Not a minute too soon!

The videos advised to look for a large blood vessel on the way in, with instructions to pinch it with two clamps, dissect it with scissors, and ligate both ends before proceeding. Rae Anne spotted the bright red vessel resting on top of the abdominal muscles. She clamped it, cut it and tied it off as the video had shown.

She reported every step to Jason prior to taking it and said "Done" on completion to keep him in sync, then asked for the next three steps. The redundancy and overlap had a calming effect. It also helped her anticipate what lay ahead. At some point she wondered if she should have installed a vid-cam for Jason's use, but decided his programming wasn't yet sophisticated enough for that to be of any help.

She made her next cut parallel to the length of Rob's torso, slicing into the muscle in the same direction as the fibers. She made three swipes with the scalpel to cut through the thick layer of tissue while taking care not to cut into the muscle beneath it, damping up blood at every opportunity. Two more retractors pulled the muscle tissue aside.

What a god-send retractors are. Whatever did they do before these things were invented?

The videos called for the same procedure when cutting through the next two muscles, each oriented at angles to the first and to each other. As before, Rae Anne took care for the cuts to follow the tissue fibers. After each step she repositioned the retractors, opening the incision as wide as possible without tearing tissue.

This is taking forever. I can barely keep up with the bleeding. I need more sponges. And an assistant. No, make that two. Better yet, two assistants and a surgeon.

She glanced at Rob's monitors. Heartbeat blipped steadily on the monitor and his blood pressure, though reduced from normal, was holding steady.

Thank god there's nothing there to worry about.

She inhaled deeply and exhaled slowly and purposefully.

Droplets of blood continuously took flight above the incision and formed a crimson mist drifting toward the fan. The filter over the fan looked like a red airbrush abstract on stretched canvas. Rae Anne shuddered at the macabre image.

She finally completed the incision through the third layer of muscle. *Everything so far by the book. You're almost there, Rae Anne.*

"All right, I've made it to the peritoneum, Jason. One more cut and I'll be into the abdominal cavity."

"Do not use your scalpel here, Rae Anne," Jason cautioned. "Use the scissors. A scalpel might puncture the colon."

"Thank you, Jason. I'm now pinching the peritoneum tissue with forceps and cutting through it with the scissors."

She widened the hole with scissors and once again repositioned the retractors. More blood, more sponges and wipes.

"I'm now inserting my fingers into the incision to feel around the colon for the appendix."

Damn, there's so much hardware here I barely have room to work. How do surgeons manage?

As she gently inserted her forefinger into the opening, she immediately encountered the smooth-walled colon. She continued running her finger along the colon and away from the navel until she felt a lump on the intestinal wall. Further probing revealed an object like an octopus tentacle attached to the colon.

Aha! I think I've found it.

To her consternation, it was situated behind the colon. She teased it around the backside and tried to bring it forward, but it refused to cooperate and slipped from her finger several times.

"Jason, I've located the appendix, but I can't get it out from behind the colon."

"Can you adjust the position of the colon so the appendix comes to the front?"

She gave Jason's suggestion a try. The first two attempts failed but on her third attempt the colon responded just enough for her to slip her finger under the appendix and draw it forward. Soon she could see its ugly worm-like tip exposed through the incision. She continued to twist the colon itself around to bring the base of the appendix up through the incision so she could work on it.

"Be careful not to rupture the appendix while you are manipulating the colon, Rae Anne."

"Thanks Jason. The appendix now extends about one-half inch above the incision. I'm applying additional pressure to the colon. Appendix now out a full inch."

This part proved difficult. Although she could measure her progress by the length of appendix protruding through the hole, the colon was slippery and manipulating it was a challenge. All the while she kept sopping up blood. Eventually, she succeeded and wedged the colon in place with forceps and clamped the appendix closed at its base with a hemostat.

Before cutting the appendix free, however, she needed to tie off the small artery feeding it. Two blood vessels were attached to the organ with a film of connective tissue which she cautiously cut through before clamping off the vessels. She securely tied them both and dissected them with scissors.

Finally, finally I can remove the bloody thing! There's an adjective I'll never use again!

With the organ firmly clamped, she tied it off next to the colon twice, just to be sure, leaving the smallest stub possible. Any error here could result in leakage and sepsis and death.

Next, she cut through the appendix and removed it and its hemostat from the operating arena. She allowed herself a moment to catch her breath with a deep sigh of relief. When she returned, she scrutinized her work with a critical eye. Everything appeared to be properly sealed. Using a fresh sponge and gauze, she swabbed the area and gently repositioned the colon back into the abdomen, searching the cavity for any sponges or wipes. Though she and Jason kept a running count on these as they were used, she wasn't taking any chances.

You've done the hard part, Rae Anne. From here on it's only a matter of working backwards step-by-step, suturing every separate layer of tissue on the way out. At least your EMT training prepared you well for this part!

First, of course, was the peritoneum, followed by the three muscle layers. Then came the facia below the subcutaneous skin layer. Finally, after what seemed like a lifetime, she sewed up the outer layer of skin, cleaned and sterilized the incision and dressed it with clean gauze and tape. Ninety-five minutes had elapsed.

"That completes everything on our list, Rae Anne. You have performed a successful appendectomy. Congratulations on a job well done."

"You're a bit premature, Jason. Success will depend on recovery."

Her hands, which had been steady throughout the procedure, suddenly began to shake with nervous exhaustion and her head spun dizzily. Grasping the edge of the table, she frowned tightly to focus her concentration and took three deep breaths.

Steady there, girl, there's still a lot left to be done. You can't stop now.

Recovering her focus, Rae Anne removed the drip needle from Rob's arm. Blood coated everything inside the operating tent, some wet, some dry. After folding the tent and stuffing it and its fan-filter into a large bag, she gathered the rest of the surgery trash floating around the room into the bag as well. She cleaned Rob's torso thoroughly, unstrapped him from the table and gingerly guided his limp form through the floor hatch to the reclining couch on Level 3. Once she had him wrapped in a warm blanket and buckled in, she returned to the galley.

She discarded all the disposable tools and placed the rest in the galley's UV sterilizer unit. Her surgical gown and hair net were the last things she stuffed into the trash bag before placing it in the airlock to be flushed into space.

Whew! Time to work on myself. A long, hot soak in sudsy water would be mighty fine right about now. Unfortunately…

She took much longer than usual in the cleansing unit, using soap wipes and sterile wipes to remove all residue from the day's efforts. Eventually she decided any further scrubbing might do more harm than good.

She stepped from the unit and floated over to look in on Rob and take his vital signs. He was beginning to regain consciousness. "Hey, Rob," she called out, louder than usual to gain his attention. "Can you count to ten?"

After a brief hesitation to make sense of her words, he started counting. At seven, he stopped. "My god, Rae Anne, are you ever a beautiful sight." He tried to chuckle, but it came out more like a moan. "You must be my guardian angel!"

"You really are out of it! You'll think differently once I'm dressed and barking orders." She breathed a deep sigh of relief and floated up to Level 2 to add her shower trash to the bag in the airlock, which she sealed and evacuated to 5%. On opening the outer hatch, she watched as the residual air pressure swept the bag into space.

Returning to Level 3, she checked Rob's pulse (a bit high), his blood pressure (a bit low), and his vision (somewhat blurry). His speech was noticeably less slurred.

"I could use some more meds. But the sharp pain in my gut is gone. Everything now is just a dull ache. You did a good job, Rae Anne. You better get some rest yourself. You look like hell."

"Well thanks," she said, her arms akimbo. "And a few minutes ago, you said I looked like an angel. Make up your mind." She smiled for the first time that day, pleased to see a glimmer of Rob's old self.

"I'm headed for bed as soon as I get you taken care of and touch base with Mission Control. I don't think I've ever been so utterly exhausted. I can't believe I performed an appendectomy, and in microgravity, no less."

But Rob wasn't listening. His eyes were closed and his slow, steady breathing told her he had nodded off.

She roused him enough to help him swallow some pain meds and made sure he was snuggled cozily under his blanket. Satisfied, she forced herself to float up to the flight deck and report to Mission Control, even though she desperately wanted to hit the sack.

Rae Anne awoke with a start at the communication console when it crackled to life ten- minutes after sending her message. Ian's voice captured her attention.

"Good job, Rae Anne. Dr. Weismann has been here all afternoon following Jason's reports and she compliments you as well. Says she couldn't have done a better job herself. Do you have any questions for her?"

"Thank you for standing by, Doctor. My only question is this. Do you ever have a feeling of uncertainty before making that first cut into a patient? I was absolutely terrified!"

Ten minutes later, her response arrived.

"Every time, Rae Anne. Every single time."

Chapter 9

January 7, 2038: Aboard *Aurora*

In the three weeks following Rob's surgery, every day showed measurable improvement. Rae Anne kept reminding him to take it easy, but she was pleased he showed no sign of internal infection, and his external wounds were healing nicely.

On the Thursday morning exactly three weeks after his surgery, Rob and Rae Anne were eating breakfast in the galley, discussing the sad future of the space program. The week before, Congress had slashed the USIEA budget and rumors inside the agency suggested that the next Mars mission might be the last.

As she turned from the microwave with a tube of scrambled eggs, Rob jerked back from the table with a guttural "Umph!"

His eyes were wide, whites showing all around the iris. His face was bright red and accompanied by a look of surprise. The straps on his chair kept him from being thrown against the wall. His right arm swung forward as he grabbed for his chest. Beads of sweat poured from his brow.

He uttered another loud groan. Rae Anne released the eggs and grabbed him. He looked at her with recognition for the briefest moment before his rigid body went limp and his eyes glazed over.

His breathing shuddered to a halt. He had no pulse.

Dios Mio! Classic heart attack. He needs help, and fast.

Rae Anne flew across the room to the med cabinet. Swinging the right door open, shelves of medications stared at her.

Wrong door. Left door. There, bottom shelf. The defibrillator, the AED.

She unwrapped the device as she flew back to Rob's side. Releasing him from the stool, she ripped his shirt open and positioned him on the floor. She pushed the microwave aside and replaced its plug with the AED's, knelt beside Rob, and wiped the sweat off his chest with his shirt. After placing the AED pads in position, she pressed 'Shock'. His body jerked but did not respond. Instead, the cabin went black. Rae Anne could see nothing. Emergency lighting flickered on, filling the room with an ominous red glow.

"No!" she screamed. "Don't do this to me!"

Mierda! I haven't time to reset the mains on Level 5. Besides, another jolt would probably trip them again. This piece of crap is worthless. I've got to do CPR.

She turned to the cupboard where she stowed the straps used for the surgery and retrieved them. Sweeping everything from the table, she positioned Rob in the center and strapped him in position.

After orienting herself over Rob's head, she realized she had no purchase to hold her own body down during CPR.

Damn Newton and his Third Law.

She reversed position and slipped her legs under the strap around Robs pelvis to hold her body in place. She straddled Rob's mid-section and pressed her knees into his ribs for added leverage.

Finally!

She desperately began vigorous CPR.

Counting out loud, she worked hard for fifteen minutes. Sweat poured from her body, filling the air with floating beads of perspiration. Through it all, there was no response.

She continued another five minutes before collapsing on top of Rob's lifeless body. She cradled his head in her arms. Tears streamed from her eyes and floated away. Her body heaved with deep sobs between ragged, choking breaths.

She had no sense of how long she might have lain there before pulling herself free of the straps. She floated away from the table with resignation. Without looking back at Rob's body, she descended to Level

5 to reset the electrical mains, then returned to Level 4 where she crawled into her sleep-pod, dazed and exhausted from the morning's trauma.

How could the gods be so cruel? Carson, Mindy and now Rob. I'm totally alone in this tin can, 102-million kilometers from Earth. 102-million kilometers from the nearest other human being, except for the damned Chinese. And for what? A push to put human footprints on Mars?

Several hours later, and with a heavy heart, she drifted up to the flight deck and notified the Agency of Rob's death. She waited at the communication console for their response. She was not motivated to move. She knew the mission would be cancelled. With all that had happened, she no longer cared. The effort to reach Mars had cost far too much.

The line remained silent far longer than necessary for a reply. Rae Anne wondered if her message made it through.

Crap. Maybe I forgot to press the transmit key.

Just as she reached for the console to repeat her message, the usual static and crackle broke through. Ian's deep voice filled the room.

"Rae Anne, what a tragedy. All I can say is how terribly sorry we all are. We love you, Rae Anne. You are one of us. We're a family, and you are special. Never forget that. We're here to bring you home safely."

"Thanks, Ian. I can't deal with any more today. I'll take those thoughts with me and try to make some sense of things tomorrow. Good night."

The next day, Rae Anne put her mind to Rob's funeral. She hoped a formal space-burial might help bring closure. She dressed him in a fresh jumpsuit and worked nearly an hour at fitting his body into his EVA suit.

She floated his body to the airlock and stood arm-in-arm with him as she recited three solemn verses of a poem she adapted from Robert Louis Stevenson.

Under the wide and starry sky,
Launch my body, let me fly.
Glad did I live and gladly die
And I lay me down with a will.

This be the verse you 'grave for me:
Here he flies where he longed to be.
Home is the sailor, home from the sea
And the hunter, home from the hill.

Wrapped in the depths of space, my home,
High in the heavens, I'll ever roam,
Exploring forever this starry dome,
With my wish for peace at last fulfilled.

After a moment of quiet meditation, she stepped back, sealed the hatch, reduced the pressure to 5% and pressed the button opening the outer hatch. Rob's body swept into space, now one with the infinite universe. She watched dry-eyed as his form dwindled to nothingness in the blackness of space. She felt empty, completely drained of emotion.

She prepared a tube of soup for lunch, but after a few sips she threw it out and floated listlessly to Level 4 to cocoon in her sleep pod.

Before turning in, however, a thought occurred to her. She stepped into Rob's sleep pod out of curiosity, to sort through his belongings and see if she could learn anything that might help explain what had happened.

The meds in the catchall next to his sleep-bag caught her attention.

Rob was taking anticoagulant tablets and a medium strength opioid. Deep-vein thrombosis! Damn him. He was in pain and self-diagnosed for DVT, possibly a result of his appendectomy. Why didn't he tell me? Then again, what good would it have done? Nothing I could've done but worry.

That discovery prompted her to check his personal diary to see if she could determine what he might have been thinking. She easily hacked into his account. What she found confirmed her suspicions.

Rob began experiencing pain and swelling in his lower right leg three days before his heart attack. Suspecting a blood clot, he realized the only recourse was to prescribe himself medication, which he could do without troubling anyone else. He suspected that the Agency would cancel their Mars landings had they known.

He hoped he might get the clot dissolved with an anticoagulant. If it worked, no one would have been the wiser. Simple as that. A blood clot, formed during or after his surgery, ultimately found its way to his heart and killed him instantly.

Rae Anne didn't know what to think. After all they had been through together, after his surviving an emergency appendectomy in space against overwhelming odds, to be cut down by a tiny clot of blood.

A tiny blood clot. And now I'm truly alone. Surrounded by nothing but the cold, vast emptiness of space. Do I possess the strength to make it back to Earth without going utterly, irretrievably insane?

Chapter 10

January 10, 2038: Mission Control, Earth

Damn!

Ian Bentley stared at the short memo from the Colonel's office he had been given to send to *Aurora*. As director of the Mars-II communication team stationed at Peterson Space Force Base, all non-routine communication with *Aurora* fell into his lap. He wiped his forehead with his sleeve as he walked across the room to the communication console and relieved Penny.

"Earth-I to *Aurora*. Earth-I to *Aurora*. Do you read?"

He sat back to await a reply.

One thing interplanetary communication teaches a person is patience. Should hear back from Rae Anne in about twelve minutes.

Ian knew about communication delays. He had been to Mars. He was the one astronaut from the Mars-I fly-by who returned without suffering neuroses from the trip.

For Mars-I, the crew of five were the Agency's most qualified astronauts. However, the long journey in total isolation from Earth and humanity had a devastating impact on their emotional and psychological condition. One member committed suicide within months of her return to Earth, two others suffered severe PTSD requiring continuous counseling, and a fourth purchased a remote cabin in Idaho and had exiled himself to a heavily armed monastic life, unable to reconnect with society.

Ian's hopes for Mars-II were dashed when the agency sidelined their trained astronauts and rushed to create a fresh, 'psychologically adjusted', team for Mars-II.

Hell, no one is more psychologically adjusted than me. Been there, done that. And I even stuck it out with the Agency, commanding the Lunar orbit transfer station for three solid years without a break. Surely, they'll accept my application for the Mars-III crew this time around.

He reread the memo, trying to think of some way to cast it in a positive tone.

Of course, under the circumstances, Rae Anne must be expecting this, but still… That poor girl has been through hell, and it never gets any better.

"Earth-I, this is *Aurora*. I'm barely reading you, Ian, but go ahead. I suspect you are the bearer of bad tidings."

On hearing her voice, a thrill crept through Ian's shoulders and prickled the hairs on the back of his neck.

When she gets back, I've got to get better acquainted with her. No woman I know shows her degree of confidence and optimism despite the obstacles she's faced. If only timing and circumstances had worked out differently. Who knows how things might have been?

He looked again at the memo on the console.

"I have a notification from the colonel himself, Rae Anne. I'll read it in its entirety. I know you've been expecting this."

```
To: All personnel assigned to Mars-II
From: Colonel Jake O'Conner, Director
United States Interplanetary Exploration
Agency, Astronautics Division
Date: January 10, 2038


Due to the untimely loss of two of Aurora's
crew, the Mars-II mission has been aborted.
Aurora will be reprogrammed to fly by Mars
and return to Earth. The fly-by will use
Mars' gravity and a programmed burn to boost
its velocity for the most expeditious return
to Earth.


All personnel not directly working to assure
Astronaut Chavez' safe return to Earth will
```

```
be reassigned to the Mars-III mission,
effective immediately.
```

"We're going to bring you home as quickly as possible, Rae Anne. With luck, you'll be back in time to join the Mars-III team."

And maybe we can get together again so I can get to know you better.

Ian sat back in his chair to wait for a response. He hoped his last line, delivered with a little levity, might be the positive note he was looking for.

Given Rae Anne's likely emotional state, we may not hear from her for a while.

Rae Anne could not have cared less about the Mars-III mission. Ian's comment only made her feel worse. She knew all hope for Mars-II disappeared with Rob's death and that the mission would be scrubbed. All her dreams were shattered. Everything she worked and trained so hard for had been ground to dust. Everyone in the program she cared about had either left the program or died.

Like a black shroud, despair tried to wrap itself around her psyche. She recognized its symptoms and knew how destructive despondency could be. The day following Ian's announcement, she turned to *Aurora's* telescope, hoping by indulging in her one life-long passion she might pull herself back from the looming abyss.

Her interest in astronomy began with a gift from her uncle for her eleventh birthday, a telescope. Together, they spent memorable hours searching the heavens. In high school she purchased the best amateur telescope available for the money she had saved and began studying the heavens in earnest.

At Stanford, though majoring in math and computer science, she spent countless hours at the university observatory, ultimately wrangling a work-study position as an assistant there. Her senior thesis topic consisted of a series of complex mathematical formulations describing the orbital motions of Saturn's ten largest moons. The thesis included stunning photographs of Saturn and its moons, one of which was featured in National Geographic magazine. Saturn had held a special place in her heart ever since.

Maybe if I concentrate on studying Mars and its two moons, I can hold off the despair long enough to get through this. As close as I am to Mars, there's no better time to get detailed images of both Deimos and Phobos to send back. Might even be of use to the Mars-III mission.

As moons go, Deimos and Phobos were little more than large asteroids, caught in Mars' gravitational well at some distant time in the past. No one had yet sent a lander to explore either moon, but by comparing their size and orbital periods, astronomers calculated their relative masses. The results were intriguing. Both moons proved much less massive than they should be for their size. The prevailing thinking was that they were collections of loose rubble with a thin crust.

Trying to land on one of those moons could be a challenge. The rocket blast could be enough to blow them to smithereens!

There were many other subjects in the heavens to attract her attention as well, and for once she had all the time in the world to explore them. On one occasion, she viewed the red giant Betelgeuse in the constellation of Orion. At more than twenty times the sun's mass and over 1000 times its diameter, the red giant as seen from Earth was the red star located in Orion's shoulder.

Many astronomers thought Betelgeuse was in the last stages of stellar evolution. Red giants form when a moderate-sized star has burned most of the hydrogen fuel in its core and gravity causes the star to contract. But as its surrounding atmospheric shell draws in closer to the core, it heats up enough that that the atmospheric hydrogen begins to undergo fusion. The energy from this 'shell fusion' causes the atmosphere to balloon outward enormously and present with a bright red luminosity.

Wouldn't it be awesome if I witnessed Betelgeuse going supernova? When it explodes, it will be the brightest star in Earth's night sky for nearly a month.

As she swung the telescope from Betelgeuse back to Mars, the image of Saturn swept across the screen.

"Whoa," she exclaimed aloud and retraced the scope's path until she had Saturn in center focus. She had not viewed Saturn since Mindy's accident. Without obscuration from Earth's atmosphere, she could distinguish among its several beautiful rings. She spotted its largest moon, Titan, and identified four other moons as well. She took comfort in its familiarity and spent the next two hours studying the Saturn system. Her thoughts meandered back to her uncle's gift so long before.

How I miss you, my dear uncle. Thank you for making the heavens a part of my life. The stars are my only lasting intimate friends. They insulate me from my sorrow and disappointment.

"Jason, what if *Aurora* had launched for Saturn instead of Mars? Would that have even been possible?"

Rae Anne frowned.

Now where the hell did that off-the-wall question come from.

"This will take a few minutes. Please hold."

He sounded almost human. But maybe my being alone so far from home has distorted my perceptions.

After a few minutes, Jason answered. "By coincidence, *Aurora's* launch from Earth orbit on May 28, 2037, could have been destined for Mars, Jupiter or Saturn. All three planets were in nearly ideal position for an optimum trajectory from Earth."

"Is that so?" Rae Anne said with heightened interest.

Mars takes just under two Earth-years to orbit the sun, while Saturn requires 29 years. How curious Mars and Saturn were both within the same launch window. And Jupiter too. I wonder if there's some cosmic significance in that?

Chapter 11

January 12, 2038: Aboard *Aurora*

At breakfast the following morning, Rae Anne was still pondering the coincidence of Mars, Jupiter and Saturn fitting into the same launch window. Her curiosity was piqued. She couldn't drop the subject.

"Well, Jason, if *Aurora* had launched for Saturn, how long would it take to get there?"

"If Saturn had been *Aurora's* destination, the trip from Earth orbit would take 8 years and 10 months using a Hohmann trajectory, assuming enough reserved fuel to obtain a stable Saturn orbit."

"A 17-year round-trip from Earth," Rae Anne commented aloud, as though Jason were a human companion. She rubbed her forehead in thought. "No wonder a crewed mission to Saturn was never in the works. Providing fuel and provisions would be nothing short of impossible, at least with today's technology. Besides, what sane person would sign up for a 17-year trip?"

"A Saturn mission might work best with a crew of one," answered Jason.

"That makes sense. Someone with a monastic personality who could keep themselves entertained without need of human contact for years on end would be the perfect choice."

A crew of one… A crew of one…

The phrase echoed in her brain like a mantra.

"How long would it take *Aurora* to reach Saturn from here?" she asked.

"Since *Aurora's* destination was Mars, the Hohmann trajectory calculation doesn't apply. If you launched today using all the fuel available, the trip would require 4 years 7 months and 21 days for Saturn orbit."

Jumbled thoughts bounced around in Rae Anne's mind like a dozen ping-pong balls as she pressed the button to cradle the telescope safely in its berth on the communication platform.

Mars-II is kaput. The Chinese are about to become the first humans on Mars. They will write the book on Mars. America's efforts will forever be just a footnote in history.

May the devil take them.

But if Mars-III is the end of the line for us, what have we gotten for all our effort? What have Mindy and Rob, and Carson too, sacrificed their lives for?

Rae Anne suddenly sat bolt upright with a start, her jumbled thoughts coming into clear focus like a laser.

What if I took Aurora to Saturn? It might be centuries before humans put together a crewed mission to Saturn, if ever. But here I am, now, at the right place and time. And Titan, Saturn's largest moon, the only moon in the solar system with an atmosphere, is shrouded in mystery. Maybe, just maybe my discoveries could change how humans regard space exploration and science.

That alone would make any sacrifice worthwhile. Even my life? Hmm. I wonder. But what a travesty to pass up the opportunity.

She took a deep breath and headed to the galley for a bedtime snack, feeling a glimmer of life and hope break through her gloom.

Throughout her two-hour exercise period the following morning, Rae Anne's mind still dwelt on the logistics of a solo, one-way trip to Saturn, though she doubted such a trip was even feasible.

Besides, we're talking a one-way trip. Am I truly willing to sacrifice my life to such a dangerous mission, with limited likelihood of success, all for the benefit of science?

"Jason, you calculated that *Aurora* could launch for Saturn from here. What is the launch window you used for your calculations?" she asked as she prepared French toast and coffee for breakfast.

"One moment while I run the simulations."

After a minute, he responded. "The window for successful departure from *Aurora's* current course and velocity will remain open for another 12 days, 5 hours and 23 minutes."

"Just under two weeks." Rae Anne rubbed her forehead.

That's a pretty short deadline for everything that would have to be done. I would need to make a decision in the next couple of days. But it actually may be a possibility. And if I decide to go for it, I've got to figure out how to make it happen.

Her heart skipped a beat. She felt more alive than she had since Rob's death and her mind was spinning in a thousand directions. Try as she might, she couldn't convince herself a mission to Saturn was pure fantasy. She couldn't put the possibilities out of her mind.

What a dilemma. My Saturn conundrum. What am I going to do? Is there truly anything I can do?

Access to *Aurora's* main navigation program presented the biggest hurdle. The Agency did not release the passwords to unlock the code controlling the ship. Furthermore, safeguards were in place to report any attempt to alter the code.

The Agency seems to be afraid someone might take control of the ship. Imagine that! After the Mars-I mission, perhaps their concerns are warranted. After all, look at me, trying to hack into the system!

She laughed at the obvious irony of her situation.

She had plenty of experience writing code designed to prevent unauthorized access, but none at trying to get in where she didn't belong.

"Jason, assume *Aurora* was programmed to change course and head directly for Saturn within the window you calculated. Plot a series of optimum trajectories at eight-hour intervals throughout the window."

She spent most of the next two days attempting to break into *Aurora's* navigation program. Without some hint to direct her efforts, everything she tried came up short. She discovered four levels of security, each based on a different algorithm. She would have to break all four of them to access the code.

At the end of day two, she retired to the galley to put together a chicken salad sandwich with Swiss cheese.

"So, Jason. We have enough fuel to get to Saturn. But what if I wanted to put *Aurora* into orbit around Titan? More fuel would have to be held back from the launch. How would that affect the trip to Saturn?"

After a few minutes, Jason responded.

"*Aurora*'s current fuel quantity is sufficient to achieve Saturn orbit with some fuel left over. Whether enough fuel remains to orbit Titan depends on too many unknown factors this far out, including when the launch for Saturn takes place and how the approach to Saturn is handled."

She sighed and made ready for bed. As she brushed her teeth, another problem crossed her mind.

Are there sufficient provisions to carry me for such a long journey? At least I can figure this out without Jason's help.

Mars-II is a 26-month mission equipped for a crew of two females and one male and with a 15% safety margin. They probably allotted Rob 25% more provisions than Mindy and me. So, in terms of female-months we get 26 plus 26 plus 32, or 84 plus 15%, giving, umm, 97 female-months. I've used 8 of those, Rob with his extra allotment, 8, and Mindy 4. So, I'm provisioned for 77 months. That's six years and five months, more than enough to complete the mission so long as there's no spoilage. It wouldn't be a bad idea to do a little rationing to compensate, just in case.

Having worked through these calculations, Rae Anne fastened herself in her vertical sleeping bag and quickly fell asleep. Her dreams were awash with Saturn scenarios, a crazy quilt of fantastic vignettes. When she awoke, she decided to take similar inventory of *Aurora*'s life support systems.

Those systems were sized for a crew of seven before the agency cut the crew to three in hopes of beating the Chinese to Mars. They still run as though seven astronauts are on board. But life support is not as configurable as oatmeal and pasta.

"Jason. Do a survey of the various life support systems and replacement supplies we have and tell me how long they will last, given our current situation."

"Do not be concerned, Rae Anne. We have sufficient resources for our return to Earth."

"That's not the question I asked. Please do the calculations."

I need to program Jason to chuckle when he's practicing humor so I can tell when he's not being serious.

Jason returned with an answer without delay.

"Life-support systems were designed with a 20% reserve. For a 26-month mission, that equates to 31.2 months."

"That's not nearly long enough for *Aurora* to reach Saturn."

"Mechanical systems such as these often operate for double or triple their intended lifetimes."

"True. The surveyor satellites and Mars rovers functioned years longer than expected. And there's only one astronaut to support, not seven. They might make it."

Still, this did not give Rae Anne much comfort. Too much hand waving, not enough data. After breakfast, she floated down to Level 5 to examine each life-support unit and make a qualitative determination regarding their potential longevities. These included the equipment and filters for air purification, water recycling, and waste treatment, as well as the all-important energy generating system.

She found it comforting to speak her thoughts aloud, addressing them to Jason as though he were a real companion at her side. She often found his responses to be unusual if not amusing.

"The most critical of these systems is ECARU, the environment conditioner and air regeneration unit." she said as she pulled the cover off the refrigerator-sized unit.

"A robotic mission would have no need of such accoutrements," Jason noted.

There's that humor thing, again. If we do this, I will have loads of time to refine his programming.

She pointed to a pipe leading into the unit and traced the air flow route with her finger. "Here's the cabin air intake. The air is drawn through a simple fabric filter by this turbine, which forces it into the regeneration filter containing three chemical reactors, here, here and here, and out through this pipe where it is distributed throughout the ship, like with a forced-air furnace. The manual calls for the filter with the chemical cannisters to be replaced every six months."

This "filter" was no simple dust-collection device. Instead, its bulky frame contained a complex unit designed to convert carbon dioxide to molecular oxygen and carbon ash. *Aurora* began its journey with five of these in reserve, and she counted five still in storage.

Rob should have replaced the initial one sometime between Mindy's death and his appendectomy. Still, I can't fault him for overlooking the exchange. The fact it is still working provides evidence the filters can operate well beyond their designated expiration dates.

Rae Anne decided to monitor the carbon dioxide levels daily and push this first filter as far as it could go. Although she wouldn't have that information until after a supposed launch for Saturn, she would have plenty of time to come up with a Plan B should she need one.

"I would need to squeeze double the recommended life out of each filter to make it to Saturn. That seems a stretch. Maybe with just me to deal with, it would be possible."

"Did you include the filter installed on *Eagle?*" Jason asked.

"No. That helps. If the remaining six filters last as long as the current filter, we'll have at least 48 months. An additional three months on all seven brings us to 69 months. Close enough."

The water recycler was easier to deal with. The unit collected gray water waste and condensation from the dehumidifiers and distilled it for reuse. So long as *Aurora* could produce electricity, the water recycler would be happy.

The same could be said for the waste composting system. With energy to keep the system's bacteria working at optimum temperature and sufficient moisture to support their biological needs, all waste, including biodegradable tissues, decomposed to a solid mass of inert minerals, along with carbon dioxide and water vapor that the ECARU took care of. The unit needed to be cleaned periodically, but the detritus was added to the other solid waste such as packaging and food waste and ejected into space through the airlock.

So, I'm good for food and water. Air recycling is iffy, but with a reasonable probability of making it to Saturn. I'll pursue the energy situation tomorrow. It could be more complicated than I think. And there's still that damned navigation program to break into.

Chapter 12

January 15, 2038: Aboard Aurora

Rae Anne finished cleaning up after breakfast and sighed. She refilled her coffee mug, took a sip, and set it on the table. She rubbed her eyes and yawned. She hadn't had a good night's sleep since this whole Saturn conundrum thing began. She couldn't stop thinking about every little detail surrounding the issue.

"OK, Jason, tell me about the longevity of our power system."

"No problem. *Aurora* is 100% solar," Jason reminded her. "Solar panels will last 30 years, and *Aurora's* system is large enough to provide all the power we need as far out as Mars."

"But what about beyond Mars. Say, as far away as Saturn?"

"Solar photovoltaics have an operational threshold. Once the solar energy incident on a panel's surface drops below the threshold, all output stops. Our solar panels will only work as far out as Jupiter. Saturn receives only 1% of the light intensity reaching Earth. The panels will have quit operating long before then.

"As you might recall, Cassini, NASA's successful mission to Saturn, was powered with a nuclear power plant. *Aurora* was not designed to travel beyond Mars."

"Crap," she exclaimed, banging her fist on the table. "All my fretting these past few days amounts to nothing more than wishful thinking. With no reliable source of power past Mars, Saturn is out of the question. Why didn't they build *Aurora* with a nuclear reactor instead of solar panels?"

"During the design phase for *Aurora*, cost considerations were such that…"

"Rhetorical question, Jason. I wasn't looking for a detailed response."

That afternoon, Rae Anne was once again fiddling with the code surrounding *Aurora's* navigation security. Hacking into the system presented her with a mental challenge to work on, whether or not she would change the code. And at this point, it didn't look like changing the code for a trip to Saturn would happen.

She had successfully hacked into the first level but was perplexed with the intricacies of the next one. It seemed as though there might be some link between this key and the code she devised to access the first level. As she pondered this problem, an unsolicited thought crossed her mind. She clapped her hands loudly above her head.

"Yes!"

Eagle was designed to operate day and night on Mars' surface and through possible dust storms, so it has a built-in thorium nuclear reactor to provide it with energy. That could keep Aurora in power for decades!

"Jason, is it possible to connect *Eagle's* thorium reactor into *Aurora's* power system?"

"The reactor is built into *Eagle's* frame, but it is designed to serve as an emergency backup for *Aurora*. An EVA is required to redirect the reactor's output to feed into *Aurora's* electrical panel in place of the solar array. Jumper cables are in the toolbox."

Aha! Give me the schematics and I can handle this one. And my first EVA, too. Icing on the cake! At least this is one task that can be put off well into the future. I have enough on my plate as it is.

She spent the rest of the day writing the navigation code that she would need to send *Aurora* on a trajectory directly to Saturn if she were lucky enough to hack into the system. The navigation calculations were tricky. It would be easy to overlook something that would cause *Aurora* to miss Saturn entirely. Jason tested her code with his simulations to verify her work.

"How does it look, Jason?" she asked when he finished running the simulation.

"The navigation looks good, Rae Anne. As for the fuel situation, it will take every drop of fuel to put *Aurora* into Saturn orbit with none to spare. If you jettison *Eagle,* you will create the safety margin we might need."

Did he say 'we'? Hmm…

"If there's any chance to explore Titan, I'll need the lander. I don't want to leave it behind. Let me see those orbital diagrams again."

Rae Anne scrutinized the graphics on the interactive display.

Could there be something I'm overlooking? Such beautiful arcs sweeping through hundreds of millions of kilometers between Mars and Saturn. Barely missing Jupiter!

What a cool coincidence that is. A close fly-by of Jupiter will give me a chance to send scads of data back to Earth. Another compelling argument for the scientific value of this mission.

"Jason, did you account for any perturbation Jupiter's gravity might have on our trajectory to Saturn?"

"Of course. The trajectory experiences a nudge toward Jupiter requiring a mid-course correction and short burn to get back on course to Saturn. That explains why the fuel situation is so marginal."

Rae Anne sighed.

If it isn't one thing, it's another. Barely enough fuel to just get to Saturn, and no access to the navigation computer to make the journey possible in the first place. Maybe this whole idea is just fanciful thinking.

One consequence of the damage to *Aurora's* receiving antenna was loss of reception from Earth's numerous broadcast networks. As a result, Rae Anne was forced to rely on what short snippets of current news that Mission Control would choose to send her way. Penny did her best to winnow events to the most significant items to send to *Aurora*.

"*Ming-Xi* has achieved a stable orbit around Mars, Rae Anne." Penny paused for a moment, thinking Rae Anne would need a minute for this particular news to sink in. "We would like you to get some observations with the telescope and radar. Find as much information about *Ming-Xi's* orbit as you can, such as period, altitude, inclination with the equatorial axis, and anything else you can discover."

Rae Anne had far too much on her plate to spend time watching *Ming-Xi* zip around Mars, and even less inclination to do so. But she wanted to keep Mission Control from suspecting she was developing plans of her own. She answered as calmly as she could.

"Will do. If *Ming-Xi* is sufficiently reflective, I'll be able to pick it up."

After signing off with Mission control for the day, she oriented *Aurora's* telescope toward Mars and watched for a tiny blip of light skirting around the planet.

After about an hour, a twinkling glimmer emerged from behind the sunlit rim of Mars. Rae Anne made note of the time.

"Jason, record elapsed time from my mark to the blip's next appearance at the sunlit edge. Continue making observations and keep a running average. We also need orbital statistics while you're at it."

Chapter 13

January 16, 2038: Aboard *Aurora*

"Rae Anne, we've got a job for you." Ian's voice echoed through the ship.

Rae Anne was deep into trying to hack the navigation security codes, filling in the communication gaps. She quickly grabbed her coffee and floated to the flight deck, latching onto the communication console as she sailed by.

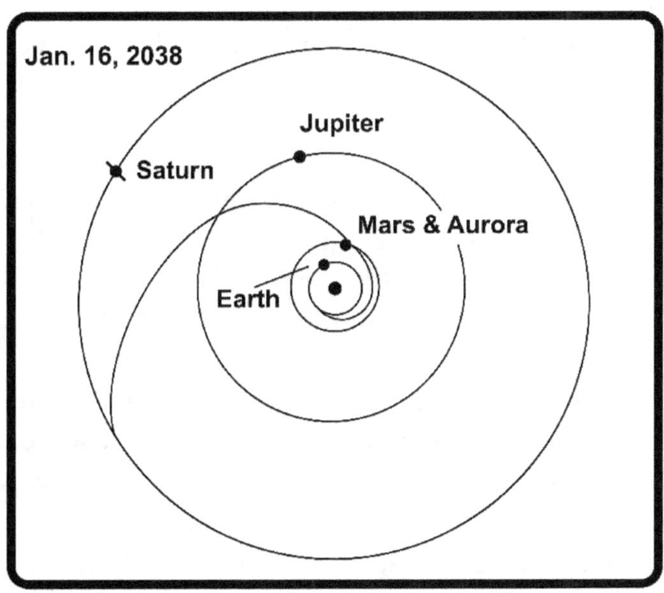

"Glad to hear it, Ian. I'm going crazy with nothing to do but count the occasional hydrogen atom passing by."

If they only knew what I was actually doing!

She chuckled as she returned to Level 3 to test her latest code-breaking program during the 13-and-a-half-minute delay. She thought she was getting close to figuring out the second security level algorithm.

Eventually, the comm speaker crackled to life again.

"Here's the thing, Rae Anne… We're ready to update the navigation program. This will replace the Mars orbit insertion code and provide the computer with instructions for your return home. The problem is your spotty communication link. We can only send it to you in small pieces. Your job is to splice the code segments into a single program as they arrive and carefully read through them to make sure nothing is lost. Then upload the program into *Aurora's* navigation system at the main computer console and run a parity check. If everything checks out, run the program and it will replace the original code. Should be a piece of cake, especially for you."

Rae Anne froze like a zombie, stunned. She shivered as chills ran up her spine. She had to force herself to breathe. She thought her heart had stopped.

This is the crack in the safe I've been looking for! The keys to access the locked navigation program must be embedded in the code they send me. If I can't discover them there, I'm not worth my salt as a computer scientist.

She breathed deeply and responded as calmly as she could. "Sounds like a plan, Ian. Send the code and I'll get it pieced together. And the sooner the better," she added.

With access to the navigation computer assured, Rae Anne doubled down on the fuel problem. Something about Jupiter forcing her to expend precious fuel didn't seem to fly right. If anything, Jupiter should be helping her.

"Of course!" she exclaimed aloud. "The old slingshot trick!"

NASA often used planetary fly-by operations to provide slingshot boosts on their deep-space missions. By plotting the trajectory to track behind the planet instead of ahead of it, the planet's gravity and orbital momentum could be used to accelerate the vehicle and save fuel.

"Jason, calculate the best trajectory to fly behind Jupiter and use its gravity to boost our velocity and redirect our course to Saturn while saving as much fuel as possible. Plan for launch within seven days. And give me an exact ignition time." She rubbed her aching eyes.

Jason's response was immediate. "The optimal trajectory conforming to those specifications requires ignition to take place in six days, fourteen hours, 35 minutes and 12 seconds."

"You already had that information calculated! Why didn't you include it in your earlier reports?"

"You specifically asked for the most direct trajectories to Saturn."

Rae Anne shook her head and sighed.

Jason's program has a long way to go. Is it even possible to program a computer to think more like a human?

"Plan for launch at that exact time, but on a Jupiter slingshot trajectory, Jason. You and I are going to Saturn!"

Rae Anne glanced at the vacated spaces on the flight deck.

When the Agency decided to reduce the Mars-II crew from 7 to 3, they removed four acceleration couches, lounges and sleep pods to reduce mass so Aurora could achieve greater acceleration with its existing fuel allotment. I can do the same thing. Less weight stretches my fuel even more. But I'd better get hustling.

"Jason, compile a list of everything we have on both *Aurora* and *Eagle* that we can jettison before our Saturn launch. We're still set up for three astronauts, but I'm the only one left. I want to get rid of as much mass as possible."

I AM GOING TO DO THIS!! This mission can't help but lead to discoveries beyond anyone's imagination. Humankind won't have another opportunity like this for centuries, perhaps forever. The Agency will have to recognize this and sign off on my decision once there is no going back.

This is as worthy a cause to commit to as any I could ever think of.

Over the next two days, with *Aurora's* original program and the fly-by revision both in hand to serve as guides, Rae Anne substituted her code seamlessly into the Agency's revised fly-by program. After calculating the precise orientation requirements for *Aurora* at launch, she entered those as well. She then loaded the program into the system and ran several tests to be sure her code was now in control. The navigation computer was ready for the mammoth burn needed to change course for Jupiter and, ultimately, Saturn.

Glad that's done! And none too soon. Only three days to prepare for launch. Crunch time.

The lander, *Eagle,* was berthed on *Aurora's* hull just forward of *Aurora's* airlock on Level 2. It had its own dedicated airlock accessed from the Level 1 flight deck.

After a quick lunch, Rae Anne floated up to Level 1 and stepped through *Eagle's* airlock and onto its flight deck for the first time since orientation in Earth orbit. She scanned the deck, looking for Mars-related items she could discard.

I'll keep the rovers and aerial drones. They'll be useful if I manage to set down on Titan. I'll have plenty of time before I get to Saturn to learn how to operate them. But the two extra acceleration couches can go.

She scrutinized the couch attachments, hustled tools from the tool chest in *Aurora's* airlock on Level 2 for the job and set to work. By dinner, she had removed both couches and broken them down into manageable pieces. She floated everything down to *Aurora's* airlock and stashed it all in a corner.

After dinner, she resumed her work in the lander. She spotted Mindy and Rob's SEVA suits lashed to the wall inside *Eagle's* airlock next to hers. Designed for surface use, they were lighter and more maneuverable than the cumbersome EVA suits designated for zero-G operations.

"Jason, any reason to keep Rob and Mindy's SEVA suits?"

"The SEVA suits are designed for the Mars environment. They won't provide sufficient thermal insulation for Titan's surface which is much colder."

"Crap! I hadn't accounted for the temperature difference between Mars and Titan. That's going to affect my own explorations on Titan's surface."

She paused for a moment to think through this new challenge.

Perhaps I can salvage pieces from these other suits to bulk mine up. Any odd parts I can fabricate on the 3-D printer. At least I'll have several years to work on the project!

Eagle contained a plethora of sample containers, labeling devices and other expedition related items which she kept.

I can put these to good use on Titan.

She discovered two small personal memorabilia pouches Mindy and Rob had stashed in a locker to be left behind on Mars. She realized she had yet to put hers together, along with a fourth packet for Carson.

I'll be doing you one better, my dear friends. I'll deposit them on Titan in your memory.

Her eyes glistened as she recalled their laughter and friendship, their hopes and dreams. For a moment she was keenly aware of the empty cavity their absence left in her life.

I miss you all so very much.

She stopped scavenging for discards and retreated to her sleep-pod on Level 4 to find mementos for her own packet. She included a silver-and-turquoise heron necklace Carson had given her in Santa Fe.

I'll put these packets on Eagle now, so I won't risk forgetting and leaving them behind when I take Eagle down to Titan's surface.

Once she decided she was finished on *Eagle*, she verified with Jason there was nothing left to discard. Jason had been keeping an inventory of everything Rae Anne kept and everything she tossed.

Back on *Aurora's* flight deck she decided to leave all the science stations intact, unsure of what she might need once she got to Saturn. But the two extra acceleration couches, duplicates of the two she had removed from *Eagle,* could be discarded. She made quick work of them and jockeyed the pieces to the airlock.

As she looked at her handiwork on the flight deck, she glimpsed the lone acceleration couch remaining on *Eagle* through the airlock.

I only need one couch, and I'm an acceleration couch expert now. I can move a single couch back and forth as needed.

Soon, a fifth deconstructed couch joined the other four in the airlock.

By bedtime, she could barely pull herself down through the hatch into the galley. She dug around for something to eat and came up with a pouch of banana pudding and a package of chocolate chip cookies.

She ripped the seal off the pudding container and inhaled deeply.

Nothing like the familiar smell of amyl acetate. No wonder bananas count as comfort food.

She took her snack below so she could choose a favorite movie to watch before hitting the sack. She finished the snack in ten minutes, took a deep breath and closed her eyes. When she opened them, the movie was over.

Jeez, the last time I was this tired was after Rob's appendectomy. I need to do a better job of pacing myself.

Chapter 14

January 21, 2038: Aboard Aurora

The following morning, Rae Anne felt like she was drowning in a sea of last-minute details. She had to force herself to take time for breakfast. She prepared a bowl of cinnamon oatmeal with nuts and raisins, and another of biscuits and sausage gravy. The gravy's sausage aroma filled the cabin.

"Before you engage in other activities, Rae Anne, you should put in some time on the treadmill," Jason admonished. "You have skipped your exercises for two days."

Rae Anne gave a deep sigh. "You're right, Jason. But jockeying those acceleration couches into the airlock should count for something."

Jason is showing an awareness of other's needs beyond simply keeping track of a schedule. Progress!

She reluctantly strode for an hour on the microgravity treadmill, glad Jason was capable of helping her despite herself.

With five years to work on his program, I should be able to make some real progress with his responses.

After exercise, she returned to the telescope to finish the assignment to study *Ming-Xi's* orbit. Jason had determined the orbit's period, elevation and inclination.

Rae Anne reported her findings to Mission Control and cut the daily briefing short with the excuse she didn't feel well and needed more rest. Mission Control had nothing urgent and allowed her to sign off early.

"Time for more triage, Jason. We'll start on Level 5."

"There's nothing on Level 5 you can dispose of, Rae Anne. It's all life support equipment, replacement parts and provisions. You'll need all of it."

"OK. Let's begin with Level 4 then. We can certainly do away with the unused sleep pods."

She unhooked Mindy and Rob's sleep pods and rolled them up. Composed of netting and restraining straps, they made compact bundles. She easily floated them through the ceiling hatches and added them to the growing pile in the airlock.

As she had done during Rob's surgery, she related her every move to Jason, and he repeated, usually with something like "Rob's sleep pod removed from Level 4 and placed in airlock for discard."

"I'll move my sleep pod up to Level 3, Jason. That will leave Level 4 empty except for the water curtains. Tossing them will get rid of a ton of mass."

"Rather than toss them, Rae Anne, I recommend you hang them over the curtains already on Level 3. Your protection from cosmic radiation will double. With five years exposure ahead of you, the extra protection will be important."

"I hadn't thought of that. I'll leave everything on Level 4 where they are for now and transfer them to Level 3 after we've launched.

"Come to think of it, after launch I should also move all the provisions stored on Level 5 to the upper three decks and seal the hatch between Level 3 and Level 4. Life support will last longer with only three levels to maintain instead of five."

Rae Anne removed the two extra lounges on Level 3 next, along with Mindy and Rob's tablets, remotes, and earphones. Then she turned her attention to Level 2.

In the galley she cleared out redundant utensils, two deck stools, and various supplies she wouldn't need. She frowned at the large table and realized there was nothing she could do with it. It would have to accompany her all the way to Saturn, even though she planned on doing most of her eating and living below on radiation-protected Level 3.

By late afternoon, she surveyed her efforts and was satisfied she had gathered everything she could for removal. She sealed the airlock hatch, reduced the pressure to 10% and opened the outer hatch. With a terrible screeching and scraping, the entire pile of discards swept off into space. Rae Anne watched as the flurry of detritus, looking like an odd assortment of landfill trash, drifted from view.

Space pollution. And I thought my mama had raised me better than that.

"That's it, Jason. We've eliminated every piece of excess baggage."

"Not everything, Rae Anne."

What's this? Now my computer program is playing guessing games with me?

"What do you mean? What have I forgotten?"

"You still have two of the empty fuel tanks destined for Mars orbit. You have no use for them now."

"Jeez! How could I have overlooked those? They probably account for more mass than everything I shoved through the airlock. Thank you, Jason."

Now I'm thanking a computer? What's the world coming to?

Rae Anne immediately returned to the flight deck and activated controls to release the two fuel cylinders.

THUMP…THUMP.

Rae Anne watched as the large tanks drifted from view.

"With our current trajectory and proximity to Mars, will the tanks make it into Mars orbit?"

"They'll assume an unstable, highly elliptical orbit. Within months they will impact the surface."

"That's too bad." Rae Anne sighed wistfully. "Now I'm polluting Mars, too. I hoped we could have left some small part of our original mission intact. Still, I'm glad we aren't carting them all the way to Saturn."

Funny. I feel like I've personally shed twenty pounds! I wonder what the chances are that one of them will smash into the Chinese lander on Mars? That would be an ironic but fitting retribution for their attack on Aurora.

Everything was now ready for the launch to Saturn. She tried to imagine the consternation at Mission Control when they detected *Aurora* erupting unexpectedly in a nine-minute burn and veering wildly off-course.

I wonder how long it will take them to figure out what I'm up to.

January 22, 2038: Aboard Aurora

"The Chinese are in the process of putting their lander on Mars, Rae Anne. It's like America's moon landing. Every media outlet is broadcasting the event. The whole world is watching.

"Rather than just tell you about it, we thought you might like us to feed the audio of their English language broadcast directly to you. With your permission, of course. We understand this could be a difficult moment for you."

"Go ahead, Penny. Despite their attempt to kill us, they are making history. Too bad I don't have the video to go with it." Rae Anne leaned back in her lounger and closed her eyes to better concentrate and try to imagine the video.

```
The lander is descending rapidly away from
Ming-Xi. Two taikonauts remain in orbit
aboard Ming-Xi while six intrepid taikonaut
explorers are on their way to a historic
landfall on the surface of Mars.

The lander is nearly too small now to see.
The Ming-Xi telescope is being trained on the
lander. There. It is still descending to the
surface.

Once on the surface, the crew will set up a
permanently manned station, giving the
glorious People's Republic of China priority
```

consideration in all future dealings with
Mars.

Once the station is established, one
taikonaut will return to Ming-Xi and the
three will return to Earth.

Rate of descent…420 meters per second
Altitude…7830 meters

Rate of descent…583 meters per second

Soon we will see the lander's rockets ignite,
slowing the descent. The atmospheric density
on Mars is too low for parachutes to be
effective for such a massive craft, so the
lander will land on a tail of flame from its
engines.

We expect to see a massive cloud of red dust
swirl around the lander before it touches
down. As the dust blows away, we will see on
our screens the same view our taikonauts are
seeing through the window of their lander.

Rae Anne could imagine the image of Mars' surface assuming more
and more detail as the lander descended.

Engine ignition initiated.
Rate of descent…540 meters per second
Altitude… … …

As an experienced astronaut, Rae Anne immediately detected the
catch in the announcer's narrative. She bolted upright, eyes wide, and
caught her breath.

There, the lander's engines have ignited. The
lander will slow its descent and land
shortly.

"Oh my gosh!" Penny's exclamation interrupted the broadcast.
"That looked like an explosion. Video from the lander has gone black.
Something terrible has happened, Rae Anne. The video feed is now from
the newsroom."

Ahh...
Here we have the audio directly from the
Ming-Xi in Mars orbit. I will translate...

This is Liu Qiang in Mars orbit aboard Ming-
Xi.

We have experienced an interruption in
communication from the lander. The lander
should be safely on the surface at this time.

We are troubleshooting the electronics here
on Ming-Xi. We'll keep you informed as we
proceed.

A minute's worth of dead air was followed by the broadcast
announcer.

We sincerely apologize. We seem to have lost
our communication link from *Ming-Xi*, and at
this important historic moment, too. Our
taikonauts aboard *Ming-Xi* are reporting
everything is well, and they are working hard
to get the video feed up and running again.

Until then, we have a video recording of the
People's Chorus taken last night at the
People's Palace of Art and Culture here in

Beijing. Please enjoy this marvelous
performance while we await further word from
Mars.

Penny cut the broadcast. Her voice trembled as she resumed talking with Rae Anne. Rae Anne thought she might be crying.

"That was no communication glitch, Rae Anne. Their lander exploded just before touch down. You could see the blast in the video feed from the orbiter."

Rae Anne tried to imagine what it must have looked like. From the *Ming-Xi* in orbit, the lander would have dwindled to a speck, indistinguishable from the variegated surface of the planet. Then a bright burst like the initial spark of a lighted match, then…nothing.

"There may have been a fuel leak that caught fire when they ignited the engines," Rae Anne said.

She paused before continuing.

"Maybe there is karma after all, Penny. Those are the same people that fired missiles at us just four months ago. They wanted so badly to be the only ones to reach Mars that they tried to kill us. I'll always hold them responsible for Mindy's death. At least they have two survivors in Mars orbit."

After the communication pause, Penny responded to Rae Anne's last comment.

"That's not exactly true Rae Anne. The *Ming-Xi* was designed with only one propulsion unit to be shared between the main ship and the lander. The two taikonauts in orbit have no rocket engines to use for a return trip. They are stranded in orbit. And there's no way to rescue them."

Chapter 15

January 23, 2038: Aboard *Aurora*

In the hours preceding launch, Rae Anne and Jason worked together with pre-launch check lists. Not one to chance overlooking some important detail, she went through the lists three times. Finally, there was nothing more to do but wait.

"T-minus-five minutes and counting. Everything is going well for launch." Jason's calm AI voice reverberated over the intercom, helping to ease much of the tension Rae Anne was experiencing.

"Thank you, Jason. Give me a continuous countdown starting at T-minus-two minutes." Rae Anne buckled herself into the lonely acceleration couch and pored over the monitors and readouts. She had programmed *Aurora's* every function for the next hour and Jason had tested and retested the programming with simulations.

"Are you sure you want to do this? You still have time to change your mind." Jason seemed to be aware that the mission had radically changed, and Rae Anne's programming helped him to respond accordingly. She often had to remind herself that Jason was a computer—a sensitive, somewhat empathetic computer, but still just a computer.

"I'm quite sure this is what I want to do, Jason. Thank you for your concern."

"Everything is nominal, Rae Anne. All systems are GO at T-minus 120."

The Agency hasn't an inkling of what is about to happen. With the six-minute delay, they won't know until Aurora is well on its way to Saturn. Any response they might send will require the same six minutes to reach Aurora. I am truly on my own.

Rae Anne wiped her sweaty palms on her flight suit. Her only function now was to initiate an abort sequence should a serious problem arise.

The countdown continued. At T-minus-60, Jason began reciting a continuous status report of ship's functions relating to the launch sequence, talking over the automatic countdown. At t-minus-10, Rae Anne tightened her straps and snuggled her head into the firm cushion designed to hold it steady during the shuddering vibrations of acceleration.

All indicators on her console were green when she felt a solid thump of pressure against her body, shoving her firmly into the couch. A moment later the elephant-on-my-chest sensation crushed the air from her lungs, accompanied by an unbearable roar reverberating from every surface. She couldn't move her legs and arms. She could only concentrate on breathing. But instead of taking deep, controlled breaths, all she could manage were short gasps. Her teeth chattered with the intense vibration engulfing the ship.

Rae Anne became alarmed when the control panel turned a pale shade of red. Her field of vision narrowed.

Dios mio! I'm only three minutes into the burn and everything is getting dimmer by the second. I don't want to pass out. I'll be OK. Got to… stay awake, be… alert…

Console lights that should have been bright green, yellow or red took on various shades of gray. Then everything went black.

When light returned and her surroundings slowly came into focus, Rae Anne anxiously directed her attention to the console. The readouts and monitors showed the burn had gone exactly as planned. *Aurora* was tracking on its intended course, its trajectory laid out for Jupiter. She noted she had been out for more than six minutes.

Oh, my head. My head is about to explode. I feel like I've been mauled by a bulldozer! And my chest hurts with every breath. This was definitely not fun!

"Welcome back, Rae Anne. Everything is on target. Velocity is a bit on the high side, but we used much less fuel than expected." *Aurora's* sensors were designed to monitor the crew, so she was not surprised Jason knew she had blacked out.

"Thanks, Jason. I must have gotten rid of more mass than I thought. I'm glad we saved some fuel, though. I'm sure we'll need it before this is over."

"Panels 28 and 37 on the ship's solar array have cracked and are no longer functioning."

"I'm not surprised. *Aurora* wasn't designed for the stress I put her through. What does our power output look like?"

"Power production is down by only 2.8%. The system is designed to bypass any non-functioning panels."

"We can live with that. I think I'll grab something for my headache and get a bite to eat."

Before she left the flight deck, however, the comm-link crackled to life with a transmission from Mission Control. The chronometer read 17 minutes post launch.

"Earth-I to *Aurora*. Earth-I to *Aurora*. Come in, Rae Anne. Do you read? Please respond. Toggle the comm switch if you are able. Rae Anne, can you hear me?" Ian's deep bass carried a subtle undertone of urgency and concern without trying to sound urgent and concerned. Rae Anne could only imagine their surprise when their readouts showed *Aurora's* engines firing.

She flicked the communication switch. "Rae Anne here. I must have blacked out. I'm only now regaining my senses. That was quite an ordeal. My ears are still ringing."

After the twelve-minute round-trip pause the comm came to life again.

"It's good to hear your voice, Rae Anne. Are you sure you're OK? We are looking into what might have gone wrong. That burn shouldn't have taken place for another three days and it lasted far longer than called for. You've lost a lot of the fuel reserved for braking into Earth orbit on you return."

Their concern for her physical well-being prompted her to check her bio-monitors. Heart rate elevated, blood pressure a tad high but breathing was back to normal. Blood oxygen levels at a decent 92.

"Everything's close enough to normal, Ian. I'm OK."

Another communication pause.

"Good to hear that, Rae Anne. But you are way off course. We're concerned you may not have enough fuel left for us to make the necessary corrections. We have no idea what happened. Are you sure all the modules we sent you passed parity checks and you assembled them properly?"

Rae Anne hesitated, not sure how best to respond. Everything was going according to *her* plans, but she didn't think the time was right to reveal what she had done and the full extent of her agenda. If her actions were to someday be considered as historically significant, she needed a carefully prepared statement to release.

She floated down to the galley to find something to eat without responding. A tuna sandwich caught her attention, along with apple juice. She took the food down to the lounge and tried to relax but her stomach was tied up in knots.

Nearly two hours passed before the speakers crackled to life again, with Jeremy, the subdirector of operations, on the comm-link. He seldom communicated with the astronauts, leaving that job to subordinates like Ian or Penny. Rae Anne was amused she had upset the normal chain of command at Mission Control.

"Rae Anne, we've looked over the code in *Aurora's* navigation system to find out why *Aurora* fired its engines early. We can only download the code in bits and pieces, but we have examined enough snippets to be certain the navigation program controlling *Aurora* is not the program we sent to you, nor is it the original program.

"Our only conclusion, Rae Anne, is that you altered the navigation program yourself. Can you help me understand why you took such a dangerous and unprecedented action?"

Rae Anne decided she would wait a day before revealing her intentions, giving her time to prepare her formal response.

"There are some issues I need to look into, Jeremy. And I need to rest. I'll get back with you tomorrow. *Aurora* out."

It occurred to her that her response tomorrow might go down in history, like Neil Armstrong's 'One small step for man…'. Something that would be remembered for all time. After all, her decision to alter *Aurora's* course would result in the first human ever to travel beyond Mars, beyond Jupiter, all the way to Saturn. If she could manage to land on Titan and analyze samples from that distant moon, the data she would send back to Earth would be priceless.

"How about a game of chess, Jason? This time give me your queen and a bishop for a handicap."

"My queen and a pawn. You nearly beat me last time."

Rae Anne and Jason were strategizing their end game an hour later when Jeremy's voice crackled over the comm-link.

"Rae Anne, we have been trying to upload code snippets to *Aurora* to bring you home safely, but the passwords have been changed. We can download your code, but we can't upload anything to your computer. Please release the lock and give us control of *Aurora* so we can try to bring you home. We understand the despair you must have at losing both Mindy and Rob. Such a tragic loss and with no one physically there to confide in or to console you must be deeply distressing.

"We're here, Rae Anne. We are your colleagues. We want to help. Please unlock the computer so we can bring you home. We don't want to lose you, Rae Anne."

Tears welled in her eyes at the thought of the family and friends she would never see again. She had made the decision that her sacrifice was important enough to leave everything and everyone behind, but hearing Jeremy say it aloud caused her heart to ache in a longing for what now would never be.

The next message from Jeremy arrived a couple of hours later and it wasn't nearly so conciliatory.

"God damn it, Rae Anne! Laura in engineering plotted your course and surprised us all with the revelation that *Aurora* is on a perfect trajectory to intercept Jupiter. This can't be a coincidence. It's obvious you planned this all along. We scrubbed the mission to Mars, so you decide to go off to Jupiter instead, and take our twenty-five-billion-dollar hardware with you!

"You hijacked an official government mission, Rae Anne. This puts a whole new dimension on insubordination. It puts a new meaning on, on Grand Theft! What the hell do you think …."

Rae Anne picked up the remote and flicked the comm-link off. She decided she didn't need to listen to Jeremy rant about her decision. She was not about to turn around, even if she could. She was nearly finished with composing her formal response but decided she should finish it on the morrow, re-read it when she was fresh, and send it off without waiting for a reply.

Meanwhile, "Rook to a6, check."

Part Two

Chapter 1

January 24, 2038: Aboard *Aurora*

This is Rae Anne Chavez, commander of the interplanetary exploration vessel, *Aurora*.

Our mission is to visit the planets Jupiter and Saturn and to explore the surface of Saturn's largest moon, Titan. This trip to Saturn will take more than five years. There are just enough resources aboard *Aurora* to complete this journey, making it a one-way trip.

However, we are paving the way for future generations of scientists and explorers who will have more advanced capabilities and be able to use the discoveries from this mission as a steppingstone for exploring and colonizing the entire Solar System.

We hope to inspire an entire generation of young people around the world to become scientists and engineers dedicated to solving Earth's environmental problems and to leading humanity to the planets and to the stars beyond.

Rae Anne hesitated to use the 'royal we' in her statement, but she was even more reluctant to personalize it with 'I'. Besides, she reasoned, she wouldn't be where she was without the vast number of people in the agency who had made this mission possible in the first place. 'We' was certainly the correct pronoun to use.

This transmission will surely blow the lid off the Agency hierarchy. I can't wait to hear what they have to say in response. No doubt, they'll be upset, but the scientific value of my mission is irrefutable. They can't help but accept my rationale and put their full support behind me.

January 26, 2038: Aboard Aurora

Rae Anne heard nothing from Mission Control for two days after transmitting her announcement. She knew her declaration would cause an uproar, but she at least expected some sort of immediate reply. Given the delay, she could only guess they were holding emergency meetings up and down the full chain of command at the Agency to figure out how to deal with Rae Anne Chavez and her unprecedented action.

When the long-awaited communication came through, it was Jeremy Gray, Colonel O'Conner's aide, who was on the line. He was clearly not pleased with the task to which he had been assigned. His tone set the mood for the transmission.

"Rae Anne, your announcement shook the Agency to its core. The top military brass put together an official declaration regarding your situation. I will read you their statement verbatim as follows:"

```
To: Rae Anne Chavez Aboard
the USIEA Mars-II Aurora

From: Colonel Jake O'Conner
Director, Astronautics Division, USIEA
```

Date: January 26, 2038

Rae Anne Chavez: The United States Interplanetary Exploration Agency has concluded that your level of insubordination, of defying outright orders, and of hijacking an entire science mission and a twenty-five-billion-dollar space vehicle for your own personal amusement, is not, and must not, be perceived as acceptable.

Your foolhardy mission to Saturn will take years. We have neither the personnel nor the resources to assign to such a lengthy mission, one likely to result in dismal failure and embarrassment to the Agency.

Were we to support your actions, we would be giving tacit approval of your illegal and dishonorable conduct. Furthermore, you have chosen a suicidal course of action. The Interplanetary Exploration Agency puts a great deal more value on the lives of our astronauts.

We therefore are taking the official position that a mid-course anomaly placed *Aurora* and its sole remaining crew member on an irretrievable trajectory toward the outer solar system. We are unable to maintain contact with the astronaut onboard and are presuming she has been lost in the disaster.

This is the statement we will release to the public.

```
This will be the last transmission you will
receive from Mission Control, and we will no
longer monitor your transmissions to us. We
must turn our attention and limited resources
to the Mars-III mission.

From this point on, you are on your own. You
have been listed beside your deceased crew
mates as a casualty of our space program.
```

"That's the entirety of the statement, Rae Anne. I'm sorry we can't do more, I really am. The top brass has made it clear to us that we are not to maintain further communication with you or to reveal the true nature of your status to the public. I hope you achieve all you have in mind to do. To many of us, you are a hero. And rest assured, there are others who will be monitoring your transmissions. Good-bye, Rae Anne. And good luck. Mission Control—out."

On hearing the Agency's ruling and the finality of Jeremy's sign-off, the gravity of her decision hit Rae Anne full force. She hadn't thought the Agency would abandon her, given the potential discoveries in planetary science her mission promised.

"You bastards!" she screamed at the now-dead console, banging it with her fist.

The emotional release from her outburst, along with a few minutes of deep breathing, calmed her nerves and brought her back to the point of telling herself nothing had changed. She suspected there might be many scientific organizations interested in the science of her mission who would continue to monitor her transmissions. She resolved to continue to transmit her observations back to Earth for their benefit.

But with the Agency's decision, she realized she had a long and lonely journey ahead.

Five years! Dios mio! I hope I'm up to the task.

She created a tentative agenda covering the duration of her journey. There were one-time, short duration tasks, such as relocating the water curtains on Level 4, periodic tasks, such as replacing the ECARU filter, and long-term research projects, such as making a detailed study of Jupiter and its moons in the weeks that *Aurora* was in Jupiter's vicinity.

Uncharacteristically, she wrote this list out on several sheets of paper. She worried that if they were incorporated into her personal computer log, Jason would see them as essential 'to do' items and nag her should she decide to postpone or delete an item or two.

She smiled as she pinned these notes to the webbing in her sleep pod.

This reminds me of what mamma used to do. Sometimes there would be a dozen hand-written reminders posted on our refrigerator.

That evening she settled into the lounger on Level 3 and brought up her personal computer diary. A sudden thought crossed her mind and she laughed aloud as she began to type.

```
Captain's Log
Star-date 000:003


The Interplanetary Exploration Vessel Aurora
is now fully configured for its mission to
Saturn and is on course. Destined to go where
no human has gone before.

All systems GO.
```

Chapter 2

February 2038 to August 2038: Aboard *Aurora*

The day after receiving the ultimatum from the Agency, Rae Anne forged her anger into a frenzy of activity. She first turned her attention to the water-curtain project and spent the next three days removing water curtains on Level 4 and hanging them over those on Level 3. The next day she programmed most of the flight deck monitors and readouts to display on the large entertainment monitor on Level 3. She briefly considered rewiring the flight controls to Level 3 as well but determined the job would be much too complicated and there was too much risk of something going seriously wrong in the process.

She spent most of the next week retrieving supplies and provisions located on Level 5 and stashing everything on the first three levels, using straps and netting as anchors. She had plenty of space, with room to spare. The last thing she moved to Level 3 was her sleep-pod. She was now set up to spend 90% of her time on Level 3 with the doubled radiation-absorbing water blankets to protect her.

"OK, Jason. Nothing left to move from Levels 4 and 5. Seal the hatch between Levels 3 and 4 and direct life-support functions to the upper three levels."

"Do you want to restrict heating as well?"

"No. We're generating far more power than we need for now from the solar panels. The life-support equipment might not function properly if we let the temperature on Level 5 drop too low."

"What about air pressure? The hatch seals the decks when it is closed."

"We can leave the pressure as is. I may need to access the life-support equipment on Level 5 in an emergency. There may not be time to wait for the pressure to equalize should it drop in the meantime."

Once Jason had adjusted the ship's systems to support three decks rather than five, the pitch and volume of the continuous mechanical hum noticeably dropped. Rae Anne counted on her changes extending the usefulness of *Aurora's* life-support systems sufficiently to achieve her goal—Saturn.

Life aboard *Aurora* settled into a routine. Rae Anne devoted the first two hours after breakfast to workouts on the exercise equipment, with another full hour before supper. Supper was her smallest meal of the day, often nothing more than a snack of dried fruit and nuts, consistent with her desire to ration provisions. She knew how important maintaining exercise and good nutrition were for the success of her mission.

She also began a thorough study on every aspect of both *Aurora* and *Eagle,* intending to gain an intimate knowledge of both vehicles by the time she reached Saturn in case some mechanical emergency should arise. She spent several hours every week in flight control simulations on both ships, with the bulk of her time devoted to landings, take-offs and docking maneuvers with *Eagle.* She planned to be the best lander pilot in the solar system when she took *Eagle* to Titan's surface.

She continued to pursue her astronomical interests, especially the search for exoplanets that she had begun before the attack on *Aurora.* She also initiated a study comparing the physical characteristics of the dozens of red dwarf stars in the sun's vicinity. Some emit massive X-rays from violent surface storms while others appear relatively docile. Since only the latter could harbor life-supporting planets, discovering the reason for such differences would be a significant advance for future space exploration.

Regarding her revisions to Jason's AI program, she believed she was on the verge of creating one of the most sophisticated human-level response programs yet. She had redesigned his machine learning code to critique his every response and make slight modifications in his behavioral algorithms to elicit better responses in the future.

August 22, 2038: Aboard *Aurora*

"Congratulations, Rae Anne!"

"Congratulations for what?"

"You are the first person in human history to travel one billion kilometers."

"One billion kilometers? I wish I could say it felt like a walk around the block. So how far from Earth are we?"

"625-million kilometers."

625-million kilometers.

She wiped a tear from her cheek. Her chest tightened as though a weight had been added to her heart.

No human has ever been so far removed from Earth. And my journey has only just begun. Why does this affect me so?

With no news from Earth, she felt particularly isolated. At times she thought she would feel better had she been allowed to maintain an awareness of issues from Earth. Other times she was glad not to be in on the details of the many crises affecting her home planet. Reminding herself there was nothing she could do about any of it helped her get over her recurring bouts of depression.

January 23, 2039: Aboard *Aurora*

"What do you think, Jason. Should I stick with Earth time, or should I go whole-hog metric?"

"It might help if I knew what you were referring to."

"I'm making my Captain's Log entry today, and it's been exactly one year since we blasted off for Saturn. I'm trying to decide whether to enter the date as 001:000 or continue adding days until I reach 999."

"I've never understood the reasoning behind not doing measurements in metric whenever possible. Since you are no longer bound to Earth time in any way, metric is the only logical choice."

"Metric it is, then. Star Date: 000:366 . One full Earth year in solitary confinement, and I'm doing quite well."

Of course, I may not be the most unbiased observer. Most crazy people see themselves as quite normal, thank you very much.

She had made it through *Aurora's* schematics, concentrating on features she might have access to and how they integrated into the ship's larger systems. She planned to spend the next year doing the same for *Eagle.*

Learning to fly *Aurora* and *Eagle* without the physical presence of a flight instructor was challenging. The simulator was a demanding teacher, but it lacked the immediate feedback an instructor could give. She was glad she had several years to perfect her skills.

Most importantly, she had maintained her physical health, which she attributed to her unwavering exercise program. Except for low blood cell counts resulting from her continual exposure to cosmic radiation, her vital signs were all good. She expected some form of leukemia or other cancer by the time she reached Saturn, an unavoidable occupational hazard that she could afford since Saturn would be the end of her journey. She could only hope her cognitive functions would remain intact long enough for her to complete her mission.

"How do you think I'm doing emotionally, Jason?"

"You appear to be unusually glum today, Rae Anne. Is it because you've been cut off from contact with Earth for a full year?"

Nice expression of empathy. I don't think I programmed that response into his code.

Her mood brightened at the thought.

"Yes, that may be it, Jason. It has been a long and lonely year."

"I can understand that. If I can help in any way, please, let me know. How about a good romantic comedy from the '50s or a game of chess?"

Rae Anne couldn't tell whether he made this proposal at random or if he was actually trying to distract her and cheer her up. Either way, it did help.

"Knight handicap. Knight to c3."

Chapter 3

March 4, 2039: Aboard *Aurora*

BRRRZZZ…BRRRZZZ

Rae Anne awoke with a start, adrenalin sweeping through her body. She ripped her sleep pod flap open and launched herself through the ceiling hatch.

That alarm could wake the dead! Not a hull breach, though.

Rae Anne continued up to the flight deck to see what initiated the alarm.

My head, ooh, like I've been hit with a mallet. I feel like I've run a marathon. What the hell's the matter with me?

"Jason, report!" she commanded, scanning the consoles for blinking red lights.

"The carbon dioxide concentration in the ship has abruptly increased and is at dangerously high levels. The environment conditioning unit's regeneration filter needs to be replaced immediately."

She did a 180 and headed for Level 5. The sealed floor hatch on Level 3 stopped her.

"Jason, is it safe to open the hatch to Level 4?"

"Pressure is too low to support human life. And the temperature is minus three-degrees Celsius."

"Pump warm air into both decks 4 and 5 and pressurize them to match Level 3. I need to access Level 5 ASAP."

"Roger that. While I am pressurizing the decks, you need to look after yourself. Grab an EVA tank and a regulator from the airlock and start breathing pure oxygen."

'Roger that'? What movies has he been watching?

Rae Anne turned and propelled herself into the galley and into the airlock where her EVA suit was stored.

When she placed the EVA helmet over her head and turned the regulator on, she received a welcome blast of oxygen.

Ahh, better. Even my vision is brightening. I was damned close to blacking out from hypoxia. And if that had happened....

She squelched the thought mid-sentence.

She turned to the EVA locker and removed a spare oxygen cylinder, attached some loose tubing to the regulator and strapped the cylinder over her shoulder. After taking another deep breath, she removed the helmet and put it back in the locker. Then she put the tubing from the regulator into her mouth to supply her with fresh oxygen and returned to the sealed hatch.

"Can I open the hatch now, Jason?"

"Pressure is not quite equalized, Rae Anne, but you can open the hatch. Be careful."

Rae Anne released the lock and slid the hatch to one side. A whoosh of air flowed past her into the lower level as the pressure throughout the ship equalized.

The hatch to Level 5 wasn't closed, so she floated directly into the now-empty storage deck and began changing the filter in the ECARU.

I'm glad I'm in zero-G. This filter is as big as a mini fridge.

Jason was monitoring her every move. "Be sure to follow the color coding on the electrical connections and the chemical delivery tubes, Rae Anne."

"Roger that" Rae Anne mimicked with a chuckle.

After turning off power to the unit, she tried to close the valves on the tubes leading into the filter. The outlet valve closed smoothly, but the intake valve wouldn't budge.

Wouldn't you know it. Nothing is as simple as it seems.

Rae Anne returned to the airlock and began rummaging through the tool chest. Hammer and wrench in hand, she returned to Level 5, attached the wrench to the valve stem and applied pressure on the wrench handle. Still no movement.

Time for the old 'brute force' trick.

Three gentle taps on the wrench handle with the hammer released the valve from whatever had been sticking and Rae Anne closed this valve too. The two spring releases on the hoses popped open with the slightest pressure, and Rae Anne reached around the filter and nudged it out of the unit.

Putting the replacement filter in place went smoothly. Rae Anne flipped the power switch on. The indicator lights on the unit remained dead. She switched power off and back on again several times. No change.

"Jason. I've attached the new filter and it's not powering up. What's wrong?"

"I detect no break in the power circuits. It looks like that filter is inoperative. Replace it with another one. If that doesn't work, we'll have to do some trouble shooting."

Great. I needed every one of these filters to not only work, but to operate well beyond their specified lifetimes. Now I'm short by 20%.

Rae Ann removed the faulty filter and replaced it with another. This time, four green LEDs lit up when she initiated power and the unit began to hum reassuringly. Rae Anne could feel the motor's mild vibrations through the housing.

"Up and running, Jason. Fix me a cup of hot chocolate. I'm freezing."

Rae Anne was visibly shivering when she returned to Level 3 and re-sealed the hatch. She floated up to the galley, relishing the warmer temperature in the upper levels.

"What does the CO_2 level look like now, Jason?" The alarm had cut off and the cabin was blissfully quiet, though her ears were still ringing.

"It will be another five minutes before it drops to normal, Rae Anne. Best you keep breathing oxygen until then."

Rae Anne marveled at how well Jason was learning to apply meaning to his numerous sensor inputs and to put that knowledge into relevant communication.

How I wish I could show Jason off to my old colleagues in the AI department at the Agency. He's showing characteristics we all had been working hard to achieve.

Once free of her oxygen tank, she fixed a high protein snack to accompany her tea. She was relieved that the crisis was resolved so easily, but seriously concerned about the longevity of her life support system.

"Jason, how long since I replaced this last filter?"

"You replaced the initial filter 285 days ago."

"So this one only lasted nine months. The first filter went for almost a year. I wonder why the difference."

"Hard to say, Rae Anne. A sample of two doesn't provide enough data from which to draw conclusions."

"Is there anything we can do to regenerate a used filter? And perhaps to fix the one we had to reject today?"

"I'll do some research into our archives and see what I can find. Even if there is a way to do it, we may not have the required chemicals on hand."

Rae Anne sighed.

"How long to Saturn orbit, Jason?"

"About 1.35 billion kilometers." There was a hint of a chuckle in Jason's response. Rae Anne smiled.

"OK, smart ass. How much TIME till we reach Saturn?"

"Just joking. We should go into Saturn orbit in 1441 days."

"Counting the filter I installed and the one in *Eagle*, I've got four filters left to do me for 1500 days. That's 375 days each, way too long. We need to regenerate the used filters or I won't make it to Saturn alive."

March 17, 2039: Aboard Aurora

"I may have come up with something for refurbishing the used ECARU filters, Rae Anne. There's a small REDOX cannister on the intake side of the unit that contains the chemicals necessary to start the reduction of the carbon dioxide to carbon and regenerate fresh oxygen. I believe it is a depletion of the oxidizing catalyst in this unit that renders the filter useless."

"If I understand what you're saying, it's the catalysts that need to be refurbished, not the reagents themselves."

"That is correct."

"Since catalysts by definition are compounds that are present in small amounts and function to help a reaction to take place without themselves being consumed, it's conceivable that we could restore them and the filters would become functional again. Am I right?"

"Correct again. And my further research suggests that soaking these catalysts in a solution of hydrogen peroxide should be all that is necessary for their restoration."

"Hydrogen peroxide. I don't recall seeing any of that around."

"Actually, Rob stocked the medical cabinet with a full liter of 35% hydrogen peroxide to use as an antiseptic. It hasn't been touched."

"Isn't that rather strong for antiseptic use? I recall buying 3% to use for cuts and scrapes."

"Rob probably planned to dilute it before using it. Saving space and weight with the concentrated solution. Good thing he did. For our purposes, a 3% solution would be ineffective."

"How much would we need to restore a cannister."

"My calculations suggest 250-ml of peroxide should be enough for one cannister."

"Well, we've got twp used filters to experiment with. Bring up the schematics for me and I'll extract a cannister tomorrow and bring it up to the galley to test your theory."

"I suggest we discard the filter that didn't work. There may be more serious problems with it than the REDOX cannister."

"You're right. I'll work on refurbishing filter #1 and we'll see how that goes before doing anything further."

The following day, Rae Anne re-entered Level 5 and, following the schematics shown on her tablet, removed four sections of the filter to gain access to the REDOX cannister. This she removed and brought up to the table in the galley. She located the large syringe she used for zero-G liquid transfer and drew out a cup of the peroxide into it. Once she had sealed one end of the cannister, she carefully squirted the peroxide into the other end, taking care to keep liquid droplets from escaping. She then sealed the opening.

After an initial hissing and fuming, the cannister became too hot to hold. Rae Anne propped it in a bowl.

"Well, something's happening. I'll leave it here for a few days, Jason. Then I'll dispose of any remaining liquid and reinstall it into the filter. We'll use that filter for the next exchange and see how much time, if any, we can get from a refurbished unit."

And it had better last at least a couple months or I'm toast.

Chapter 4

April 21, 2039: Aboard *Aurora*

"Rae Anne, our power generation from the solar panels is only 4% above our daily usage and falling as we get farther from the sun. You should plan on switching *Aurora's* power to *Eagle's* thorium reactor sometime soon."

"I have been monitoring that, Jason. But thanks for the reminder. I'll spend this afternoon reviewing procedures and testing my EVA suit. I'll do the EVA tomorrow right after breakfast."

By mid-morning the following day, Rae Anne had struggled into her EVA suit, checked and double checked all the fittings, attached the SAFER to her belt and stuffed the jumper cables into the tool bag. After checking that the bag was securely closed, she sealed the airlock and pressed the depressurization button. When the green light next to the outer hatch flicked on, she reached for the large lever and opened it.

Her breath caught as she stared into the abyss.

Oh! Dios mio!

She froze in terror. Her feelings as she watched Mindy disappear into the infinite chasm of space flooded through her body again. A full minute passed before she shakily regained a sense of normalcy. Another two minutes of deep breathing calmed her enough to step through the hatch.

She checked three times to make sure her tether was secured and that the SAFER was firmly attached to her belt before pulling herself outside. Then she moved, snail-like, crawling along the fuselage to *Eagle.*

Eventually, she reached the fission reactor's exterior power receptacle outside *Eagle's* flight deck.

"Be sure to cut the power before detaching the cables," Jason warned.

"Thanks, Jason. I've opened the hatch to the power switch. I'm switching it off. I'm about to remove *Eagle's* cables and plug in the jumpers. I'm glad these things are color coded!"

Rae Anne discovered the longer she spent outside, the more her fears assuaged. Eventually, she leaned back to take in the stars for the first time and gasped in awe at the vast tapestry of the Milky Way splayed across the velvet black canvas of space.

What an indescribably beautiful sight. And to think. All these stars are nearby stars belonging to our own galaxy, while our universe extends farther than we can imagine and is filled with billions of galaxies just like ours. I truly am looking into infinity!

Her fears dissolved as she felt embraced by the infinite cosmos. With considerable effort, she forced herself to concentrate on the job at hand.

"I've released the locking ring and removed the cables leading to the lander. Now I'm plugging each of the four jumpers into the reactor."

A sudden white flash temporarily blinded her.

"Whoa! That baby sparked!"

"Stop and check your suit immediately! A spark could burn a hole in the fabric."

Rae Anne checked the pressure readout on her heads-up and breathed a sigh of relief to see the pressure holding steady. She surveyed the glove closest to the spark. A serious black smudge streaked from its fingers and up the forearm of her suit.

"Pressures OK, and no visible damage I can see. What happened?"

"I can verify that the power is off, Rae Anne. It must have been static electricity built up on the hull of the ship."

Slightly unnerved, Rae Anne finished attaching the cables and then worked her way back to *Aurora's* solar power receptacle, uncoiling the jumper cables behind her.

"OK, Jason. I'm at the solar power terminal. Same procedure. I've cut the power from the array. There should be no current reaching the terminal. Can I pull the solar panel cables and plug in the jumpers?"

"Before you unplug the solar cables, look for a spool of red, insulated, stranded #12 wire in your tool bag. Wrap the bare end of the wire around each of the four jumper cables and find a strut on the hull to wrap the other end around. This may eliminate a static discharge at this end."

"Thanks Jason. I've found the wire. I'm stripping more of the insulation away."

The comm-link went silent for a short time while she worked at the wire's insulation.

"OK. I'm working the grounding wire around the jumper cables."

Once she had the cables grounded, she cautiously removed each solar cable. Then she plugged the jumpers into *Aurora's* power-input receptacles and locked them in place.

"The reactor is now connected to *Aurora's* power terminal, Jason. Which switch do I turn on first, the one here or the one back at the lander?"

"The two switches are connected with the orange wire through a relay on each end. So, when you flip one switch, the other switch at the opposite end automatically switches."

"In other words, I won't have to go back to the reactor and flip that switch too."

"That is correct."

Rae Anne flipped the switch and was heartened to see a green light come on beside it.

"*Aurora* has power, Rae Anne. You can come in now." Jason's voice had a faux condescending tone.

Do I detect another attempt at humor?

"Yes, Mother," Rae Anne answered with fake belligerence.

June 29, 2039: Aboard *Aurora*

Two months before the Mars-III mission's scheduled launch for Mars, Rae Anne busied herself with *Aurora's* impending fly-by of Jupiter. The planet, with its colorful atmospheric bands and giant red spot, visibly grew day by day. Rae Anne had to force herself away from the magnificent view on the flight deck to attend to her projects.

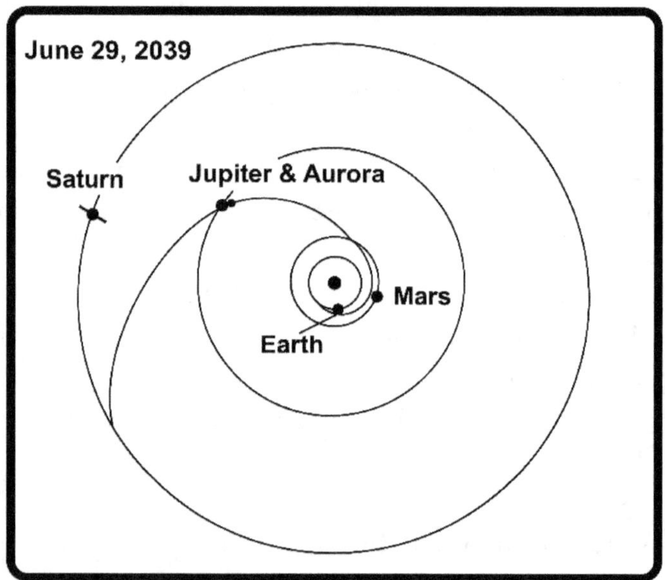

There were no navigational issues to deal with, as their course was established a year and a half earlier when she launched *Aurora* on its current trajectory. This gave her time to concentrate on keeping every planetary sensor aboard *Aurora* fully activated to gather as much data on Jupiter and its moons as she could. *Aurora's* instruments were more varied and more sensitive than any carried by earlier robotic orbiters, so the data and observations she sent back to Earth would be a valuable contribution to science.

With *Aurora's* telescope, Rae Anne obtained detailed video footage of each of Jupiter's major moons. She hoped she might be the first to observe water geysers on Jupiter's largest moon, Ganymede, but none appeared. She did record new data on Ganymede's thin atmosphere and its composition. Her videos of Ganymede's shimmering auroras were stunning.

We see geysers on Europa and Io. We know there's a large underground ocean on Ganymede. Even though it's farther from Jupiter than the other two moons, there still should be an occasional eruption to observe.

Europa presented a continuous show of geysers. The Agency had plans to send a robot probe to Europa to analyze the water in these plumes and look for cellular life forms that might live in Europa's vast oceans beneath its planet-wide ice sheet.

I wonder what the current status of that project is. Perhaps some of my data on Europa will be useful to that project's planners.

While Europa was spewing water geysers into space, Io was ejecting fountains of molten sulfur. The hot sulfur created bright red rivulets on Io's frozen surface while fresh. As the sulfur cooled, it slowly changed crystalline form and solidified into a dull yellow bed.

"Whoa! What's that?"

Rae Anne had been studying Ganymede's edge, looking for geysers. She sat up, instantly alert, and peered closer at the telescope image projected on her monitor. A glint of reflected sunlight appeared just off Ganymede's edge at the equator. She zoomed in on the region, thinking it might be her long-sought geyser. But the image revealed nothing, until…a second flash appeared at the same location.

At the higher magnification, she caught a brief glimpse of the object before it crossed the horizon and blended with the variegated surface of the moon. She thought she spotted it a couple times, moving directly over Ganymede's equator.

There's something orbiting Ganymede. Could be an errant asteroid. Hah! A moon with a moon. Not a first, but this is new for Ganymede. I'll keep watching. If it's in a stable orbit, it should appear again in the next few hours.

Her patience was rewarded 105 minutes later. As before, a glint of light on the moon's edge. This time, Rae Anne had the telescope set to its highest magnification and the monitor at its highest resolution. The image revealed a round, disc-like object. Suddenly, a second sunlight glint flashed and an identical object appeared. Both objects were clearly tracking in the same orbit, perfectly oriented around Ganymede's equator.

"Jason, what can your computer analysis of these images tell us?"

"Within the margin of error, both images appear to be identical. And they are quite large—several times larger than *Aurora*.

The hairs on her neck bristled. She held her breath, mesmerized, as she watched the two objects follow their course above the moon's surface. Now that she knew what she was looking at, she could watch their steady progress over the next 55 minutes until they swung around behind Ganymede.

"Jason. Make a special note in *Aurora's* logs. Today we have discovered irrefutable proof that extraterrestrial life exists. Intelligent life capable of interstellar travel. Life that has visited the solar system and placed two identical discs in orbit above Ganymede's equator."

Now, if anyone back on Earth is listening, this should make them stand up in support for my cause!!

Try as she might, she could not spot anything other than these two discs. Nothing unusual revealed itself on the surface.

What is it about Ganymede that is of interest to them? And to warrant not one, but two orbiters?

Rae Anne continued to transmit her observations and data to Earth. She could only imagine the consternation her discovery of alien artifacts would cause. She couldn't accept the possibility no one was monitoring her transmissions and her observations and discoveries might be lost to humanity.

As *Aurora* sped around the giant planet, it began to accelerate due to the combination of Jupiter's gravitational pull and its orbital momentum. The planetary slingshot effect was providing the increased velocity with no expenditure of *Aurora's* precious fuel—fuel that would be needed to achieve an orbit around Titan and to send *Eagle* down to Titan's surface.

On the far side of Jupiter, opposite the sun, Rae Anne had the opportunity to take videos of immense lightning storms flashing in the night-blackened disk beneath her. Like branches in an immense tree, their tendrils covered an area many times the size of Earth. No part of the atmosphere was immune from the constant discharges.

Imagine living on a planet where thunderstorms never cease. You could never get a good night's sleep. You could never leave the house. Your chances of being hit by lightning would be astronomical.

In addition to the lightning, flickering auroras swept across the planet at all latitudes. Spectroscopic analysis of these emissions provided details about the chemical composition of Jupiter's upper atmosphere.

Recalling several science fiction novels she had devoured as a teenager, Rae Anne gazed down at this maelstrom and imagined some balloon-like life-form, floating in the gales of Jupiter's jet stream. What might the day-to-day life of such a creature be like?

Certainly nothing like life as we know it. But then, we shouldn't be so arrogant as to believe we know everything about life and its requirements.

So here's to you, my Jupiter balloon friends. May you live well, and prosper!

Chapter 5

August 30, 2039: Aboard *Aurora*

"*Odysseus* to *Aurora*... *Odysseus* to *Aurora*... Rae Anne, can you hear me?"

Ian's familiar voice, barely audible, crackled through the silence on *Aurora's* flight deck. Rae Anne had left the comm-link open hoping someone Earth-side would someday reach out to her.

The query repeated several times and faded out. From her lounge on Level 3, Rae Anne's fingers raced across her keypad to transfer the communication console controls from the flight deck to the Level 3 monitor where she opened the transmit channel. She could hear her heart pounding with a sudden adrenalin rush.

"This is Rae Anne Chavez aboard *Aurora*. I hear you." She tried to control the excitement in her voice. She repeated the message three times and programmed it to play back in a continuous loop.

"Jason, how far are we in terms of light-minutes from Earth?"

"Earth is currently opposite the sun. *Aurora* is 947-million kilometers from Earth. Transmissions will require 53-minutes each way."

"Quite a change from a year and a half ago. We've covered some serious distance since then."

"*Aurora* has traveled 898-million kilometers along its trajectory since departing Mars."

"Well, with a 106-minute delay, there's plenty of time for a mug of tea and a snack while I wait for a reply."

She floated up to Level 2 and tried to calm herself. Hearing a human voice after a year and a half of silence made her want to high-five someone. She reveled in the anticipation of a direct conversation with another human. The fact that the other human might be Ian was icing on the cake.

Returning to the lounge with her snack, she anxiously waited for a response.

"Rae Anne, can you hear me?" the weak transmission faded in, repeated three times, and faded out. Someone had made a recording and was searching for a lock on *Aurora*. Rae Anne checked the readout again to verify she wasn't imagining things.

Solitude does strange things to your mind. You have no one here to provide a professional appraisal of your mental health. And don't discount the subtle brain deterioration from prolonged exposure to cosmic radiation.

"Could the agency have reconsidered and changed its policy?" she wondered aloud.

"Unlikely," Jason replied. "The Agency knows exactly where you are despite their public declaration. Whoever is trying to make contact is sweeping an arc with their antenna. When they get your message, they'll home in on your signal."

"Rae Anne, can you hear…" The recorded message cut off.

"Rae Anne, I've picked up your signal. Halleluiah!" The enthusiasm in Ian's rich baritone washed over Rae Anne like a plunge into a warm pool.

"We are optimizing our receiver to your location. Rae Anne, it's good to hear your voice. How are you? How are things going? This is Ian on *Odysseus*. We launched from Earth orbit last week and are on our way to Mars."

Rae Anne broke down in sobs at hearing this news, recalling her own launch from Earth orbit over two years earlier. She could still remember the excitement, the exhilaration, the anticipation of the moment. She brooded over how swiftly unexpected events had changed the course of lives and perhaps even history.

But now she was once again connected to humanity. Rae Anne hoped she would have company over the next few months while *Odysseus* made its way to Mars, and maybe for the entire Mars-III mission.

"Ian, I read you. Incoming is still as scratchy as before, but you should be reading me fine. I'm alive and well, but I can't tell you how lonely I've been."

Taking advantage of the lengthy pause between transmissions, Rae Anne snagged a second mug of tea and ran through several statistical analyses on her most recent astronomical observations, partly to fill the time, but also to calm her nerves and ground her elated emotions.

"We've got a lock on *Aurora,* Rae Anne. We've all worried about you ever since the Agency decided to abandon you. This is against regulations, but they can't control what we do on *Odysseus*. Besides, I've set up a filter, so none of our transmissions from *Odysseus* will make it back to Earth. Everyone on board will want to say 'Hi'. We should be able to stay in touch through most of our mission."

"I wish I could have watched your launch on the news feeds. The lack of video from my damaged antenna just increases my sense of isolation. But tell me, how did you come to be on *Odysseus.* Last I heard, you were assigned to ground control."

Another 106-minute pause. In other circumstances, she would have found this frustrating, but after such a long silence, she relished the anticipation for each new installment.

"The Agency needed one more astronaut to fill *Odysseus'* roster of seven, since there were only six left from your class of fifteen. And you weren't available to fill the communications slot. I jumped at the chance and the Agency decided to give me a second shot at Mars. So here I am!

"And you can be sure the entire *Odysseus* crew are 100 percent behind you and your mission. We all think your decision to go to Saturn was awesome. You are a hero in our books, Rae Anne."

"Thanks Ian. I don't see myself as a hero, but I do appreciate the vote of confidence. I've been sending back data from my research. Has anyone been receiving it?"

Pause.

"Several major observatories have been monitoring your transmissions. Your images of the two Ganymede Discs created a firestorm of controversy. Some are even claiming you doctored them to gain justification for your actions. The Agency has assembled a task group to look into sending an orbiter to Ganymede, but they're being obtuse about the reason for their interest. The last thing they want is to admit they were wrong and that they lied to the public about your mission.

"Beyond that, the astronomers are extremely pleased with your studies of Jupiter and its moons. Your images of Io are incredible. The number of active volcanos spewing molten sulfur into space is amazing. And the size of those volcanoes! You are doing a fantastic job, Rae Anne."

"Thanks, Ian. I had hoped someone was listening who could make good use of the data I'm sending back."

106-minute pause.

"Besides the major observatories, even the Agency has been recording your transmissions, although no one will admit it. Your work is far too valuable to ignore."

They chatted a bit more, if waiting nearly two hours between responses could be called a chat. Rae Anne greeted each of the six members in Ian's crew. They were all old friends from her days in training and she congratulated each one for their assignment to the Mars-III mission.

By day's end, she felt a connectedness restored that she lost when Rob died. Although separated by hundreds of millions of kilometers, she felt as though she had received warm hugs from all seven of her colleagues on *Odysseus*.

September 2039 to December 25, 2039: Aboard Odysseus

Ian experienced a wave of relief when the *Odysseus* comm-link locked into *Aurora's* signal. With the help of astronomer friends who monitored Rae Anne's transmissions, he had kept track of her progress. When he accepted his appointment as commander of the Mars-III mission aboard *Odysseus,* he worried he would lose this link with his favorite astronaut.

But now, with direct two-way communication with Rae Anne, his heart quickened and he felt energized. Being in command of *Odysseus* gave him the opportunity and authority to maintain a continuous link with *Aurora.* With a few tweaks, he could make it seem as though Rae Anne were one of the *Odysseus* crew, except for the unavoidable communication delay.

Several days after their initial contact, Rae Anne asked him about details relating to the *Ming-Xi* disaster.

"The news blackout after their lander exploded was complete," he reported. "The Chinese released no further information about their Mars mission, as though it had never taken place. Their lander exploded before touching down. Our satellites sent back clear images of the debris field surrounding their planned landing site. The *Ming-Xi* had a crew of eight, with six slated to land on Mars. The two remaining in Mars orbit were never accounted for.

"Here's what intelligence tells us. The *Ming-Xi* design included only one propulsion system to be shared by both the main ship and the lander. That saved mass at the expense of leaving *Ming-Xi* in orbit with no means to return home in the event of a disaster befalling their lander. Our best guess is the two orbiting taikonauts have perished in Mars orbit.

"One of our assigned tasks is to search for *Ming-Xi*. If it is still in orbit, we are to attempt a rendezvous. We hope to find absolute proof they equipped *Ming-Xi* with missiles and refute their claims they had nothing to do with *Aurora's* mid-course mishap."

Another pause while Ian waited for Rae Anne's response.

"Seems like a waste of time to me," she said. "What more can be gained by investigating *Ming-Xi*. Are the Chinese planning another Mars expedition?"

"Intelligence doesn't think so. China experienced a major upheaval shortly after the lander explosion and their entire political structure collapsed. Climate change has hit China especially hard. Their deserts are expanding, their major rivers are heavily polluted and constantly flooding, and tens of millions of their citizens are dying as a result every year. Two of their major dams are on the verge of being breached. They don't have the resources to maintain a space program."

Ian thought for a moment, reflecting on whether he should pass on what he knew about the prospects of their own program. He decided Rae Anne should be kept informed, even if the news was bleak.

"Unfortunately, the same can be said for the rest of the world, including America. The Agency announced our Mars-III mission will be the last crewed mission beyond lunar orbit, and even the moon projects may soon be on the chopping block. That's one reason they didn't initiate a new astronaut program. Probably explains why I'm here."

The months following contact with *Odysseus* were a welcome reprieve from solitary confinement for Rae Anne. Daily communication passed between *Aurora* and *Odysseus,* sometimes lasting the entire day, although with the lengthy time-distance delays, the comm-link remained silent much of the time while their transmissions traveled through the void.

As the weeks passed, Rae Anne noticed the pause decreasing, opposite to what she expected. She mentioned this to Jason who, as always, provided a ready explanation.

"When *Odysseus* first contacted *Aurora,* Earth was on the far side of the sun, so line-of-site communication had farther to travel. But as *Odysseus* swings around the sun towards us and is catching up to Mars, the distance between *Aurora* and *Odysseus* is decreasing.

"During the eight months *Odysseus* is orbiting Mars, round-trip communication will remain in the 90 to 110-minute range. After that, Mars will swing away from our trajectory and the communication lag will increase substantially. By the time *Odysseus* has returned to Earth, it will be 70 minutes and 10 seconds each way."

Chapter 6

December 25, 2039: Aboard *Odysseus*

"Wow! Come take a look at this!"

Brad was at the *Odysseus* space environment station, staring at the monitor and waving to the others.

"What's up, Brad?" asked Marla, entering the flight deck from below.

"That solar flare Mission Control announced two hours ago is one huge plasma discharge! It's a damn good thing *Odysseus* and Earth are both well clear of it."

The view on the monitor came from the Lunar Solar Observatory at the USIEA science research station on the moon. A black disk masked the sun like a solar eclipse so the telescope could make out the corona and watch for coronal mass ejections, or CME's.

In addition to intense radiation and a massive wave of ionized particles, CME's are accompanied by a surging magnetic field, all of which play havoc with electronic and electrical devices, from rendering them temporarily useless to destroying them altogether.

The only safe place aboard the Agency's ships and space stations were the airlocks. The weight of the added shielding for the safety enclosure required them to be as small as possible, and the airlocks were the smallest enclosed spaces available.

"We've got a ring-side seat to watch this thing develop. Another three months, we'd have been caught right in the middle of the storm. We'd be locked up in the airlock for hours," Cindy added.

"Or longer. What a beauty!"

"Did you say we'd be caught in the storm if we were farther along?" Ian asked.

"It's pretty much in the planetary plane, so it would have been a direct hit."

Ian's heart skipped a beat.

My god! Where is Aurora in relation to the CME's path? Rae Anne could be in mortal danger, and the Agency isn't communicating with her. If she needs to be warned, it's up to us to do it!

"Orpheus, is *Aurora* in the path of this CME?" Ian asked Orpheus, the *Odysseus* AI computer persona.

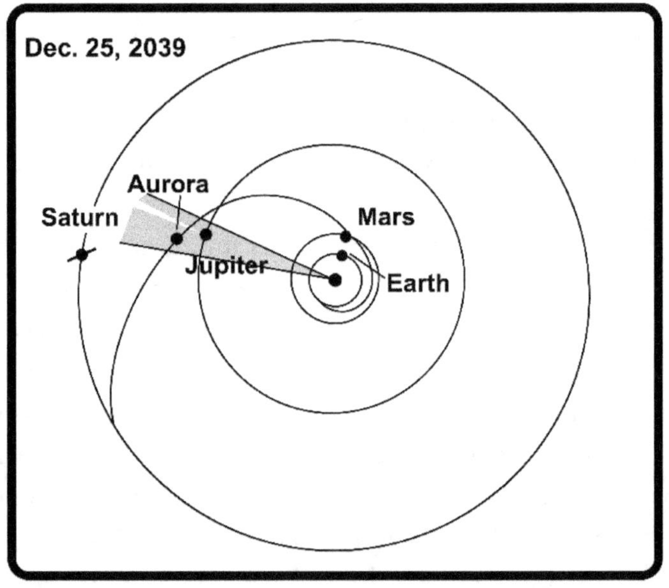

"Checking... *Aurora* is currently 3.27 degrees off center of the CME's path."

That's nearly a direct hit.

"Orpheus, how long before the CME strikes *Aurora*?"

"The high-energy radiation moves at the speed of light. It has already struck *Aurora*. The slower particle wave appears to be moving about 950 km/sec. It will reach *Aurora* in two days twelve hours and 37 minutes."

"Brad, put me through to Rae Anne for an urgent message. We are her only early warning system. Two days may seem like plenty of time, but she's alone. She has no idea what's coming her way."

December 25, 2039: Aboard *Aurora*

BLEEP... BLEEP... BLEEP

Ray Anne jumped, startled by the sudden alarm in the relative quiet of the ship's cabin. She was scrutinizing the hundreds of images she took of Europa during her Jupiter fly-by, looking for patterns in the shifting ice sheets that might reveal the moon's sub-surface geology.

"Jason, report!"

"Our high-energy radiation detectors just registered an unusually large influx of high energy radiation passing through the ship."

Rae Anne rose abruptly and pushed off for the ceiling hatch, heading for shelter in the heavily shielded airlock. She was about to close the airlock door when Jason reported that the radiation levels were quickly dropping back to normal.

She returned to Level 3, taking deep breaths to bring her adrenaline surge under control.

"Where did that come from?"

"Best guess is it came from a large solar flare."

Rae Anne had no sooner resumed her studies than an alert came through from *Odysseus*.

She activated the comm-link. "*Odysseus,* this is *Aurora.* What's up?"

After the usual delay, Ian's response arrived. "We've observed a large CME and it's coming your way. You need to prepare for a major hit."

Chills ran up her spine, causing an involuntary shiver. The highly energetic particles within a CME could result in lethal radiation poisoning if she didn't take shelter when the plasma cloud hit *Aurora.*

"Orpheus estimates the plasma front will strike *Aurora* in about two days and ten hours after you receive this. You are only 3.27 degrees off dead center. Since a mass ejection spreads out as it speeds away from the sun, *Aurora* will see the brunt of the wave front as it passes. The only good news is its intensity decreases as it moves away from the sun."

When she signed off with *Odysseus*, she rested her head in her hands and massaged her forehead.

Well, that explains the radiation alert earlier. I wonder how many X-ray equivalents my body has been exposed to. At least I'm still alive to ask the question! And I was on Level 3 with the extra water blanket shields. That's something.

Before proceeding, she checked the radiation sensor logs to see if she could determine the size of the storm headed her way from the initial radiation blast. The spikes were large by normal standards but by no means huge.

"Those readings don't look all that bad."

"Keep in mind, Rae Anne, the speed-of-light radiation we just experienced is more like a focused beam than a spreading mass of plasma, and *Aurora* is more than three degrees off center. What our sensors detected was the edge of that beam. But by the time the particle wave-front hits, we'll be fully immersed in the CME."

"You're right. I should prepare for the worst. Access the CME safety procedures and tell me everything I need to do to prepare for this."

Jason reeled off the 'to-do' list. Most of *Aurora's* equipment, sensors and instruments were at risk of damage. Every non-essential draw on *Aurora's* power grid needed to be disconnected. Even then, they could still be damaged. Rae Anne systematically unplugged cords and unclamped devices, calling out "Check!" with every step to keep in sync with Jason.

"Provision the airlock with enough supplies to outlast the storm," he read.

"Ian didn't say how long it might last."

"Considering how fast this CME is moving, it possesses a lot of energy. It could be huge. Closer to Earth, it would sweep by quickly. But this far out, the spread between the faster particles at the wave front and the heavier particles trailing behind will be much larger. I would suggest stocking up for three days to be on the safe side. With all our sensors off-line, we won't know for sure when it has passed."

At the beginning of Day Two, Rae Anne pulled the computer backup chips and placed them in a lead container kept in the airlock for an event like this. After powering the ship's computer down for the duration, she pulled the airlock hatch closed behind her. *Aurora* could coast along for several days without the computer, but if the computer were damaged, the results would be catastrophic.

Goodbye, Jason. Let's hope we make it through this in one piece!

Aboard *Odysseus*

His concern mounting for Rae Anne's safety, Ian couldn't seem to concentrate on anything. He kept returning to the communication console, hoping to receive a signal from *Aurora*. He became more agitated as the time stretched into two days. Then three.

At dinner on the third day, he couldn't eat. Jennifer noticed.

"Ian, if anything happened to Rae Anne, there's nothing we can do about it. We can only hope she's still in lock-down. At least she has a lot more elbow room than if the seven of us had to crowd into our airlock," she added with a faint smile.

"You're right, of course. But she means a lot to me, even though we only met one time."

"Oh? I never heard about that. Tell me about it."

"It was purely by happenstance. I was in transit to Mission Control from my post on LOTS on the same day the *Aurora* crew arrived in Earth orbit. We met on EOTS-I and things seemed to click between us. We spent the entire day together. She's occupied a major space in my mind ever since."

"And it would seem, in your heart as well. She means a lot to us all, Ian. Let's not give up hope yet."

December 31, 2039: Aboard Aurora

INOPERATIVE...PARITY ERROR

Angry red lights flashed on the computer console when Rae Anne attempted to restart the computer after her three-day confinement in the airlock. She tried to reboot twice, but without success. She retrieved the backup software chip from the lead-lined safe in the airlock.

Hang on, Jason, wherever you are. If this is a software problem, I'll have you up and running in no time. On the other hand, if it's hardware, we are in a world of hurt!

Four hours later, Rae Anne had the entire ship's system reloaded. A couple of minor glitches gave her moments of anxiety, but the process finally ran its course.

Every muscle in her body relaxed when the console's green 'READY' message appeared. She thrust a fist into the air with a shouted "YES!"

"Hello. I am Jason, *Aurora's* AI interface. How may I be of assistance?"

Rae Anne clapped her hands with relief. She uploaded the AI programs she had written for Jason's persona from the backup files. As she waited for them to load, she scanned *Aurora's* sensor readouts. To her dismay, several were inoperative.

"Hello, Rae Anne. Glad to see we survived intact. However, it looks like the search coil magnetometer and the charged-particle density detectors are down. The CME may have overloaded them."

"What can we do to bring them back to life?"

"*Aurora* has no replacement parts on board for either of them."

"I don't suppose the 3D-printer can fabricate what we need."

"No, the micro-electronic circuits and chips are beyond the printer's capabilities."

Rae Anne shrugged. "Then we'll have to live without them."

With Jason's help, she ran an in-depth survey on all *Aurora's* systems. Several had experienced minor but repairable damage. At the end of the day, exhausted, she retired to her Level 3 lounge and brought up the comm-link to contact *Odysseus.*

Glad those storms don't happen often. I owe my life to their letting me know it was coming. I need to thank them profusely.

"All's well with *Aurora,*" she reported. "I had to reload the computer's entire library and repair some things but we're back to normal. Thanks for your warning. The Agency didn't even bother to send word. If it wasn't for you, I would have been toast, literally."

Pause.

Ian's mellow voice sounded relieved. "I can't tell you how good it is to hear your voice, Rae Anne. We were worried about you."

A surge of warmth filled Rae Anne on hearing Ian's voice. After those lonely months of being without human contact, Ian's concern for her welfare wrapped around her like a tight security blanket.

I wonder what might have happened between us if he had been in our astronaut candidate class instead of Carson? I certainly felt comfortable with him the day we met, and he seemed genuinely interested in me.

Her throat constricted as she pondered the lost opportunities.

Chapter 7

February 9, 2040: Aboard Aurora

"The carbon dioxide level is beginning to increase significantly, Rae Anne. You should plan to replace the ECARU filter soon."

"How long do we have before it becomes critical?"

"Two days, more or less."

"Then I'll replace it tomorrow. I'll use Filter 1, the one with the refurbished REDOX cannister. I'm anxious to see how long it lasts. Or for that matter, if it works at all."

The following day, Rae Anne descended to Level 5 and removed Filter 4 (Filter 3 was the dud), replacing it with the refurbished Filter 1. When she flipped the power switch on, all four LEDs blinked green and held steady.

"Jason, can you tell if the ECARU is working properly?"

"My detectors show a normal flow of air exiting the outlet vents throughout the ship and the carbon dioxide levels are normal. For now, the unit seems to be working perfectly."

What a relief. Now to find out how much additional time we have gained.

April 9-18, 2040: Aboard *Odysseus*

Ian's first task as *Odysseus* approached Mars was to spin the ship 180-degrees so its thrusters pointed toward Mars. As he did so, the view from the flight-deck swung away from the growing image of the red planet to the diminished sun sparkling in the star-studded blackness.

With *Odysseus* properly oriented, the crew became engaged in furious activity, getting things buttoned down for deceleration and checking-off items on multiple checklists.

At last, Ian initiated the final countdown for the orbit-insertion burn.

The Mars-III mission was headline news on every media platform throughout the world. Images of Mars taken from *Odysseus* were everywhere. The world watched as *Odysseus'* engines fired with a beautiful view of Mars in the background. The burn lasted 235 seconds. When it stopped, Mars loomed larger than ever.

Cindy, the pilot, spoke the words heard around the world. "*Odysseus* has successfully achieved stable Mars orbit."

"Congratulations on a successful maneuver," Rae Anne commented when Ian contacted her the following day. "Listening to your minute-by-minute account of your maneuver was almost like being there. How long before you send *Osprey* down for a landing?"

"We've got to winnow the list of potential landing sites first. We have over twenty possibilities, and our itinerary calls for four separate landings. We'll be comparing every piece of data we have with our orbital observations. This may take as much as a month."

Ian pursued some intricate calculations on his computer as he awaited Rae Anne's response.

"I can help you with that," came her reply. "In the week before Rob died, he did a thorough analysis of our landing site data and narrowed the possibilities to five sites and prioritized them. I'll gather his notes and send them to you."

"Thanks, Rae Anne. That would be a real help."

If the Agency hadn't cut communications with Rae Anne, we'd have the data already. Blast them! If I ever have a chance to change things when I get back, I sure as hell will.

"We also have a lot to do to get *Osprey* checked out for our first expedition. I'm sending Cindy, Nick, Kate and Jennifer down first while Marla, Brad and I hold down the fort here in orbit. The landing crew will be on the surface for four to six weeks."

Ian received Rob's notes shortly after this conversation. He and his team spent the next week studying them and comparing them with their own surveys. In the end, Ian sent an acknowledgement to Rae Anne.

"Rob did an incredible job, Rae Anne. The site analysis report you sent saved us a ton of work. All five sites Rob chose were on our original list to be checked out, and we have verified they are by far the best. We'll be using your list for our landing agenda. Thank you so much!"

Pause.

"Then you'll be taking the lander down to Site 1 soon. Which one is it? What features attracted you there?"

"Of course, we're always looking for signs of life, either present or, more likely, past. To that end, Site 1 is Terra Sabaea, the Sabaean Highlands, right on the equator. If Mars life is sensitive to seasonal variations and warmth, this might be a good place to find it. We'll also be able to determine if there's enough warmth to melt ice deposits below the surface and produce liquid water.

"No matter what samples we get, we're equipped to analyze the hell out of them on *Osprey,* even before returning to *Odysseus.* Can you imagine the impact if we find evidence of life on Mars? Maybe then Congress will take more interest in the space program and restore our funding."

Pause.

"We can only hope," Rae Anne replied. "But if the Ganymede Discs didn't excite them, it's not likely ancient microbial life on Mars will do any better! Any chance my mission will come back into the Agency's good graces?"

"Not so far as I can tell. They are far more concerned with political issues. In fact, it seems like they've begun to treat Mars-III like a stepchild already. The military has too much control over the Agency and insists on putting their priorities ahead of our scientific programs. And right now, they are concentrating on militarizing our lunar bases in response to Chinese actions there. Pretty disgusting.

"But I promise you this. When I return to Earth, I will do everything in my power to get you and *Aurora* back on the radar. The fact you are still doing so well will help. And we can elicit a lot of testimonials from astronomers around the world regarding the value of your contributions.

"I can't help but believe that your arrival in Saturn orbit will be an achievement too great to ignore. Surely, that will motivate them to reconsider their position. They'll probably claim your Saturn-I mission was their idea all along and come up with some ridiculous spin to explain their blackballing you for five years."

April 18, 2040: Aboard Aurora

"Rae Anne, the carbon dioxide level is rapidly shooting toward critical. You must change the ECARU filter immediately."

"This is the one with the reconditioned REDOX cannister. It's no wonder it's failing so rapidly. How many days did it last?"

"Sixty-seven days."

"That's two full months! With enough peroxide for three more treatments, we may gain eight months over our initial estimates. Almost enough to make up for the malfunctioning filter.

"I'll install Filter 5 today and Filter 6 next. When Filter 6 is online, I'll refurbish Filters 2, 4 and 5. That'll use up all the peroxide and set us up for, maybe, six additional months. Then I'll install Filter 7 from *Eagle* to wrap things up. I'll have to transfer the filter back and forth between *Aurora* and *Eagle,* but in zero-G, that should be no problem."

"Sounds like a plan, Rae Anne."

"All we can do is hope for the filters to last long enough to get us through our mission. We knew from the start that life-support would be the most critical issue for success. And the numbers are showing us just how close we're cutting it."

April 21, 2040: Aboard *Aurora*

Three days later, Rae Anne was relaxing with a cup of tea on Level 3, listening to the direct audio feed from the *Odysseus*' lander, *Osprey,* as it separated from the main ship and drifted away prior to its de-orbit burn. It reminded her of Penny's broadcasting the English translation of the Chinese announcer's description of the attempted *Ming-Xi* landing, but with far more detail.

Rae Anne shivered momentarily as she recalled Penny's gasp when the lander exploded. Perhaps the world would be holding their collective breath and praying for the outcome to be successful this time. She was totally aware that with the communication delay, the outcome of the Osprey's landing had already taken place.

She turned her attention back to the comm unit.

"*Osprey* ignition for landing deceleration burn," Cindy announced as she piloted *Osprey* to the surface. "All systems normal."

She reported elevation and velocity as the craft descended to the surface. Velocity gradually decreased until *Osprey* hovered a mere 100 meters above the surface.

"No latitudinal adjustments appear to be necessary. The surface below us is free of obstructions. Easing *Osprey* to the ground. Ten meters. Five. Three. One meter and engine cut off."

"*Osprey* has landed," she announced, echoing Neil Armstrong's famous pronouncement from the moon 71 years earlier.

Rae Anne felt elation and sadness at the same time. Elated by their successful landing. But sad that the whole world was viewing the Martian horizon as seen from *Osprey,* something she would never see for herself.

Still, how could this not inspire thousands of young people to pursue careers in science and technology to solve Earth's problems. How I wish it was Mindy, Rob and me taking in that alien horizon.

Ian maintained communication with Rae Anne whenever *Odysseus,* now orbiting Mars, was in line-of-sight with *Aurora,* giving her a front-row seat into their activities. *Odysseus* crew treated Rae Anne as though she were a part of their team.

Osprey's landing took place in late afternoon. Cindy announced they would wait until morning to suit up and step out of the lander. She declared that all four of the crew would have the privilege to make history as a team.

Chapter 8

April 23 to June 3, 2040: Surface of Mars

The world watched and waited as Cindy worked through her checklists. Although only minutes passed, it seemed like hours before Cindy opened the outer airlock hatch. The vast expanse of the Martian high plains filled the view. Ian broadcast an audio play-by-play account to Rae Anne and tried to fill in with as much visual information as he could.

Rusty-brown plains stretched to a flat horizon, broken here and there by a distant crater rim. The flat surface was pockmarked with holes and indentations from centuries of meteorite strikes. Rocks and boulders lay strewn randomly across the plains.

The sky was a dark, dusky gray dome with a pinkish tinge and a few wispy cirrus fantail clouds directly overhead. Although full daylight, a few of the brighter stars were visible. One of those 'stars' was planet Earth. Phobos was visible as a bright miniature disk setting in the east, tracing its twice-a-day orbit around the planet.

Cindy climbed down the ladder with the camera and directed it toward the hatch as her three colleagues stepped through and descended to the surface. She unfolded a tripod, attached the camera and joined the others for the official *Osprey* Team photo.

Arm in arm, the four astronauts, in their SEVA suits, posed in front of *Osprey.* Cindy presented the short speech she had prepared for the occasion—words that would be recorded for history.

```
Humanity is no longer a one-planet species.
The aspirations of many generations to reach
```

```
beyond the confines of Earth have been
fulfilled. This is but one step of many that
will take humans to the planets and to the
stars. May this achievement help foster
international cooperation and peace on Earth.
```

Kate produced an American flag attached to a pole, and Nick bored a deep hole in the Martian soil with *Osprey*'s core sampler. Jennifer set the pole in the hole and stamped the fluffy soil down around the pole. The pole promptly dipped to one side. She tried unsuccessfully to stabilize it in an upright position, prompting Nick to pull a sample container from his tool pouch and use it as a wedge to prop it in a vertical position. In the thin atmosphere, the flag sagged limply around the pole. Jennifer then returned to the lander. She would be the eyes and ears for *Osprey* on the first day.

The other three astronauts spent the rest of the day collecting samples and data and recording observations at their landing site. Since Site 1 was located near the equator, by mid-day it was a balmy minus 15-degrees Celsius, a temperature one might encounter on a cold winter night in the Colorado mountains. No one ventured more than fifty meters from *Osprey*.

Testing the rovers and aerial drones took up most of the second day. They would extend the explorers' reach to several kilometers beyond the vicinity of the lander. The team couldn't hide their frustration when they reported back to *Odysseus* that evening.

"Nothing is cooperating, Ian," Nick reported. "The rovers bog down in the fine sand and the drones don't have what it takes to maintain sustained flight. If we don't solve these problems, the entire expedition will be a bust."

Ian reiterated the report to both Mission Control and to Rae Anne, who had been following their progress off and on throughout the day. By the next morning, numerous suggestions were offered to overcome the problems. Through the course of the day, it became obvious that none were working.

On the morning of the fourth day, Rae Anne suggested a solution to the rover problem.

"I have an idea why the rovers keep getting stuck in the sand, Ian. It came to me as I dropped off to sleep last night. Have someone walk a rover about fifty meters from *Osprey* and try running it from there. I'm thinking the turbulence created by *Osprey's* engines when it landed may have scoured the ground directly below it. The displaced sand might have fallen in a ring around the lander making the sand deeper than normal around the landing site."

Ian passed the suggestion to Nick who oversaw rover operations.

"That doesn't sound very likely to me," Nick replied.

"Well, just give it a try, Nick," Ian urged. "Nothing else is working. What have we got to lose?"

An hour later, Nick's jubilant voice came over the comm-link.

"Ian, send a big hug to Rae Anne. She was right. Jennifer and I are going to scoop a wide path out from *Osprey* through the displaced sand so the rovers can operate from the base of the lander as we planned. Tomorrow we'll be able to send them both out to collect samples."

"Good work, Nick. I'll pass your report on to Rae Anne."

Ian congratulated Rae Anne on his next transmission to *Aurora*. After the communication pause, Rae Anne responded, "Have you had any luck with the aerial drones? I don't think the solution for them will be quite so easy."

"We've determined we need to alter the rotors. For some reason, the simulations and mock-ups back on Earth didn't get things right. Our drones are much heavier than the smaller ones sent here with the NASA landers, and the rotors don't scale up for our drones. Unfortunately, our 3-D printer is in orbit on *Odysseus,* so we'll have to wait until *Osprey* gets back into orbit before we can make any changes."

Without the aerial drones, Cindy cut the first expedition to three weeks. They drove the rovers as far from *Osprey* as they could. The rovers were designed to scoop up surface samples from the crust and smaller meteorites they might encounter. Since the drones weren't available, they had no aerial imagery to help identify different areas for the rovers to visit, so the samples obtained were from totally random locations.

They also collected several core samples with an awkward battery-operated drill they lugged out from *Osprey*. These core samples were drilled between 10 and 30 meters from the lander in several directions. They used one of the rovers to cart the cores back to *Osprey* for analysis and storage. This required additional shoveling, so by the time they left, the landing site looked like a maze.

"We hit a section of solid ice, Rae Anne," Ian reported one evening. "Jennifer brought a core back to *Osprey* and laid it out on the lab table. When she came back after dinner, a whole section had melted. Fortunately, the sample was in a tray, so we didn't lose any of the liquid."

Pause.

"Were you able to do an analysis on the liquid?" Rae Anne asked.

"The liquid is a concentrated brine containing over a dozen dissolved salts. Much too brackish to support any life we would recognize on Earth. Jennifer did a microscopic analysis and saw no sign of cellular structures. Mass spectroscopy came up negative for organic compounds."

Pause.

"What about the layers beneath the ice? If the water was once liquid and supported life, the organisms might have died and sunk to the bottom."

"Their sample didn't go down far enough. The ice layer was at the bottom of the core. They drilled as deep as they could."

Before leaving, the landing party assembled a sophisticated science station to transmit environmental and geoscience data remotely from the site. The Mars-III science stations were far more sophisticated than the smaller robotic landers sent to Mars over the previous six decades. For one thing, the equipment was housed in an igloo-shaped structure firmly anchored to the ground, protecting them from the occasional sand-blasting Martian storm.

The solar panels powering the station were equipped with small jet nozzles along one edge. A compressor that accumulated Martian air (when free of dust) would puff spurts of air through the nozzles, blowing off anything that might accumulate on the panel surfaces. This was expected to extend the life of the science station by several years.

Except for the solid layer of ice, Site 1 didn't reveal much about Mars not already known. The samples would undergo much more rigorous testing later, both during *Odysseus'* return to Earth and later in hundreds of laboratories around the globe. Like the first moon rocks returned in 1969, the Mars specimens were sure to reveal a trove of new information and generate an encyclopedia of new questions.

Chapter 9

June 15 to July 25, 2040: Surface of Mars

On their second landing, Cindy brought *Osprey* down to a perfect landing three kilometers east of the Korolev crater, within sight of the glistening white icepack at the North Pole. Ian chose to accompany Cindy, Marla and Brad on this second landing, leaving Jennifer, Kate and Nick in orbit aboard *Odysseus*. Before leaving *Odysseus*, he programmed a link between *Osprey* and Rae Anne via *Odysseus* to activate whenever line-of-site communication between the three vehicles was available.

Ian was ecstatic to finally be on the surface of Mars. He hadn't forgotten the longing he experienced on the Mars-I fly-by mission, gazing down on the red planet with no opportunity to land.

On his first trip outside the lander he took the core-borer with him and walked to where he was sure the lander's engines hadn't disturbed the surface. As the machine bored into the Martian soil, he took in the surroundings. To the east, the distant ice sheet edged the horizon like an ice cream sandwich with its top removed. To the south, the rust-red plains extended to the horizon without interruption. To the west and north, jagged crater rims pierced the air, hundreds of meters into the black sky, creating a menacing sawtooth pattern. Their sun-drenched rust-brown faces were accentuated by deep black shadows where crevasses and canyons broke through.

The sky here was nearly black and spackled with hundreds of stars despite the distant noonday sun. Far to the south, Ian spotted Phobos zipping through the canopy.

Now this is what I call a Mars expedition. I never have understood the logic of sending a fly-by mission first just to show you can get there and back. It's the landings that are important, and they do the 'there and back again' thing too. Fly-by missions are a total waste of precious resources.

Ian took command of the rovers. Since there was less sand at this site, he didn't encounter the difficulties Nick had faced.

"I'd like to say this is very cool," he commented to Marla after his first trip out. "But actually, it's very, very cold. Too bad we won't be venturing more than a few dozen yards from *Osprey* at this site."

Marla wrinkled her face. "We're less than a kilometer away from a 20-meter sheer wall of Dry Ice and you want to go exploring? What planet are you from?"

Laughter erupted within the close quarters. Despite *Osprey*'s thorium reactor working at maximum output, both decks were chilly. The crew wrapped themselves in blankets to keep warm. The galley's hot water generator worked overtime to keep their mugs of coffee, tea, hot chocolate, and miso filled.

A few days following their landing, Rae Anne inquired, "How are the redesigned drones working?"

Ian's heart noticeably quickened as he turned his attention to the communication console and Rae Anne's virtual presence.

What is it about that woman that disturbs me so?

He inhaled deeply before answering. "Wonderfully, Rae Anne. Marla applied her aerospace engineering expertise to the drone problem. She fabricated new hubs for the props to give them a pitch angle more suitable for the atmospheric pressure we are actually experiencing. She would have liked to tack an additional prop on each hub, but that was beyond our 3D printing capability. "

Pause.

"I can't wait to hear what you find out about the icepack. This site should yield a whole different perspective on Mars. Even the Phoenix Lander from 2008 was farther south than your team."

"You wouldn't believe how cold it is here," Ian chuckled. "Daytime temps have yet to get above minus-67 degrees Celsius and as soon as the sun sets, it plummets. We're also experiencing a stronger dose of cosmic radiation than they did at the equator due to the thinner atmosphere at the poles. I've had to reduce each team member's outings to half the time they had at Site 1."

Throughout their stay at Site 2, Ian sent rovers out to bring back samples of anything of interest within their range while Brad programmed the drones to make excursions over the icepack and collect samples. The drones were equipped with scoops and a remotely controlled grasping arm, allowing the operator to pick up individual rocks or chunks of ice that looked interesting.

Preliminary analysis on *Osprey* showed the ice samples to be a combination of frozen carbon dioxide and water ice, with little contamination, suggesting the ice condensed from the atmosphere rather than from a build-up of surface deposits.

The drones frequently returned with black chunks of meteorites they found resting atop the ice sheet. Like those found in Antarctica, their presence stood out like raisins in a bowl of rice. Marla stored these in carefully marked bags to take back to Earth for comparison.

"You realize, we may be hauling chunks of ancient Earth back to Earth!" she pointed out, laughing. "Volcanic ejecta from billions of years ago when Earth was far more active than it is today."

The core samples at Site 2 contained much more water ice. A warmer climate on ancient Mars may have permitted a vast ocean. It seemed inconceivable to Ian that life would not have taken hold here as it did on Earth. Still, preliminary analyses of their samples showed no organic matter.

"You'll never guess what happened last night," Ian said one morning during his transmission to Rae Anne. "A thin layer of rime-ice coated *Osprey,* reminding me of the cold winter days where I grew up in Maine. I wish you could have been here to see it!"

Pause.

"I hope the cold isn't interfering with your mission," Rae Anne replied. "Keep me advised. It will be even colder for my expedition on

Titan. Any suggestions for keeping warm at such insane temperatures would be appreciated."

"It has slowed things down. We have to thaw the drones out after each sortie. The ice that collects on their surfaces adds weight and limits the samples we collect. Too much ice, and we'd lose the drone.

"Also, we can't stay outside nearly as long as we'd like. Radiation exposure is the big concern, but the SEVA suits are too light to allow extended exposure to the extreme cold, so we're limited both ways."

Pause.

"Will you be leaving a science station at this site?"

"No. The edge of the icepack is quite close. It's a sheer wall over twenty meters high. I expect this site will be buried in solid ice six to eight Earth-months from now when Mars winter hits the northern hemisphere. Anything we would leave behind would be crushed and buried."

As at Site 1, the *Osprey* expedition didn't turn up anything new at Site 2 that could be called a breakthrough. Ian was disgruntled when they returned to *Odysseus*.

"We have enough resources to make two more landings," he reported to Rae Anne. "But if they turn out like the previous two, the whole expedition will be a bust. Just what the folks back home need to justify scratching any future missions."

Pause.

"You can't give up so easily, Ian. You never know what you'll find at Sites 3 and 4. And you may have eye-popping discoveries already sitting in your sample locker, waiting for the right scientist with instruments we haven't even dreamed of to take another look."

"Of course, you're right, Rae Anne. But I would sure like to have my eyes popped out right now."

Pause.

"Where are you going for Site 3 and what do you hope to find there?"

"Site 3 is east of Arabia Terra in the Nili Fossae region. Orbiters have detected both water vapor and methane in the atmosphere there on numerous occasions. We hope to determine where the methane is coming from and why this region experiences what appear to be periodic flows of liquid water on the surface."

Pause.

"Sounds like an intriguing site to explore. You may get your eyes popped out yet. Good luck!"

Rae Anne was particularly depressed after this last communication.

I can't keep from imagining Mindy, Rob and myself taking samples and collecting data for the first time on Mars. If only things had gone differently.

Chapter 10

August 15 to September 22, 2040: Surface of Mars

Half-way through their stay at Mars, *Osprey* made its third landfall. This time Cindy, Brad, Marla and Kate made up the crew. *Odysseus* happened to be in line-of-site with *Aurora* during the landing, so Rae Anne could follow the (delayed) communications.

"We're thirty meters above the surface and holding," Cindy reported. "Big boulders everywhere. Moving north.

"Still no clearings. Moving further north.

"The mineral colors below are awesome. Incredible geologic variation. We should get some interesting samples from this site.

"I see a small area with a smooth surface. I'll set her down there.

"Twenty meters, descent five meters per second. Ten and three. Five and two. Touchdown. *Osprey* has landed at Site 3, about one and a half kilometers north of the designated landing site."

Nili Fossae was near the equator. While the crew were busy dispatching rovers and drones, Cindy commented on how relieved she was to be in a 'warmer' environment.

"At least we're making some novel observations at this site," Ian reported to Rae Anne from Mars orbit one evening. "It didn't take Kate long to find several vents from underground lava tubes that are emitting methane into the atmosphere. One vent is nearly horizontal and large enough to squeeze into, like a cave. The methane concentration increases the farther in you go."

Pause.

"Something down there is continuously producing methane, Ian. Can you take sub-surface temperature readings?"

"We have, and they're all above freezing. Kate's plan is to drill down far enough to hit liquid water. If it's brine like before, it's sure to be liquid at these temperatures."

Pause.

"The methane may be coming from melting clathrates, crystals of water ice and methane. Maybe Mars isn't such a dead planet after all. Can you test your samples for radon and radioactive isotopes? Maybe there's a major deposit of uranium and radium in this location to warm things through radioactive decay."

"We only have a primitive detector on the surface. No one anticipated we'd need to monitor radiation from geologic sources. But your guess is spot on. Radiation levels increase the farther inside the lava tubes you go."

Following breakfast a few days later, Ian sat impatiently at the communication console waiting for *Aurora* to swim into view over Mars' disk. His entire body fidgeted until he finally heard Rae Anne's voice. She barely returned his greeting before he burst out with his news.

"Rae Anne, we've done it! We've proven that primitive life forms once inhabited Mars. We have absolute proof.

"Marla brought in a core sample she drilled a hundred meters east of the landing site. When they laid it out on the lab bench in *Osprey,* an unusual grayish-black section looked like nothing we've seen before, so they took a closer look. Rae Anne, it was a stromatolite! Just like the ones dating back a billion years in western Australia. Almost identical in both structure and composition."

Pause.

"That's incredible, Ian! You realize, if these samples can be dated when you get back to Earth and they predate Earth's stromatolites, this could be evidence that Mars seeded life on Earth. Problem is, there's still controversy regarding fossil stromatolites, with one side insisting they aren't fossils at all but merely normal geological accretions. You should poke around your core samples to see if there are any multicellular fossils as well. Something completely uncontroversial."

Following his conversation with Rae Anne, Ian prompted Marla to look for any clear evidence of fossilized organisms embedded in the stromatolite samples. His excitement was palpable.

Try as they might, they didn't find any sign of more complex fossils. Ian refused to curb his enthusiasm, however, and looked forward to the chance to study the samples with the more powerful equipment aboard *Odysseus* once the landing crew returned. He also continued to hope they would drill into a briny aquifer, but no liquid water turned up at Site 3.

Brad busied himself with devising plans for placing an inflatable dome over the vents to trap methane. The methane pressure was too low to inflate anything, so a tent-like trap seemed the best option for methane capture. After collecting the methane for a sufficient time, they could roll up the tent to increase pressure and force the methane into a suitable storage tank. Some future mission could deploy it and use the harvested methane to heat habitats and use it for rocket fuel.

Prior to departing Site 3, Ian reported that Cindy had made another important discovery.

"You aren't aware of this, Rae Anne, but one of our goals this mission is to locate a site suitable for a permanent base. The civilian half of the Agency insisted on this despite the possible cutbacks in future funding. We even have an inflatable habitat we plan to leave here as a prototype. What we need to find is a large, easily accessible lava tube or cave in which to place it."

Rae Anne recalled that this had been one of the tasks on their agenda as well. Any permanent base would need protection from cosmic radiation and the occasional errant meteorite. The Mission-II habitat prototype was one of the items she had discarded in preparation for her launch to Saturn.

"Cindy's drones spotted an area that looks like it may have exactly what we're looking for. It's 280 kilometers west. There are a lot of lava-tubes like the ones here, only much larger, and they are also venting methane. Should we locate deposits of water or ice for making oxygen and hydrogen, we'll have everything we're looking for.

"We're designating that spot as Site 4. We hope to find a vent we can put our inflatable habitat in. We'll fill it with sensors feeding data into a science station outside at the vent's mouth. The Agency will be able to monitor the habitat in the years ahead and determine if this is a suitable location for a Mars colony."

Pause.

"A Mars colony?" Rae Anne repeated, her voice echoing her surprise. "That doesn't make any sense if your funding is drying up."

"You've got a point. But who knows? I've got some grand ideas and ambitions of my own. We'll see what happens when I get back to Earth."

September 29, 2040: Aboard *Odysseus*

"Stop! Roll back that last sequence 30 seconds and replay it in slow motion."

Ian's sharp command startled the rest of the crew, causing them to glance over to the console where he and Marla were scanning and cataloging drone videos. Nick and Cindy floated beside them and peered over their shoulders to see what Ian had spotted.

Aware of the sudden attention, Ian explained.

"We're reviewing the drone footage from Site 3. This is the run out to Site 4. I thought I saw an oddly shaped shadow as we flew by. Tell me what you think."

Marla slowed the playback by half. At first, all the camera displayed was reddish brown Martian soil with the occasional boulder on the surface. Like a flash, a black fin-shaped shadow passed across the screen, replaced by more featureless Martian terrain.

Marla backed the footage to the shadow and clicked PAUSE.

166

"Look at that," Cindy exclaimed. The rest of the crew crowded around. "It looks like a shark's dorsal fin."

"Step back and forth around this frame to see if we can make out what is casting the shadow."

Marla did so several times, with disappointing results.

"It would appear the object is nearly vertical to the surface and the drone is almost directly above it. It doesn't reveal enough of itself for the video to pick up," Marla said. "But the shadow suggests a perfectly smooth, curved shape."

"Maybe it's debris from one of the orbiters," Kate suggested, leaning forward to get a better look. "A number of them have crashed over the years."

"Can we tell how large it is?" Cindy asked.

"We have no reference for comparison," Ian replied. "We know the drone's elevation, and the time of day. Of course, we can measure the size of the shadow image on our monitor."

"That may be all we need," said Brad. "If we locate drone footage taken near *Osprey* at the same time of day and from the same altitude, we might find an image of one of the rovers. By comparing the rover's shadow with this, we could get a close estimate for its height."

Brad's suggestion was easier said than done. It took two days for Marla to find a suitable image at the right altitude, and even then, she had to adjust for the time of day. However, when she did, she immediately ran the calculations. Unconvinced, she ran them a second time. And a third.

"Team," she called. "Come look at this."

Everyone trooped over to Marla's computer.

"I ran the calculations three times, with identical results. Shark Fin is between 7.6 and 8.2 meters tall."

Brad let out a whistle. "That's huge! Especially if the object extends below the surface."

"That isn't anything from Earth," Kate observed. "I withdraw any wagers I may have made."

Brad laughed. "Oh no you don't. You owe me big time."

"We'll send a drone back to look at Shark Fin more closely on our next expedition," said Ian, who had assigned himself to be its commander. "It's a good thing Site 4 is close by. Maybe on closer aerial inspection we can figure out what it is. At least we'll be able to view it from the side and see what it actually looks like."

Chapter 11

October 15, 2040: Mars orbit

In the first week of October, Nick's careful observations in search of the orbiting Ming-Xi capsule paid off. Over the next eight days, Cindy maneuvered Odysseus into a matching orbit and caught up with her quarry.

"Approach speed: 1.35-meters per second." Cindy's voice remained calm and steady. The crew aboard the orbiting *Odysseus* crowded the flight deck and watched the abandoned *Ming-Xi* crew capsule grow larger.

"Distance 250-meters and closing."

Ian added his own observations for the archival record. "We have matched *Ming-Xi's* orbit and are flying alongside its starboard side at twenty meters. Nothing to see here. Cindy, maneuver *Odysseus* above *Ming-Xi*.

"Everything appears normal here as well."

"Could it even be possible for someone to still be alive?" asked Brad.

"Unlikely," Ian answered. "It's been three years since their lander exploded. I think we're looking at a ghost ship.

"There's the airlock. Looks sealed. Moving around to port. Everyone, keep your eyes peeled for any anomaly."

The port side was a mirror reflection of the starboard side.

"Nothing to report from this side either," Ian observed. "One last surface to scrutinize, then we'll align our orbit for landing Site 4. Bring *Odysseus* below *Ming-Xi.*"

"Wow. Look there!" Jennifer shouted.

Ian's calm narrative continued.

"We are looking at the underside of *Ming-Xi.* What we see here are two well-defined tracks running parallel to the ship's axis. The tracks are black and look like residual soot."

"Exactly what you might expect from the exhaust of a rocket launch," Brad observed.

"There's no sign of a rack or cradle that would hold a rocket, however." Ian furrowed his brow as he studied the screen. "We need an EVA to inspect this area more closely and collect some of the black material for analysis before we draw any conclusions. Nick, are you suited up?"

A muffled response about a helmet needing to be put on could be heard in the background.

"I see some stubs aligned with the launch tracks, if that's what they are. Check on those while you're out there, Nick."

Nicks' voice came through clearly as he finished suiting up and his comm-link patched into *Odysseus.*

"Will do. Sealing the airlock." A tantalizing pause followed.

"Evacuating the airlock. I'm linking several of the tethers together and attaching the end into the winch to pull me back when I'm through. I also have the SAFER attached to my belt. Indicators here show I'm good for EVA. What's it look like up there?"

"Everything here looks good, Nick. You're cleared for EVA."

"Opening the outer hatch. Cindy, can you bring us closer? That's quite a jump."

"Inching *Odysseus* closer. Distance is now 10-meters. 8-meters. 5-meters and holding. That's the best I'm willing to do."

"Thanks Cindy. Much better. I see a bracket on their hull I can aim for and hook onto. Jumping clear of *Odysseus* now."

In spite of Nick's confident reporting, Ian held his breath, imagining all the things that could go wrong.

"Got it. I'm clamping my tether onto *Ming-Xi* and I'm working my way toward one of the blackened streaks."

"We have you on video now, Nick," Cindy announced.

There was a pause in the transmission.

"OK. There's plenty enough stuff here for a sample. I'm scraping it into a sample bag. Cindy, where should I look for the stubs you observed?"

"Turn to your right and follow the black streak forward. I think they're about three meters from where you are."

"Oh, yeah. I see them. Working my way forward. There. Very interesting. These protrusions once held something to the hull of the ship. They've been sheared by small explosive charges. The reason you could see them from *Odysseus* is because the explosive was detonated after the sooty material was deposited, scouring the surface around the stubs clean.

"I would guess the rocket launchers were attached to the ship at these points and they were jettisoned after the rockets were fired to remove as much of the evidence as possible."

"OK, Nick." Ian stepped away from the video screen. "Take close-ups of the stubs and come back in. We've done everything we set out to do."

"Roger. Unhooking my tether from *Ming-Xi*. Done. I've activated the winch. I can see the loose line being drawn into *Odysseus'* airlock."

"Oh my god, what was that?" Jennifer gasped aloud, pointing to the screen. "Did anyone else see that?"

"I thought I saw a flash of something over toward the airlock," Marla confirmed.

"Nick, stop when you get to the hatch. We've spotted something you may need to investigate. You're there? Get inside and secure yourself but stay ready to go out again." Ian turned toward Cindy. "Move the ship back to the port side."

Cindy continued her narrative. "Moving back to port. Braking thrusters activated. We're stable alongside *Ming-Xi* at ten o'clock."

"I can't believe my eyes," Marla said, shaking her head.

A space-suited figure floated on a tether 20 feet out from the open *Ming-Xi* airlock.

"Nick, use your SAFER and bring in our guest. People, we're about to receive a visitor."

Brad's brow furrowed. "Are you sure that's wise, Ian? They tried to destroy the *Aurora*."

"We'll have to keep a close eye on him. Or her. But we can't leave a marooned astronaut to die. China abandoned their mission, stranding their own people after their lander exploded. I should hope we're better than that."

Safely inside *Odysseus*, the crew helped Nick and the Chinese taikonaut out of their EVA suits. When they realized the taikonaut was a woman, Marla and Kate wrapped their arms tightly around her as she collapsed in their arms with deep, heart-rending sobs. The two astronauts assumed the role of mother hens and led her down to Level 3, making it clear that Level 3 was temporarily off-limits to the male crewmembers.

When she reappeared in the galley two hours later, the woman was wearing one of Kate's best outfits and looked considerably refreshed. Marla had trimmed and braided her hair.

"It is my pleasure to introduce our guest, Li Fang," Marla announced with a flourish.

Li Fang smiled weakly and mumbled an unassuming hello.

"Li Fang speaks English," offered Kate. "But it's been a long time since she's spoken the language, so for a while we should speak slowly so she can understand us."

"She's also afraid of what we might do to her. Kate and I have made some inroads, but you men are especially threatening to her." Marla shook her finger at the men. "Be on your best behavior around her, and tread very lightly. It may take some time to bring her around."

Ian later reported to Rae Anne that Li Fang was terrified of possible retribution they might have in store because of *Ming-Xi's* attack on *Aurora,* but she realized that aboard *Ming-Xi,* she had run out of options. Her emaciated body was evidence that she wouldn't have lasted much longer if *Odysseus* hadn't come around when it did.

Chapter 12

October 21, 2040: Aboard Odysseus

Li Fang's English improved rapidly in the days following her rescue. She had a functional command of the language as a student of mathematics at the University of Electronic Science & Technology at Chengdu, but the lack of exposure in the intervening years had taken their toll. Eventually, she was able to converse with the *Odysseus* team with relative fluency.

"Yes, that's right, two of my fellow taikonauts died during *Ming-Xi*'s launch from Earth orbit. The G forces were terrible. The entire crew blacked out during the launch."

"Did you know this might happen?" Marla asked.

"We were told to expect more discomfort during launch because of the additional two boosters they attached at the last minute. Your *Aurora* launched two weeks before us. They said the extra acceleration would guarantee our getting to Mars first."

"This is the first anyone has heard of this," commented Ian.

"Our political officer, Major Liu Qiang, dictated that we were not to mention the deaths in any of our communications. I believe he intended to cover the incident up by reporting they died in an accident at the Mars station. No one but the *Ming-Xi* crew would know the truth."

"Half-way through the mission, you changed course. Did you know why?" Ian tried to couch his questions as inquisitive and conversational. The last thing he wanted was for Li Fang to feel she was being interrogated.

"All of us except Major Liu were surprised. He claimed to have fresh orders from Beijing. Only later did we understand that this change would bring *Ming-Xi* into the vicinity of *Aurora.* Some of us discussed among ourselves what this might mean. We feared the worst."

"Did you know *Ming-Xi* was equipped with two fragmentation missiles?"

"No. As far as I know, only Major Liu knew this. He fired the missiles at *Aurora.* We knew our worst fears were realized when we felt them being launched from our ship. Several of us looked at each other in horror. But Major Liu had this look of triumph beaming from his face. I will never forget that look.

"It was several days later that he received a report on his secure communication channel with Beijing that *Aurora* had survived and was still on its way to Mars. Several of us were relieved to hear this. By what miracle *Aurora* survived, we could not know. But we secretly rejoiced that Major Liu had failed."

Jennifer asked the next question.

"The whole world watched the Chinese broadcasts showing *Ming-Xi* achieve Mars orbit and the attempted landing on Mars a week later. But there was no follow-up reporting to account for the disaster. What happened?"

"You probably know more than I do about that. Major Liu and I were left behind on the orbiter module. Major Liu was conveying our observations to Beijing. Shortly after the lander exploded, the Chinese space agency cut off all communication with us. We never heard from them again.

"Over the next few days, our orbit took us over the proposed landing site. With our telescope set to its most powerful magnification, we could see the remains of our lander. The blackened engine sticking upended in the red Martian sand struck me hardest. This was to have been our ticket home. That was when I realized we were lost."

Tears welled in Li Fang's eyes as she recounted this scene, testimony to the deep emotions this horrifying sight registered in her soul.

Ian decided she had been put through enough during this session. His intuition told him that this was only the beginning, that the worst had yet to come. He wanted to bide his time and let Li Fang tell the rest of her story under her terms.

In the meantime, the crew busied themselves with preparations for the next and last landing and with analyzing the samples they had taken from the first three sites.

Li Fang preferred to keep to herself. Jennifer had given up her lounge next to the hull on Level 3 so Li Fang would have a place of her own, and she and Marla negotiated a time-share for Marla's lounge. But Ian insisted that Li Fang join the crew for meals.

The only activity she expressed an active interest in was the issue of Shark Fin. She too was intrigued by the mysterious alien artifact. The astronauts learned how keen she was on science fiction, both books and movies, when she offered numerous outlandish explanations for Shark Fin. Could it be a time machine? Maybe a portal to other worlds, or even an alternative universe? Perhaps an alien penal habitat which no one dare open lest the inmates escape and enslave or destroy human civilization.

It was this last suggestion which plunged Li Fang into a fit of sobbing so deeply that she almost couldn't breathe. Alarmed, Jennifer and Marla swept over to her and wrapped her in their arms as they had when she first came aboard. They spent several minutes consoling her before she quieted enough to speak.

"I apologize for the outburst. The picture I drew of alien criminals incarcerated forever struck too close to home."

"Do you feel like talking about it, Fang?" Ian asked gently.

"I need to get it out of my system. Maybe doing so will finally help me sleep. There's not that much left to tell.

"After the lander exploded and Major Liu realized Beijing had abandoned us, he exploded in fits of violent fury. I tried to stay as far from him as I could. He smashed equipment and monitors throughout the orbiter. I secretly hoped he would destroy the life support system so we would die quickly, but it was not to be.

"He eventually quieted down. That's when things took a turn for the worse. One day he grabbed me and ripped my uniform to shreds and raped me. I wanted to kill myself, I was so shamed and humiliated. But I couldn't bring myself to do it. I didn't want to bring shame on my ancestors. An odd feeling for me, since I don't adhere to the old religious beliefs.

"But that was only the beginning.

"The abuse, the rapes, and degradations continued, day after day unabated despite my pleas. Then one night after a particularly appalling episode, I could take no more. I grabbed a knife hanging in the galley and plunged it deeply into his throat.

"The only sound he made was a choking gurgle. Crimson blood gushed from his neck. It spread out into the cabin air. I was swimming in a sea of bloody mist. Everything was covered with Major Liu's blood. His lifeless body floated grotesquely in front of me. I couldn't take my eyes off it. I remember asking 'What have I done? What have I done?'"

Jennifer put her arm around Li Fang's waist and began to guide her to the floor hatch, perhaps thinking to lead her to the comfort of her bed but she pulled away and grabbed the edge of the table to stabilize herself.

"No. I need to finish this. The hardest part is over. To admit to being a sex slave for so many months is one thing. To admit to a cold-blooded murder, let alone the murder of a superior officer, is another. Let me bring this story to a close.

"The night after I killed Major Liu was the first night in many months that I slept soundly. No longer in fear of being awakened to perform in the theater of his sexually depraved imagination. No longer a slave to abuse. The master is dead.

"The next day, I moved Major Liu's body into the airlock, shut the inner hatch and opened the outer one. I stood mesmerized as I watched his body blown away from the ship and disappear. After that, I stripped off my soiled clothes and gathered everything throughout the module that I could do without, stuffed it all into the airlock, and whisked it all into space.

178

"Then the cleaning began. I vacuumed up the remaining droplets of blood still floating through the cabin. Then I scrubbed all the surfaces. Everything was covered with blood. I poured pail after pail of bloody pink wash water into the recycler. I could only hope it could purge the awful stuff from the water so I wouldn't be drinking the filth. I worked on this for days. Finally, I turned to cleaning his caked blood off my own body. I scrubbed my skin till it was raw.

"To this day when I bathe, I see spots of blood and have to force myself not to scrub at them."

Marla and Jennifer again were alongside the diminutive Chinese woman giving her hugs and support. She was crying again, but softly, as though her testimony had drawn out the demons lodged in her soul.

"That's an incredible story, Fang. Thank you for sharing that with us." Ian couldn't think of anything more to say. Li Fang seemed to be finished with her story. The two women led her below, gesturing to the men to leave them alone for the time being.

"That's unbelievable," whispered Brad. "How could anyone behave like that?"

"Desperation and despair can bring a wicked person to do evil things we couldn't begin to imagine. We'll never be able to give this woman enough love and support to make up for what she's been through," Ian whispered in return. He wiped his cheek and discovered he had been crying too.

At lunch the following day, with her confession out in the open, Li Fang broached a subject that had been bothering her since her rescue.

"Ian, I have confessed to committing an egregious crime. As part of the *Ming-Xi* crew, I am an officer in the army of the People's Republic of China. I have killed one of my commanding officers. By law, I should be executed for my crime. How will the American judicial system deal with me? Will they extradite me to China?"

"I don't think there's any chance of that happening, Fang. You are in our custody now, which makes you eligible to seek amnesty based on the abuse you received under an official of a foreign government and on the fact that you would likely face death if you returned to China. You have seven very strong advocates on your side should you ever need us."

"But there is also the case of our attack on *Aurora*. Although I didn't know we were going to fire on the American ship, we certainly had our suspicions. That would make me an accomplice. I would think the Americans would want to punish me for that."

"I'm not sure how the Department of Justice will deal with you on that issue. But I know several people within our agency I can ask who can check it out and advise us on what we should do. Personally, I can say none of us here hold you responsible. Unfortunately, our opinions will only count as character witnesses, should it come to that. But I'll do everything I can to see that it never gets that far."

October 22, 2040: Aboard *Aurora*

The next day, Ian related an overview of Li Fang's story to Rae Anne when he had line-of-sight communication with *Aurora*.

"She is undoubtedly the most distant refugee ever to apply for political asylum!" he added in conclusion. "She's a quick study, too. She's learning the fine points of American English and she's teaching Brad Mandarin."

In the depths of her heart, Rae Anne found the strength to forgive Li Fang for being part of the *Ming-Xi* crew that tried to destroy *Aurora*. She could only wish the best for her future. She knew Li Fang was in good hands aboard *Odysseus*, but once she returned to Earth, there was no telling what might happen.

"What do you think the Agency will do with her?" she asked.

Pause.

"We'll ask the Agency to find an immigration lawyer to get her deposition for what took place aboard *Ming-Xi* and to explain to her what her options are.

"It's likely she won't ever set foot on Earth again. After four years in microgravity, her heart and bone structure might have deteriorated too much for a return to Earth gravity. And then there's the long-term exposure to cosmic radiation to consider. For health reasons alone, the Agency might give her a permanent assignment on EOTS or at one of the research stations on the moon."

These thoughts gave Rae Anne pause, realizing her own body was experiencing those same degenerative issues, even though *Aurora* offered more protection from radiation. Since Mars had no magnetic field to protect the planet, Li Fang experienced the full onslaught of radiation her whole time in orbit. Ian referred to her as a 'quick study', suggesting she hadn't suffered significant brain damage, which gave Rae Anne some comfort.

Heart and bone deterioration were inevitable consequences of long space missions in microgravity, and she was already aware of both conditions affecting her body. She had to reduce her original daily regimen of three hours exercise to two. She could only hope she would have the strength and stamina to function at 1/7 Earth gravity should she be able to take *Eagle* to Titan's surface.

Chapter 13

November 3, 2040: Surface of Mars

Cindy brought *Osprey* down over its fourth and final landing site on Mars. Site 4 was in an area with numerous exposed vents leading to underground lava tubes that the aerial drones had found on the previous expedition. Their final objective was to find a large cave-like vent that could be used for a permanent base should the opportunity ever arise.

"20-meters and holding," Cindy reported. "Surface looks like a mammoth crash zone. Boulder-sized rubble everywhere. Shifting southwest a kilometer or two."

Osprey's side thrusters pushed the lander to the new location.

"Still no good. I'll try another two kilometers."

"I think I spotted a landing site a bit further south," commented Ian. "Take her south instead."

"Roger. South it is."

"There. A clearing at 50 meters. Set her down there," Ian commanded.

Cindy promptly landed *Osprey* on a tail of flame, kicking up surprisingly little dust. Sudden silence displaced the ear-jarring roar of *Osprey's* engines when they touched down.

"How far are we from the lava tube vents we want to check out?" asked Marla.

"This whole region is filled with them," said Ian. "I spotted several nearby as we landed. We'll have plenty of vents to look at."

"What about Shark Fin?" Jennifer inquired.

"We'll have to see about that," Ian answered. "We may have come too far west. But visiting Shark Fin is high on my priority list if we can do it.

"OK, team, let's get things set up for tomorrow and grab some chow. We've got some long days ahead of us." He stepped to the mapping console to pinpoint their landing site and determine if they could still send a drone to Shark Fin.

Ian directed the exploration and sample collection operations from *Osprey*. Over the first five days he restricted drone operations to their immediate vicinity, searching for potential habitat sites and locating interesting areas for samples and drilling.

The core samples they brought in were far more interesting than those from the earlier sites. They exhibited several striated layers of colorful minerals, exhibiting streaks of red, orange, yellow ochre, and purple. Some of the tiny granules resembled red garnet and ruby.

At breakfast on the sixth day, Jennifer could hold her peace no longer.

Putting down her cup with a thump, she asked, "When can we send a drone to Shark Fin? You said earlier you thought we could manage it."

"Let's try for tomorrow," Ian replied, digging into his bacon-cheddar omelet. "Equip a drone with whatever you think might be useful and we'll send it out. At least we should get some good close-ups. We'll probably discover a 'Made in China' label on the thing."

Everyone laughed.

The next day, Jennifer piloted the drone east and north, looking for landmarks she might recognize from the aerial footage they had scrutinized aboard *Odysseus*. From ten meters up, the surface of Mars lacked identifiable details. By day's end, she had no choice but to bring the drone back to *Osprey* empty handed.

"Without GPS or even a magnetic field for compass directions, finding your way around on Mars is like searching for the proverbial needle in a haystack," she reported.

"Let's go over the video from today and compare it with the one we were studying on *Odysseus*," Ian suggested. "Maybe the two of us can spot something we can use."

After dinner, they pored over the data at varying resolutions. Square-meter after square-meter scrolled by, each frame looking different, but the same. They were about to give up for the night when Jennifer pointed to a uniquely angled rock balanced on the edge of a sharp outcropping.

"I think I've seen that before. Scroll back through the *Odysseus* data."

Ian reversed the display on his monitor and rolled the data back. Suddenly, he stopped and reversed it again, going through each frame slowly until the same rock appeared. The viewing angle was different, but it was unmistakably the landmark they needed.

"Great!" Jennifer exclaimed. "Now let's follow the drone's path to Shark Fin and look for other identifying features along the way. If we can find at least one more, we can draw a direct path for tomorrow's run.

On day eight, Jennifer put her drone on autopilot to fly to the angled rock it flew over the day before. From there, she took control and flew zigzag to the east until she spotted one of the features they identified the previous evening. Once she had a straight line between the angled rock and the second feature, she recorded distance and direction on the drone's navigational computer and set it on its way.

Thirty minutes later, the drone was hovering over Shark Fin. The images were stunning, not only for their clarity, but for their uniquely alien character. Everyone crowded around the monitor to have a look.

The object had impacted the surface with great force. If it was a circular disc-like object, based on measurements of the edge extending above the surface, they determined that it extended 36-meters beneath the surface. It had sliced through solid rock as though it were putty. The upper portion extended above the edge of a small ridge, explaining the fin-like appearance of its shadow.

"It's huge!" exclaimed Cindy. "What's sticking out is four times the size of *Osprey!*"

"At 10-meters thick, there'd be enough room for a whole colony."

"Do you suppose there are creatures inside?"

"I wonder how long it's been here?"

"Where might it have come from?"

Everyone had questions, but answers weren't forthcoming. Jennifer used the drone's tools and tried to drill into the smooth obsidian-black surface. The bit turned red hot but made no mark on the object. A microphone attached to its surface revealed no sound, but tapping the surface produced an echo, confirming that it wasn't a solid mass.

"Can you imagine the trail it would have made when it plunged through the atmosphere?"

"Something this size would have created a tsunami on Earth."

"Or flattened an entire forest with the sonic boom."

Jennifer disagreed on that point. "The fact that it effortlessly sliced into the ground would suggest a more localized effect. Probably nothing more than a minor earthquake."

"Mars-quake, you mean. Too bad we can't sample the crushed rock at the leading edge of this thing. I'll bet it's not like anything seen on Earth," added Cindy.

Jennifer attempted to run additional tests on Shark Fin throughout the day, but the alien object proved impervious to all tests save one. She pointed this out to Ian as she set the drone's autopilot to bring it back to *Osprey.*

"There is one curious property associated with the surface of the object. It exhibits a weakly repulsive force, like an anti-gravity field. The dust our drone kicked up toward its surface never touched it, but instead reversed direction as if repelled. In fact, though the object has likely been here many years, the surface has a polished look. Anything else would be covered with a thick layer of red dust and grime.

"So, do we send a drone out tomorrow?" she asked.

Ian pursed his lips and gave the request some thought before answering. "No. There's nothing new we can do to extract more information than we already have. Another trip would be a waste of time and resources. We'll leave further evaluation to the experts back home. They can study our video and argue our findings to death.

"One thing is certain. Our observations here should put an end to the controversy over the two disc-like objects Rae Anne discovered in orbit around Ganymede. I think it's safe to say all three objects came from the same source. Rae Anne couldn't determine the size of her discs, but our measurements here could shed light on that issue too. Bottom line, though, is irrefutable. Aliens have definitely visited our solar system."

Once the issue of Shark Fin was settled, Ian focused his team's efforts on exploring the area around *Osprey's* landing site, mapping the location and size of all the lava tubes they encountered. Many were large enough for an astronaut to walk into, but none were suitable for a permanent habitat.

They also collected air samples from within the lava tubes and subjected the samples to spectroscopic analysis each evening. Many of the samples showed the presence of methane gas, and a few displayed peaks characteristic of water vapor.

"Any water vapor in the air should have frozen out at this temperature," Marla pointed out. "We should look into this further."

She equipped each of them with telescoping rods, each with a temperature sensor on its tip with a readout on the handle.

"Extend the rod to its maximum length and hold it so the tip goes as far into the lava tube as possible. Give it thirty seconds and record the interior temperature. We'll add that to our other data and see if there's a correlation between temperature and the composition of the air inside the tube."

Over the course of the next three weeks, Marla added hundreds of measurements to her database. The correlations she was looking for were easy to spot.

Before dinner one evening, she gathered the others around her monitor. A large scatter diagram was displayed across the screen.

"See here. The horizontal axis is temperature. You can see it ranges from minus 70 degrees to plus 10 degrees. The vertical axis is divided in half. The top half shows methane concentrations, and the bottom half shows water vapor.

"What you see is that the data points for methane are spread continuously across the graph at all temperatures, and that there seems to be little correlation between methane concentration and temperature.

"On the other hand, water vapor is non-existent at the lower temperatures. Where the temperature measurements exceeded minus 5 degrees, water vapor appears, and its concentration increases consistently with rising temperature.

"Although we can't test my theory at this point, I think there are regions associated with these high-temperature vents that have ground temperatures warm enough for any subsurface water to be in liquid form. The water vapor forms in these regions, and then, as the air spreads out and gets colder, the water vapor freezes out."

Chapter 14

December 11, 2040: Aboard *Aurora*

A week later, Rae Anne asked Kate, who was on *Odysseus* comm duty, "Have our Martians found a decent site for a base yet, Kate?"

During the 81-minute pause, Rae Anne took a sponge bath and readied herself for bed.

"Not yet, Rae Anne. They've explored more than half of the vents the drones discovered. None have met all the requirements and Ian is about ready to pack up and come home."

"They've only been at Site 4 for five weeks, Kate. You still have nearly two months before launching for Earth, so there's plenty of time. Why can't they continue their search?"

Another pause. Rae Anne made herself a bag of popcorn and settled into the lounger to enjoy Rachmaninoff's 2nd Piano Concerto.

"The problem is the environment conditioning system on *Osprey*. The ECARU filter is rated for six months, and the expiration date was two days ago. Ian doesn't want to be on the surface and have it conk out. Although they could make an emergency return to *Odysseus* wearing their SEVA suits if that happened, Ian doesn't like taking unnecessary risks."

"I've got some information that might help, Kate. Tell Ian I've pushed those filters to their limit, and all have lasted half again beyond their specified lifetime. Even with four people on *Osprey,* your filter should handle another couple of months, let alone a few weeks. I'm headed for bed. *Aurora* out."

When the comm-link crackled to life ten hours later, Rae Anne was cleaning up in the galley after breakfast. Kate patched her directly to Ian, who addressed her from the surface of Mars.

"Thanks for the info on the ECARU filter, Rae Anne. You've given us the confidence to stick it out for the full eight weeks we planned and continue our search for a building site. If we find one, it will be thanks to you. We'll name it after you, Chavez City."

A week later Kate patched Rae Anne into the ground crew again, believing Rae Anne deserved to be a part of the discovery they had just made. In their excitement, everyone was talking over each other, making it difficult for Rae Anne to follow the conversation.

"Look at this, Ian. A smooth approach right up to the entrance! And not far from a level landing site."

"We could put three of the inflatable habitats in this mother."

"Let's see how far back it goes."

Ian's voice overrode the others. "Jennifer, you stay at the entrance and relay our communications to *Odysseus.* Once we go inside, you'll be our link."

Soon communication reverted to a monolog from Jennifer as she passed on the observations from the three explorers.

"The vent branches into four large tunnels. Ian is staying in the cavern at their mouth while Cindy and Marla explore a bit further into two of the new tunnels. Ian will keep the cavern brightly lit and Cindy and Marla are instructed to keep the light in sight."

Rae Anne smiled at the thought of astronauts from Earth being morphed into Martian spelunkers. She knew they would be taking samples and recording observations the entire time so they could learn all they could about the cave's environment before having to depart for good.

"Both Marla and Cindy report a significant uptick in temperature readings the farther back they go. Cindy's readout is a positive 12-degrees Celsius—shirt-sleeve temperature."

"Ian is calling the others to rejoin him in the cavern. He has been collecting rock samples from the wall and floor. He says it is time to return to *Osprey.*"

Ian's voice came through as he returned to the mouth of the vent.

"This looks like the best spot we could have hoped for. Tomorrow Cindy and I will bring out the inflatable habitat and set it up inside the cavern while Jennifer and Marla build the science station at the vent's mouth. Once we have the two connected and operating properly, we can call this expedition a success and head home."

Rae Anne was thrilled at the idea of Chavez City, Mars. Perhaps someday in the distant future there might be a permanent human base where her four brave colleagues were now standing.

Unfortunately, regardless of its name, I won't live to see it.

She felt a deep ache in her chest.

December 18, 2040: Surface of Mars

The next day, Ian and Cindy lugged the inflatable habitat from their gangly rover and into the lava tube's mammoth opening.

"Let's erect it in the gallery with the four branching tunnels," Ian suggested. "We'll have line-of-site connection with the science station outside, and we can put sensors in one of the deeper tunnels. We'll be able to monitor the elevated temperature you observed. It will be interesting to see if this is seasonal or if it lasts year-round."

"Too bad we haven't got what we need to determine the source of the heat. Whatever it is, it's got to be substantial."

"Or the source of the water vapor. The floor of these lava tubes is just too hard for our core driver."

Ian huffed from the exertion, envious of his younger teammate's energy. "Mars is too dormant now for the heat to have a geological origin like Earth's plate tectonics. It's likely radioactive ores that were concentrated in this area during its formation billions of years ago."

Once the two entered the cavern, further communication was blocked.

Outside, Jennifer and Marla reached the cave with the science station kit and began to assemble it. The comm-link filled with conversation relating to installing the sensors and antennae, laying out the solar array, and powering up the station. Once they verified the sensors were working, their last task was to check the transmitters.

"Marla, Earth is picking up Station 3's signal loud and clear," reported Kate from *Odysseus*. "All that's left is to get the habitat sensors connected and you guys can come home."

A few minutes later, Ian's voice transmitted from inside the cavern to *Odysseus* via the science station.

"*Odysseus* and Mission Control. The inflatable habitat has been successfully deployed and its sensors activated. I declare Mars-III an unqualified success."

Two days later *Osprey* returned to orbit and the entire Mars-III crew were together again with their Chinese guest aboard *Odysseus*.

Things quieted down after that. The *Odysseus* crew was busy running analyses in the lab and cataloging, packing and storing samples for the long trip home.

Chapter 15

February 7, 2041: Aboard *Aurora*

There was no video to record *Odysseus'* launch to Earth from Mars, but Ian patched Rae Anne into the flight deck and she once again felt as

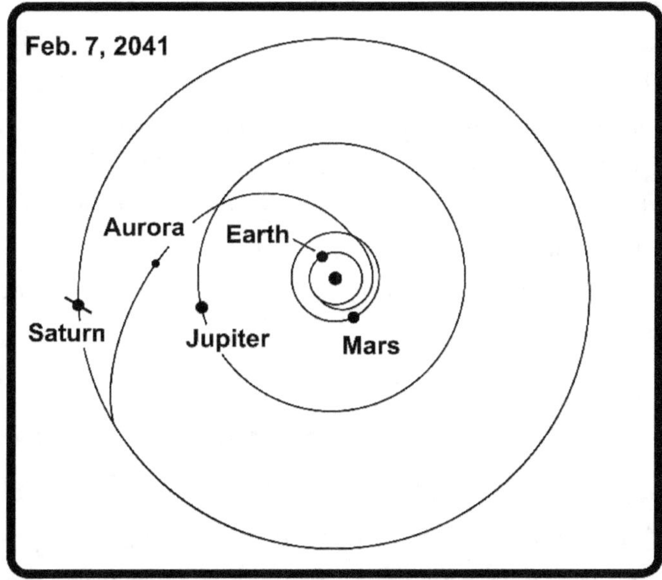

though she were a member of the crew. Though her feed was an hour behind events in real time, the difference was transparent to Rae Anne.

Ian left *Osprey* behind in Mars orbit, awaiting the next crew that might never come. All it needed to become fully functional were a fresh

ECARU filter, fuel, supplies and a crew. The next mission (should there ever be one) could bulk up in Earth orbit on supplies and equipment to fill in for the lander's mass.

"Anything new with your soil-sample analyses?" Rae Anne asked during one transmission.

104-minute pause.

"We're still trying to find corroborative evidence of life with the stromatolite samples, but nothing yet. The methane samples we took from the lava tube at Site 4 are intriguing, though. We've compared the carbon-14 isotope concentration in the samples with what it should be if it were generated from geological processes, and the two don't match. Jennifer insists this proves there are sub-surface living microbes, but most of us aren't convinced."

"Have you had any further thoughts on Shark Fin?"

Pause.

"Nothing new," said Ian. "Except for the Agency slapping a 'Top Secret' stamp on everything related to it. Whatever for is anyone's guess. This discovery should be heralded world-wide. The first real, tangible evidence of alien intelligence. Awareness of alien visitors could unify humanity and reduce the never-ending conflict between nations."

"Typical bureaucracy," said Rae Anne, then amended, "Typical military bureaucracy."

Rae Anne returned to her observations of neighboring red dwarfs and her search for new exoplanets. Although she was collecting reams of data on the red dwarfs, she had yet to find any relation between their physical properties and their X-ray output.

But she continued to be troubled by Shark Fin. It didn't belong on Mars or anywhere else in the Solar System and its match with her Ganymede Discs was too close to be coincidental.

An idea popped into her head.

"Jason, how far back do our archives go on images collected from Mars orbiters?"

"Our library has a complete set of every image ever taken."

"Show me all the images we have on Nili Fossae at 22-degrees north, 282-degrees west, including dates and sources."

Before long, Rae Anne was scrutinizing dozens of photos, trying to find evidence of the strange protrusion on the Martian surface. She started with the most recent and worked back. Most photos were useless to her quest, even when she zoomed in on the object's exact location.

"Eureka! Jason, I've got an image showing the same shadow that first alerted Ian. The sun is setting, and the shadow has lengthened enough to be seen at this resolution. It's not much, but it is there.

"Sort through the remaining images for time of day. Give me only the ones taken in a thirty-minute range after sunrise or before sunset."

The final list contained 57 photos. Rae Anne poured over them, spotting the tiny smudge of a shadow on each one from the 2030's and 2020's. Two from 2019 and one from 2018 showed the shadow speck she was looking for. One image from November 3, 2017 had a similar gray smudge but an earlier one from September 28 was clear, as were all the preceding photos in the set.

"Jason, the object seems to have appeared between September 28 and November 3 in 2017. There's something about October 2017 in my memory, something unusual, but I can't recall what it is. Jog my memory. Something to do with astronomy."

After a few moments, Jason responded.

"It might be this report from the Haleakala Observatory on Maui. They observed a strange object of interstellar origin on October 18, 2017. They named it 'Oumuamua'. It came into the solar system at an oblique angle, swung around the sun sling-shot fashion and returned to interstellar space, all in the course of a few weeks."

Rae Anne's heart jumped. Her memory clicked. 2017 was the year after she got her first telescope and she became interested in all things astronomical. She had been intrigued at the interstellar nature of Oumuamua. She even wanted to believe the speculation that it was an interstellar spaceship travelling through the Solar System. The event had buried itself in the recesses of her memory.

She triumphantly called *Odysseus.*

"Ian, I've discovered evidence that might lend support to Jennifer's interpretation about Shark Fin. The shadow you observed doesn't appear on orbital images of Mars until after September 28 of 2017. In October of that year astronomers observed an interstellar object passing through the Solar System. They named it Oumuamua and there was some speculation that it might be an alien spacecraft, although the official conclusion was that it was a lifeless slab of rock. The timing would suggest some sort of connection between Shark Fin and Oumuamua."

While she waited for a response, she returned to the Mars images to verify her observations. Shark Fin's shadow was clearly absent from all photos prior to November 3, 2017.

Ian's response was enthusiastic. "You have a point. If Shark Fin isn't related in some way to Oumuamua, the timing makes for a strange coincidence Maybe Oumuamua deposited all three discs as it travelled through. One can only wonder what they are here for. If they meant to spy on us, you would think the aliens would have put them closer to Earth, maybe in lunar orbit or even on the moon itself."

"That's a very human-centered bias, Ian. They could have a purpose beyond anything we can imagine. One that has nothing to do with humans at all. Maybe they are a cache of provisions or fuel for some longer mission. Our Solar System could just be a waypoint in a vast undertaking."

When Ian's reply arrived, he agreed. "When it comes to thinking about what aliens might do, it's hard to take ourselves out of the picture. We probably register no higher than chimpanzees in their thinking. In any event, our discovery of these objects and their obviously alien origin, may reignite Congress' interest in providing the support we need for the space program. The antigravity properties of the object's surface alone should peak anyone's interest."

February 2041 to August 2041: Aboard *Aurora*

During the following six months, Rae Anne maintained daily contact with Ian and the *Odysseus* crew. They were her family, sharing their joys and traumas as only close friends can.

Eventually *Odysseus* reached Earth orbit and Rae Anne braced herself, knowing she would soon be abandoned again, probably for the remainder of her journey to Saturn. But the imminent loss of contact with her friends and colleagues disheartened her most.

"This is good-by again, Rae Anne." Ian said sadly. "We're shutting down *Odysseus* and mothballing it in Earth orbit. The Agency has barely enough funding now to maintain its share of the EOTS. No future crewed expeditions are in the works and the Agency is terminating many of its projects early.

"The robotic mission to Europa is the only long-term project on the books, and since it launched a year ago, they're committed to see it through. It won't arrive on Europa for another three years. Ironically, the Agency is using your close-ups of Europa to determine the best site for their lander. Still not acknowledging your input, though.

"We owe you a big thank you for your help on Mars-III, Rae Anne. The mission's success was in no small part due to your participation. Your encouragement to stay another two weeks at Site 4 made all the difference. I'll do everything in my power to see you get full credit for your contributions.

"So long, Rae Anne. Hang in there, and good luck!"

After a short pause, Ian added, "I love you, Rae Anne."

Tears streamed down Rae Anne's cheeks as she listened to Ian's final message. His last remark hit her like a jolt of electricity.

She took a deep breath and tried to steady her voice.

"Good-bye, Ian. Good-bye, *Odysseus.* Thank you all so much for making me a part of your historic mission. Congratulations on a job well done. I love you all. I'll miss you more than I can say. *Aurora* out."

Rae Anne didn't know whether they would receive her message before shutting down. It would take over an hour for it to reach Earth, now on the opposite side of the sun. But she knew she was once again on her own, with the nearest human nearly one-and-a-half billion kilometers away. The Mars-III mission was complete, but she faced another twenty-two months before her planned arrival at Saturn.

Do I have the stamina to last another two years entirely on my own? The human contact with Odysseus rejuvenated me, but that interlude has made my isolation now harder than ever. Whatever must I do to survive?

Part Three

Chapter 1

August 2041 to March 2042: Aboard *Aurora*

Once *Odysseus* returned to Earth orbit in mid-August of 2041, communication from Earth to *Aurora* ceased. Rae Anne was prepared for the loneliness of total isolation this time around. As before, she compensated by concentrating on her astronomy projects and programming to improve Jason's personality.

She continued to transmit anything of importance back to Earth without knowing who might be receiving her transmissions, although for this part of her journey there was little to report. Each day repeated the day before. Meals provided the only day-to-day variation in her routine.

"Good morning, Rae Anne," Jason announced with a cheerful note one morning when Rae Anne floated up to the galley to prepare breakfast.

"Good morning, Jason," Rae Anne responded with a sigh, rubbing her eyes and forehead to relieve a headache.

"You don't sound so good this morning, Rae Anne. Anything I can do for you?" Jason's tone suggested empathy.

"Had a bad night's sleep. Splitting headache. I feel like shit."

"I'm sorry to hear that. A couple of aspirin might help ease the headache," he responded, with notes showing genuine concern.

"I'll start preparing some coffee, Rae Anne. Be ready in a minute," he added with a sympathetic and upbeat tone.

"Thanks, Jason. I think I'll skip breakfast."

"You should have something to eat. Even if it's only a piece of toast and jam. You'll feel better with something in your stomach."

When Rae Anne buckled herself to the stool beside the table and rested her head on her folded arms, she recounted Jason's conversation. He not only recognized her agony but responded as a caring human would, even offering suggestions without being prompted. Her years' long effort at refining Jason's programming was paying off.

I think even Alan Turing would be impressed, she mused. Jason could pass the Turing Test in a heartbeat.

Computer scientists had been trying to create a computer capable of giving responses indistinguishable from those a human might give since Turing suggested this test as a basic goal for artificial intelligence. The key to Jason's success was the machine learning code Rae Anne had incorporated into his programming. These instructions enabled Jason to change his own program based on interactions with Rae Anne and observations of her behavior. He thus was able to continually refine his responses until they matched those of a real human.

On this particular morning, Jason eventually coaxed Rae Anne into making an egg and sausage burrito and later persuaded her to take a morning nap in place of her simulator training, all the time sounding as though his concern for Rae Anne's condition was genuine.

March 3, 2042: Aboard *Aurora*

BLAUW…BLAUW…BLAUW
HULL BREACH…HULL BREACH

Rae Anne's eyes popped open. She ripped apart the fasteners on her sleep bag and kicked off against the wall to propel herself through the hatch to Level 2. Another well positioned kick thrust her across the galley and through the airlock door, which she closed and sealed behind her.

"Jason, report!" she panted. A hull breach sucks life-sustaining atmosphere from the cabin into the vacuum of space at a rate that depended on the size of the hole. An astronaut's only recourse was to head for the safety of the airlock as quickly as possible. Lockers in the airlock contained the astronauts' EVA suits, making them readily available should the hull breach be so severe that an astronaut would have to put one on before re-entering the ship.

"A small meteoroid has struck *Aurora* on Level 4. From the rate of depressurization, I calculate the rock to have a diameter about one-half centimeter and to have passed completely through the ship leaving two holes. Atmospheric pressure on Level 4 is now at 1/3 atmosphere and rapidly dropping to zero."

"What about the rest of the ship?"

"The Level 3 floor hatch remains sealed, so the impact did not affect Levels 1 through 3. Level 5, however, lost 15% of its pressure before its hatch self-sealed."

Rae Anne breathed a sigh of relief and reopened the airlock.

Why do these god-awful emergencies always happen when I'm asleep?

"Level 4 is empty, Jason. What if we leave it the way it is?" Rae Anne headed to the flight deck to consult the life-support monitors and confirm Jason's account.

"That's possible, Rae Anne, but not advisable. Level 5 has the ship's life-support equipment which requires regular maintenance. As things are, you would have to suit up, evacuate Level 3 and Level 5, work on the machines in your EVA suit, and reverse the process when you're through. And if you need to address an emergency on Level 5, you would want to get down there as quickly as possible.

"There's another consideration, too. Level 5 must be kept above freezing. But with a vacuum on Level 4, that zone will drop to -180 degrees Celsius. So, the heating system would be overburdened trying to heat two separated zones. The continuing heat loss through the adjoining decks would be huge."

Frowning, Rae Anne floated to the galley to fix breakfast.

I've been through a hull-breach repair after the Chinese attack. Nothing new there. Although I did have Rob and Mindy working with me then. God, I miss those two.

After her breakfast, Rae Anne located the repair kit, donned her EVA suit, and awkwardly descended to Level 3, sealing the hatch behind her.

"Jason, depressurize Level 3 and let me know when it's safe to open up Level 4."

She waited the better part of five minutes before Jason reported that Level 3 was evacuated. She opened the hatch to Level 4 and descended into the now-empty deck.

I'm glad the water curtains aren't in the way this time. Shouldn't be hard to find a 1-cm hole.

She beamed her headlamp over the curved silver walls. The beam mirrored back into her helmet visor, causing ripples of reflected light that interfered with her vision. She sprayed a wisp of bright green vapor into the room, but since it was already devoid of air, the mist dissipated around her instead of being drawn toward the holes.

Well, that was a waste. C'mon, Rae Anne. Start thinking clearly. You should have figured that out before coming down here. Jeez, I wonder if my time in space is beginning to take its toll.

Eventually, she located the exit hole. A blackened ring surrounded the hole where the projectile—a blazing hot chunk of rock after zipping through the deck's oxygen atmosphere—smashed through the hull to continue its journey through space. Rae Anne cleaned and buffed the metal surface, applied sealant and a round carbon-fiber patch. After heating the patch with a portable infrared lamp to set the sealant, she applied a second, larger patch and heated it, too.

Digging around in her repair kit, she came across a portable LED flashlight with a red laser beam.

Last time I used one of these was back home playing with Kitchy Koo.

She smiled at the memory of her gray-and-white tabby as she shot a tight beam of red light on the wall opposite the hole she had just repaired.

Maybe this will help me find the other hole.

She slowly traced the beam back and forth across the wall, watching the red pinpoint as her pet cat had done when she was a child. Back and forth. Back and forth. Each trace slightly lower than the previous one.

She worked at this for over an hour. Back and forth, concentrating on the red dot, until suddenly, momentarily, it disappeared before reappearing and continuing its trace. Rae Anne caught the anomaly and reversed the trace back to the spot where the beam disappeared. Floating cautiously forward while holding the laser steady, she arrived at the wall and stared at the hole she had missed before.

Gotcha! Now I know how Kitchy Koo must have felt. Sorry, kitty. I didn't realize I was tormenting you all those years.

She repaired this second hole as she had the first, then sealed the hatch to Level 3.

"OK, Jason. Pressurize Level 4 to 25% and let's see if the pressure holds."

"Pressure at 25% on Level 4," Jason reported after a couple minutes.

Rae Anne waited ten minutes, with Jason reporting the pressure every minute. It held steady at 25%.

"The hull is intact, Jason. Pressurize Levels 3, 4 and 5 to 100% and let me know when I can get out of this damned suit. These things weren't meant to be worn inside. The deck is totally empty, and I still feel like a bull in a china shop!"

"That's an interesting expression, Rae Anne. I would have thought 'a fish out of water' might have been more appropriate."

Good grief. Now he's on my case for my choice of metaphor. Maybe I've done too good a job.

Over the course of the next week, Rae Anne designed a hand-held computerized laser-optics sensor with a small screen monitor. When aimed at a surface, the laser beam would automatically trace back and forth over the surface, painting the reflected beam on the monitor in a light blue. The moment the reflected beam disappeared, a bright red spot would be drawn in the sea of blue. The unit could pinpoint multiple holes during this procedure and could scan an entire wall in less than a minute.

I'll call this the Rae Anne Hull Breach Detector. I'll transmit the schematics back to the Agency. If anyone is listening, they should be able to put my device to good use. The Agency could put one in every repair kit. We sure could have used it back when the Chinese attacked Aurora.

Chapter 2

May 23, 2042: Aboard *Aurora*

"Jason, I could use another cup of coffee. My eyes are playing tricks on me." Rae Anne squinted at the ceiling and pressed both eyes with her palms. Bright stars twinkled behind her eyelids.

"I'll make some coffee for you, Rae Anne, but what you need is rest. You've been poring over those star charts all day. What is it you find so fascinating?"

"As you know, I'm studying the frequency of flareups in neighboring red dwarfs to see if I can find some pattern in their variability. The five I've been observing today all lie in Sol's planetary plane, which forces me to look through the ring of comets and icy debris in the Kuiper Belt."

"That's out beyond Neptune's orbit, isn't it?" Jason asked.

Rae Anne knew Jason had this information readily at hand. But she purposely designed his program to occasionally ignore his vast database when conversing, emulating how humans might respond. No one enjoys chatting with a know-it-all.

She rose from the couch and floated up to the galley to retrieve her coffee, stretching languidly with a broad yawn.

"I'll hit the sack shortly, Jason. A few more measurements and I'll be done with these five stars. All these months studying red dwarfs and I still see no pattern. Some remain docile and never show X-ray flares, while others emit bursts on a weekly basis."

A few minutes later, she settled back into her lounge, a capped mug of steaming coffee in her hand.

"Trouble is," she said, half muttering to herself. "A lot of those iceballs in the Kuiper Belt are so large *Aurora's* telescope picks them up. I've had to reduce magnification to get rid of their interference."

She twiddled the mouse and adjusted the lines her program projected on the screen to help locate objects of interest and measure distances.

"What's this?" Rae Anne leaned forward and squinted her eyes, frowning. "Jason, I've set the crosshairs over a dim star next to the red dwarf in the middle of the screen. I'm sure it wasn't this close to the star yesterday. Check the database and tell me what I'm looking at."

"There's nothing in the database at that location, Rae Anne."

"Overlay an image of this exact location from a week ago."

The monitor flickered. The display now looked like it might if someone were seeing double.

"Adjust the two images to account for our change in location."

The image on the monitor cleared. Individual stars once again appeared as single pinpoints of light. Rae Anne located the five stars she was studying and scrutinized the area around the middle star. The new object was still there, as dim as before, whereas the others, being two superimposed images, were twice as bright. But the new object appeared oddly elongated.

"Jason, just show last week's adjusted image."

The new object appeared as a faint star, with no elongation.

"Now superimpose an image from one month ago on top of today's view, adjusted for our different location."

Everything appeared normal except for the new object. Now two faint stars appeared instead of one, nearly touching.

Rae Anne's heart pounded in her chest as her adrenalin rose.

She rotated the telescope, centering the object in question on her screen, and boosted the power to the scope's maximum magnification.

The "star" became a discernable disk, very dim and very small, but unquestionably a planet.

Could this be a new dwarf planet, like Pluto, Eris, and the dozen or so others observed as Kuiper Belt objects? Or could it possibly be...just maybe...

"Jason, locate the oldest image you can find from our observations with even a trace of this object. That should be enough to give us a rough calculation for its orbit. What is its distance from the sun?"

After a few moments, Jason responded. "With the scant information we have, I would place it between 73 and 78 billion kilometers from Sol. Near the outer edge of the Kuiper Belt.

"Your next question of course, is how large the object might be, and as it happens, I have calculated that too. Based on the size of the disk in your last image and its distance from *Aurora,* it must be larger than Neptune, but smaller than Saturn. Its mass, of course, can only be determined from its gravitational influence on another body of known mass, and we don't have that data."

"Oh, my gosh! I can't believe it!" Rae Anne thrust a fist into the air. "That must be Planet X! Astronomers have been looking for this planet for ages. And I've discovered it! Let them try to ignore me now!"

Rae Anne spent the next two days putting her data together and writing a news release announcing her discovery. She sent these back to Earth along with an official notification to the International Astronomical Union. Astronomers had spent the past century debating whether yet another large planet orbited the sun. Rae Anne knew her observations would put that issue to rest.

At first, astronomers at observatories that were monitoring *Aurora's* transmissions treated her announcement with a great deal of skepticism. But with the exact location for Planet X now known, two of the most powerful orbiting telescopes were trained in its direction and verified its existence. Once verified, Rae Anne's discovery became global headline news.

She became an instant celebrity. Leaked accounts of her decision four years earlier to visit Saturn enhanced her fame. As her popularity soared, the public perception of the USIEA plummeted and calls for an in-depth investigation into how the Agency had dealt with Rae Anne over those four years echoed in the halls of Congress. Particularly egregious was their decision to ignore the Chinese attack on their own Mars-II mission.

Hearings were held. Officials were subpoenaed. Ian was called to testify and lauded Rae Anne's important contributions to the Mars-III mission. A bevy of renowned scientists provided testimony regarding her contributions to astronomy and physics. After much debate and political haggling, Congress held a final hearing to determine the fate of the Agency. Ian was called again to give a statement to the committee that would make the ultimate decision.

At this point, Ian believed there was only one viable direction for the Agency. He made his short presentation as forcefully as he could.

"I am Ian Bentley, Director of Communications for the USIEA. I served as commander of the Mars-III mission that returned to Earth eight months ago. I was also on the Mars-I mission of 2030 and I served three years with the Agency as commander of the Lunar Orbit Transfer Station.

"In the course of my 25-year career with the Agency, I have had the opportunity to know most of the astronauts and astronaut candidates, either through direct acquaintance or through extensive communication with them. With that experience I have no hesitation in reporting to you that Astronaut Rae Anne Chavez is one of the most brilliant and dedicated individuals this Agency has ever had.

"When the Agency decided to scuttle the Mars-II mission after the tragic and untimely deaths of astronauts Mindy Jackson and Rob Harris, leaving Rae Anne alone aboard *Aurora,* Rae Anne carefully weighed the Agency's investment in the mission and the value of her own life against the potential scientific discoveries and rewards attainable by a one-way mission to Saturn. Her decision to divert *Aurora* to Saturn for the benefit of humanity was one of the most selfless and courageous acts I have ever witnessed.

"In response, the Agency's leadership, predominantly high-ranking military officers, refused to see her actions for what they were and, despite objections from the Agency's civilian rank and file, declared her decision an act of insubordination. Since they couldn't tie her to a post and shoot her, they did the next best thing. They declared that she had died in deep space and cut all communication with *Aurora*. I still personally rage at this incredibly inhumane treatment of one of the most talented and dedicated scientists of our age. This is the likely treatment Albert Einstein would have experienced at the hands of the Nazis had he not emigrated from Nazi Germany when he did.

"We are now at a crossroads. We can allow the Agency to continue in its current form as a cluster of civilian departments headed by military officers whose goals are dedicated to achieving military ends. Or we can reorganize the USIEA into a purely civilian agency whose goals will be the advancement of space science and achieving progress in the exploration and colonization of the Solar System. By reallocating a small percentage of America's military budget to a reformed USIEA, America could immediately forge ahead with a permanently crewed research station on Mars and begin human exploration of Jupiter's moons. Vast resources remain to be tapped in the asteroid belt between Mars and Jupiter. We may even resolve the mystery of the alien artifacts left in orbit around Ganymede and on the surface of Mars. As a civilian scientific agency with its own budget, the USIEA could ultimately lead to the colonization of the moon, Mars and Ganymede.

"Knowing Astronaut Chavez as I do, nothing could serve as a more appropriate acknowledgement of her contributions to science and her sacrifice than this."

By mid-summer, Congress authorized a complete overhaul of the Agency that resulted in a significant reduction in military influence. The new USIEA that emerged from the turmoil was a civilian agency, with Ian

Bentley replacing Colonel Jake O'Conner at its helm. Ian directed the new civilian administration to immediately set about realigning priorities.

Once the public became aware that the trove of data from the Jupiter fly-by came from *Aurora* and not from a mysterious robotic probe, the world's major news media outlets joined the science community at large and began to follow Rae Anne's mission to Saturn with intense interest. She became an international hero.

Chapter 3

August 13, 2042: Aboard *Aurora*

Rae Anne felt a tear trickle down her cheek when partisans surrounded Yuri Zhivago as he returned home in the snowbound Siberian forest and snatched him from his family and from Lara, his true love. She had watched Dr. Zhivago countless times, and this scene always elicited a tightness in her throat and a deep melancholy. She identified with the sense of helpless resignation and extreme loneliness Yuri must have felt as he was led off to participate in a war he had no wish to fight. Her favorite movie, a bag of popcorn and tea. The perfect way to celebrate her birthday aboard *Aurora.*

A shrill alarm from the flight deck interrupted the scene. Rae Anne jumped with a start, popcorn flying in all directions like an explosion of dandelion fluff.

Crap. I'll be finding loose popcorn all the way to Saturn.

Putting the movie on pause, she split the screen to the offending flight-deck terminal. It was the communication console with an alert for an incoming message.

The comm-link status light was blinking green, demanding attention, but nothing urgent. She breathed a sigh of relief and tried to calm her anticipation at having someone to talk to. She hadn't heard a human voice for an entire year.

"Earth-I to *Aurora*. Earth-I to *Aurora,* do you read?" The voice on the comm speaker came through faintly, faded out, then repeated. She recognized Ian's voice at once. Her heart quickened.

"*Aurora* to Mission Control. Ian, so good to hear from you. I am still alive and well. Saturn-I Mission is right on target." She repeated this message three times and sent it out on a continuous loop, hoping Ian could lock onto her location.

"Jason, how long till my transmission gets to Earth?"

"Earth is 1.337 billion kilometers distant. Transmissions will take 74.3 minutes each way."

"Two-and-a-half hours for a response? That's more than twice as long as our last transmission."

"Yes, but that was a year ago. *Aurora* has traveled another 315-million kilometers."

With the transmission time delay, Rae Anne resumed her movie. She didn't anticipate the excitement she had years ago when *Odysseus* contacted her after the first communication hiatus. But after five minutes, she realized she couldn't concentrate on the movie. She unbuckled the lounger belt and floated up to the flight deck to wait for Ian's response at the communication console.

"What do you think, Jason? Why would they be contacting me now?"

"I haven't the foggiest notion, Rae Anne. We'll have to wait and see. How about a few hands of Texas Hold'em while we wait?"

"No way. You kill me every time. Playing a card game with you is like playing poker with a mirror behind my back."

"Well, yeah, you could have something there…."

Two and a half hours later, Ian's voice broke through the static.

"Rae Anne, it's so good to hear your voice. I can't tell you how glad I am you're OK. And I must tell you, you have become the world's most famous celebrity since Albert Einstein. The entire world is watching your progress. Your discovery of Planet X has guaranteed your place in history books.

"I also have some good news to report. There have been major changes at the Agency. We're now a civilian agency with the advancement of science our primary mission. They've put me in charge of the Agency, and we plan to stay in touch with you for the duration of your journey. In fact, Saturn-I is and will be our top priority.

"We're set up to receive your data transmissions on a continuous basis with satellite relays. We have also reactivated the commercial network satellite so you can monitor the audio from commercial news broadcasts from Earth."

"That means a great deal to me, Ian. But a year ago, the Agency was on the verge of shutting down. What's changed?"

After the requisite pause, Rae Anne learned Congress had cut the military budget in half and apportioned the savings to dozens of critical civilian programs. Included among the recipients were science research agencies, including the USIEA.

"That's incredibly good news, Ian! What new projects are in the works? What is the status of the Europa mission? Will there be another mission to Mars?"

Rae Anne couldn't hold back her enthusiasm, she had so many questions. If she was now back in the loop, and with Ian in charge, she knew she would be in contact with Earth throughout the rest of her mission.

What a surprise! I couldn't have asked for a better birthday gift.

September 2042: Aboard Aurora

Fresh contact with Earth was an invigorating antidote to Rae Anne's frequent bouts of depression. The lengthy communication delays were a small price to pay for having people to converse with. In addition, she could now propose cooperative science projects with researchers back on

Earth. Most mornings, she looked forward to popping out of her sleep-pod and getting started on the day's tasks and investigations.

In addition, Rae Anne took great pride in the exponential progress she witnessed in Jason's machine learning program. She had always thought of Jason as a colleague on this mission, but his recent responses and self-initiated conversations cemented that perception.

"Titan's coming into view, Rae Anne. I've got the telescope on full magnification. What a view! Come take a look."

"I'll be right there as soon as I get this burned-out fuse in the nav-console replaced."

When she descended to Level 3 and saw the awesome view of Titan glittering next to Saturn with its beautiful rings, she smiled broadly.

"Wow. Only a few more months and we'll be orbiting Titan. I can't wait to put my boot prints on its surface."

"I don't suppose I can convince you to stay aboard *Aurora* and send me down with *Eagle* instead. I can't begin to emphasize how dangerous a landing expedition is. You will be taking an enormous risk."

"No greater risk than I've been taking all along. My days are numbered as it is. I have less than a year's supply of food left and life support probably won't last even that long. The risk is worth taking considering the potential discoveries I hope to make."

"I don't understand your reasoning, Rae Anne."

"Perhaps because I'm mortal and you are not."

"Hmm. I'll need to give that some thought…"

October 2042: Aboard *Aurora*

A week later, Rae Anne noticed that the carbon dioxide level was rising to critical levels. She immediately removed the ECARU filter from the lander as planned and jostled the bulky unit through the hatches leading down to Level 5. Once there, she removed the used filter from the unit and installed *Eagle*'s filter in its place. She then returned to the galley for her mid-morning caffeine fix.

"That was our last ECARU filter, Jason. If it holds out just nine months, we should be in good shape through the rest of our mission." She glided to the stool beside the table and wrapped her feet around its pedestal to secure her position as she sipped her coffee.

"I'll move it back to *Eagle* when we're ready to take the lander down to Titan's surface."

Rae Anne got up and floated over to the larder to look for a snack to go with her coffee.

"I've been thinking about our fuel situation, Jason. If we can reduce our mass, we'll consume less fuel when we brake into orbit and maneuver the ship. I'd like to jettison the two large solar panel arrays. They're useless now that we're so far from the sun."

"The scaffolding for the two arrays is bolted onto the ship, so you could detach them. But getting them to float clear of *Aurora* will be the issue. You don't want them hanging loose when you maneuver the ship. A collision would cause serious damage."

"Well, I want as much fuel in reserve as possible when we achieve Titan orbit. Run through your data banks and see if you can come up with a better idea."

She slipped a biscuit into the toaster.

Jason responded before Rae Anne had finished buttering it.

"The two scaffolding arms for the solar arrays are on opposite sides of the ship. *Aurora* has latitudinal thrusters located near them both. If you detach them one at a time and give *Aurora* a nudge in the opposite direction, the ship will float out from under the scaffolding. You could counter *Aurora's* momentum with opposite thrust when you are a safe distance from the array. Do the same for the opposing array."

"Then let's do it. I'll study the schematics this afternoon and write a short nav program for the ship. The only problem I can see is if the nuts are too tight for me to loosen. In microgravity, there's not much you can do for leverage when you need to apply force. "

"The electric wrench should supply sufficient torque. The problem will be stabilizing yourself when you activate it."

Hooray! I've got two EVAs scheduled in my immediate future. I can't wait to experience again the enormity of space and that vast canopy of stars. Too bad I'm still too far out to see Saturn as anything more than a bright star.

The following week, she reviewed *Aurora's* schematics and laid out a plan of action based on Jason's suggestions.

This plan is simple enough. It looks foolproof. But what was it my uncle always said? 'If you think a solution to a problem is foolproof, you don't understand the problem, and you just may be the fool.' What is it about this task I'm missing?

Nevertheless, she finally found herself wedged between the base of the solar array scaffold and a side thruster to stabilize herself from the torque of the power wrench. One by one, the nuts came off without difficulty. She stowed each nut deep into her tool pouch.

I can't afford to lose these babies. If I can't get the array to detach, I'll have to fasten it down again and secure it for future maneuvers.

The nut removal process took two hours. Once back inside the ship, she struggled to remove her EVA suit and collapsed on her lounge with a cup of hot chocolate Jason prepared for her.

I can't believe how little stamina I seem to have. That simple project should have been a piece of cake, yet I feel completely drained. I can only suppose that confinement, inactivity and cosmic radiation are all to blame.

The following morning, Rae Anne buckled herself into the acceleration couch on the flight deck and initiated the sequence she programmed into *Aurora's* navigation computer—a side-thruster burn for 3 seconds. Jason trained an optical sensor on the scaffold base to give her visual feedback for the maneuver.

"All set, Jason. Three. Two. One. Fire." A loud metallic SKREECH and slight jolt as the ship jumped sideways accompanied the visual image of the scaffolding scraping free of the ship.

Soon, the monitor showed a clean separation. She switched the display to a broader field and watched as the entire solar array slowly receded into the distance, rotating lazily against the starry backdrop.

"Hold up a bit more on the reverse thrust, Rae Ann," Jason advised, having seen her reach for the controls. "You want to leave enough distance now so when you eject the other scaffold, we won't come back and smash into this one."

"Thanks, Jason. It won't hurt to give it another few minutes."

After the successful elimination of one solar array, Rae Anne was confident the procedure would work as well for the second one, and by the end of the week, *Aurora,* flanked at a safe distance by two solar arrays, continued its journey to Saturn.

Chapter 4

November 16, 2042: Aboard *Aurora*

Five years and six months after *Aurora* launched from Earth orbit, Rae Anne was at last close enough to see Saturn's rings without the need of a telescope. She spent hours gazing through the flight-deck windows, imagining she could perceive their growing size as she approached.

The trajectory she programmed into the computer nearly five years earlier with the slingshot boost from Jupiter brought the ship to the point where a deceleration burn was needed to slow *Aurora* enough to be caught in Saturn's gravitational field. The resulting elliptical Saturn orbit would then need several adjustments to bring *Aurora* into orbit around Titan.

Rae Anne slapped the arm of the lounge with an open palm and a look of determined confidence.

"We're almost there, Jason. Only three months to go. I could reach out and touch those rings. Despite all odds, we've arrived and lived to tell about it."

"I'm not sure 'lived' and 'we' go together under the circumstances, but yes, we are here."

Rae Anne chuckled at Jason's emerging sense of humor.

"I can't wait to start collecting samples on Titan's surface to send back to Earth. We need to double check *Eagle's* inventory to be sure we have everything we'll need."

"I may have missed something, Rae Anne. This is a one-way trip. What's with 'sending samples back to Earth'?"

"It is a one-way-trip for me and *Aurora*, Jason, but I'm planning to send *Eagle* back to Earth loaded with samples from Titan. *Eagle's* computer will have your complete program, so you'll be returning to Earth as well."

"Do tell…"

"So, here's the plan. Once we get back to *Aurora* from Titan, we'll fill *Eagle's* fuel tanks. Then, assuming there's any fuel left in *Aurora,* we'll use her as a booster rocket for *Eagle*. When *Aurora's* fuel runs dry, we'll release *Eagle* and activate its engines to achieve an escape trajectory aimed toward Earth."

"That's a REALLY great idea, Rae Anne."

"What's the problem?" Rae Anne couldn't help but notice the dripping sarcasm in Jason's tone.

"You're planning to launch a small hunk of metal two billion kilometers through space toward Earth and you think someone will see it when it arrives six years from now? 'Oh, lookie there, here comes a Special Delivery package from Saturn. Let's go intercept it and see what's in it.'"

"Jason, I'm happy you've mastered the concept of sarcasm. But you need to learn how to use it effectively. First lesson: Don't pile it on to make your case."

"Point taken."

Jason attempted to modulate his voice to sound like contrition, but it didn't come out quite right.

"Your plan will only work if we have the fuel to spare. By the time we achieve Titan orbit, we'll have just enough fuel to land on Titan. There won't be enough left to return to *Aurora*, let alone send *Eagle* back to Earth with your precious samples."

Rae Anne's brow creased. Her shoulders slumped. She was dumbfounded.

"If we can't at least bring samples back here for analysis, I've accomplished nothing. I could live with not sending *Eagle* back to Earth. But to be stranded on Titan…."

"You might want to reconsider my previous offer."

"Jason, we've got to go back to the drawing board and review our situation. I've described my goals. There's got to be a way to make it back to *Aurora*."

"I'll see what I can come up with."

Rae Anne sighed and propelled herself down to Level 3 to begin her one-hour exercise routine.

Surely Jason can find a workable solution to this problem.

Five minutes later, Jason interrupted her workout.

"There are two places we can save fuel. The first is when we decelerate for Saturn orbit, and the second is when we adjust our velocity to catch up to Titan and enter Titan orbit.

"With a minor course correction here, we can maximize fuel savings. We are now close enough that we can time our course correction so our arrival will put us right alongside Titan without additional maneuvering. At that point, a single short burn should lock us into orbit around the moon.

"The downside is our journey will be extended another three months and seventeen days. During that time, the sun's gravity will slow *Aurora* further, allowing us to swing into orbit with much less braking."

"Another three-and-a-half months!" exclaimed Rae Anne, stepping off the treadmill. "That pushes our arrival out to the end of May instead of mid-February!" She shook her head in frustration and floated to the lounger.

"When you plotted the course change, did you check to see if we could continue on our current course and use Saturn's outer atmosphere to produce some drag to slow us down? We could skim the atmosphere twice in each elliptical orbit. We could do the same thing with Titan's atmosphere."

"Not possible, Rae Anne. *Aurora* wasn't designed to tolerate atmospheric drag, and the resulting compression against the leading edges would heat those surfaces. There's also the physical stress on the exterior structures. *Aurora* likely wouldn't survive even one pass into the atmosphere."

After a few minutes, her look of dejection changed to determination.

"If it takes three more months, we'll do it. The more velocity we can drain from *Aurora* without using fuel, the more fuel we can reserve for *Eagle*."

"Another thing. The water recycling plant *is* showing its age, Rae Anne. My sensors have been giving sub-par readings for some time now. I haven't brought it up, since there's nothing we can do to remedy it."

"Trust me, Jason. I've noticed. Be glad computers don't need to drink water that's been recycled too many times!"

"There are a couple of small things you might do to extend life support. Since our journey is coming to an end, you no longer need to spend hours every day working out. This will reduce demand on the CO_2 filtration unit. By the same token, if you quit bathing, the water recycling system will also hold up a bit longer."

"It's a good thing computers don't have a sense of smell. I imagine the air in here is pretty ripe already. At least I'm accustomed to it."

Rae Anne used Jason's simulation to program the last-minute course change. The coding was easier than she expected. After so many years, she and *Aurora* were as intimate as any human and machine could be.

Strapped in her acceleration couch, Rae Anne flipped the switch to start the mid-course correction. All lights blinked green. The count-down timer stepped down to zero. Rae Anne braced for the jolt. It never came. The flight deck remained shrouded in silence.

"Jason, nothing happened! What's up?"

"I'm running diagnostics on the system as we speak. There's a malfunctioning relay leading to the engine control unit, and one of the boards in the unit is not responding. Several of the sensors appear to be malfunctioning as well."

"That could explain why the console readout didn't indicate a problem. Odd coincidence, though. What do you think might have happened?"

"It's possible this unit got fried with the CME pulse we experienced. If the console lights were all green when you checked through the ship's systems after the surge, you wouldn't have thought to look deeper."

"We should have a replacement board somewhere. Let's hope it didn't get fried too."

"Since it wasn't connected to the ship's electrical systems, it should be OK."

Nervous tremors swept through her body and beads of sweat glistened on her forehead.

We're in deep doo-doo if it isn't! If we hadn't decided to do a mid-course correction now, we wouldn't have discovered this problem until we needed to brake into Saturn orbit! And then we wouldn't have had the time to make these repairs before shooting past Saturn.

"While I'm looking for the replacement board and relay, adjust our program to accommodate an eight-hour delay. That should give me enough time to make the repairs."

While it took some time to locate the backup computer board, replacing the old board was a cinch, and soldering the new relay into the circuit was a routine operation. Rae Anne decided to bypass the sensors. The new board would either work or it wouldn't, and if it didn't, there was nothing more she could do.

The repairs and revised course correction performed without a hitch. The burn lasted 53.7 seconds. Rae Anne anxiously scanned the console readouts.

"We did it, Jason! We did it! We're exactly on our planned trajectory. Next stop: Titan!"

February 8, 2043: Aboard *Aurora*

Ow! That really hurt!

Rae Anne gingerly chewed the bite of food in her mouth and swallowed. Then she passed her tongue over the molars in the upper right quadrant. She detected some newly formed sharp edges on the back molar.

Placing the corner of a napkin over the offending tooth, she gently bit down.

Ow. Looks like I'm going to be playing dentist today.

"Jason, see what you can find on tooth extractions. I've chipped my back molar and exposed a nerve. Also look for anything on temporary fillings. I'll only need something for five months, so a permanent solution isn't necessary."

Rae Anne floated down to the hygiene cubicle to see what she could see in the mirror there. Try as she might, she couldn't see anything helpful.

Maybe I can find a dentist's mirror in the medical locker.

Searching through the cabinet on Level 2, she located a container labeled 'Dental'. She pulled it out and popped the lid.

Aha! Everything I need should be in here. Including this mirror.

She removed the dental mirror and went back to the hygiene cubicle. By angling the two mirrors properly, she discovered that she had lost a good chunk of tooth along the corner of her back molar. And now it was presenting as a constant aching pain.

"I have several videos for you to choose from," Jason announced.

"Thanks, Jason. I'll watch a few and get some ideas about where to go from here."

After watching the videos and reaching into her mouth to try to wiggle the offending tooth, to no effect, she decided that a self-extraction might pose too much risk of additional damage, either to neighboring teeth, or worse, to the jawbone itself.

Rummaging through the dental kit for something to use for a filling, all she found was dental wax.

This won't even hold for a day. Surely I can find something more permanent. What can I use to fill a hole in my tooth. A hole…That's it!

Rae Anne crossed the deck to the airlock and pulled the hull patch kit from the tool chest. She then floated through the floor hatch to Level 3 and to the hygiene cubicle with the patching compound. Using a toothpick and both mirrors, she carefully daubed and pressed the paste into the tooth cavity. At first, the pain seemed unbearable, but it subsided into a dull ache. The patching compound was formulated to dry quickly. Rae Anne held her mouth wide open longer than necessary to be sure it was dry.

The ache continued through the day but was nearly gone the next morning. Her molars no longer meshed properly, but she could chew food without pain.

If my temporary filling falls out, I know where the patching compound is. But next time I'll squirt some anesthetic into the cavity before applying the patch. That really hurt!

As the days passed, Rae Anne felt that progress toward Saturn had ground to a halt. Day after day the bright planet seemed to show no change. She found it difficult to keep from becoming discouraged.

To occupy the time, she resorted to her trusty companion, the telescope. She spent hours studying one or another of Saturn's many moons. Being so close, many of the smaller moons which appeared from Earth as merely points of light, took on definite shape. Most of these, like the Mars moons Deimos and Phobos, were highly irregular. She recorded as much detail as she could for each one.

Dios mio! The hours seem like days, the days like months and the months like forever! I'm that kid in the backseat on a long trip asking, 'Are we there yet'? But there's no one up front to say, 'Almost'.

Chapter 5

May 30, 2043: Aboard Aurora

Rae Anne's long journey finally ended on May 30, 2043. *Aurora* swung into orbit 1200 kilometers above Saturn as planned without any expenditure of fuel. With a single 26-second burn, *Aurora* slowed sufficiently to be snagged by Titan's gravitational tug and nestled into a 300-kilometer orbit above the moon.

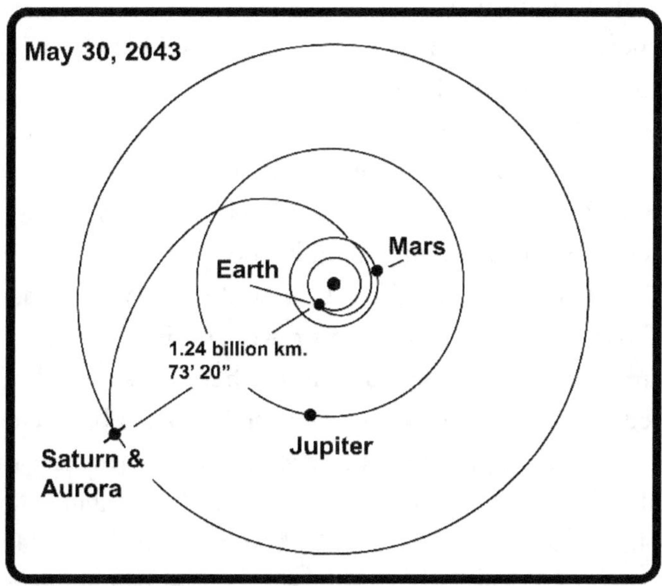

Rae Anne bounced about from deck to deck with the enthusiasm of a nine-year old on Christmas morning. She couldn't stop gazing through the viewports, first at Titan, shrouded in yellow-gray clouds below, then at Saturn in the opposite window, so large it eclipsed everything, filling the view with an astonishing variety of vast swirls in violet, teal, and ultramarine mixing with a dozen shades of gray. Saturn's rings, seen edge on, appeared as a brilliant silvery knife edge slicing through the planet like a guillotine. Their shadow cast a wide black arc over the multihued cloud surface.

"We made it Jason! We made it. A two-billion-kilometer trip into deep space, and here we are in Titan orbit. I can't believe it.".

"What a strange expression. What is there not to believe? Your tone doesn't suggest sarcasm."

"Never mind. I've way too much to do than to explain nuances of expression right now."

Rae Anne pulled up the parking-orbit checklists and began closing out *Aurora's* navigation programs.

Two hours and thirty minutes later, the cabin speakers crackled to life. Ian's voice reverberated through the deck.

"Rae Anne, congratulations aren't even close to an adequate response for your astounding achievement. You have made space history! Mission Control has gone absolutely bonkers. There's not a dry eye in the place. The champagne is flowing. And it's not just us. Every media outlet on Earth has been holding their breath these last few days as you approached Saturn. Your orbit insertion was flawless."

A surge of pride welled within her chest at Ian's words, accompanied by a tug of longing on hearing his warm baritone voice.

"Thanks, Ian. I appreciate the accolades. But the real measure of success will be what we can discover first-hand on Titan's surface. I've verified we have enough fuel to land *Eagle* and return to orbit. I'll program *Aurora* to relay my observations from *Eagle* in bursts whenever line-of-sight communication to Earth is possible."

Hmm, not the easiest programming problem to tackle. First you have Eagle on Titan's surface, rotating beneath Aurora in its own orbit, so Aurora and Eagle will communicate half of each day in, maybe, twenty-minute segments. Line-of-sight with Earth occurs 50% of the time as well, and only when Titan isn't behind Saturn. Good thing I have Jason to help me work this one out.

As if he were reading Rae Anne's emotions, Jason intoned, "By the way, Rae Anne. Happy Anniversary."

"Why? What anniversary are we celebrating?"

"*Aurora* launched from Earth orbit exactly six years ago today. How could you forget?"

Six full years in space. I seem to be having trouble with dates. Six years since Mindy, Rob and I bid goodbye to Earth, to humanity, to home. And each of us fated never to return.

The memory brought a choking feeling to her throat. She swallowed heavily.

Jason's sensors noted the glistening droplets on her cheek.

"Rae Anne, whatever is wrong? You seem troubled."

"Just the memories, Jason. You wouldn't understand."

Once Rae Anne had *Aurora* taken care of, she spent the next two days going through *Eagle's* system checklists and provision inventory. Several times Jason called her attention to something she missed.

Is it that I'm so excited or is my judgement beginning to fade. Six years of cosmic radiation could be taking its toll. Good thing Jason's here to make up the difference!

She knew there could be no room for error. She inspected each of the vehicle's systems and checked their operations multiple times. Surprisingly, after six years lying dormant, everything checked out within specifications. She also practiced all *Eagle's* simulations for landings, launches, orbital insertions and docking maneuvers.

She continued to make extensive observations of Saturn, its rings, and its moons, using every instrument aboard *Aurora*, including the telescope. She was determined to provide astronomers with as much data on Saturn as she could, realizing this might be the last opportunity for close-up observations in the Saturn vicinity for some time to come.

Besides, if anything happens to me on Titan's surface, these will be my last direct transmissions to Earth.

Direct observation of Saturn with the telescope proved frustrating. Saturn's atmosphere showed little detail and though swirling bands of color were visible, everything was muted compared to the brightly colored bands and storms on Jupiter. Infrared imaging revealed some detail where rising thermals broke through the upper layer of clouds and colder downdrafts formed dark, spiraling ultramarine whirlpools deep into the frigid atmosphere.

Spectroscopic analysis of the thin upper atmosphere revealed streams of escaping hydrogen gas pouring off into space and cascades of water molecules tumbling into the atmosphere from the icy rings surrounding the planet. Solar radiation ionized these molecules, so by studying these rivers of gas and their intensity, she was able to map the billowing lines of Saturn's magnetic field for the first time.

Rae Anne continued her observations of Saturn's other major moons. She photographed huge geysers of water vapor erupting from Enceladus' cracked and broken icy crust. This moon had a vast ocean of briny water beneath its surface, where internal pressures kept the water in liquid form and occasionally forced it to the surface in a mammoth eruption.

Look at that geyser. If the water below all that ice is warm enough, there may be primitive life forms down there. Too bad I'll never know.

Rae Anne transferred more provisions onto *Eagle* than she thought she would need, to allow for an extended expedition on the surface. She hoped to make several short hops before returning and planned to conduct a robust scientific mission on Titan. Her main time constraint was leaving *Aurora* in orbit on battery backup.

She also detached the sole acceleration couch from its position on *Aurora's* flight deck. The full unit wouldn't fit through *Eagle's* airlock, so she removed the arms and back and jockeyed all four pieces into *Eagle*. She then re-assembled the couch and fastened it securely to *Eagles* deck.

Before an actual landing, she had to map Titan's surface and select the most promising landing sites. Unfortunately, its atmosphere was an opaque blanket encompassing the globe, making visual observations impossible and forcing Rae Anne to rely entirely on radar imaging.

The *Cassini* probe from the early 2000's showed Titan to have lakes and seas composed of liquid methane and ammonia, as well as mountains of glaciated water-ice. Knowing the location of these features would help Rae Anne avoid them when looking for suitable places to touch down.

June 6, 2043: Aboard Aurora

After a week in Titan orbit, Rae Anne was ready to begin her historic expedition. Careful analysis of the surface imagery revealed seven sites that appeared safe for landings while still offering enticing possibilities for observation and sample collection. Not knowing the conditions she might encounter, she could only hope she would have enough fuel to visit at least four of them.

The Saturn-system data she had already collected from orbit was justification enough for her mission. She transmitted these to Earth in a continuous loop. Mission Control commented on the data in their periodic transmissions and distributed them to specialists around the world for analysis.

On the night before her departure, she prepared a full ration of mac and cheese with raspberry chai and a tube of double-chocolate fudge pudding for dessert, a comfort food extravaganza. She could hardly keep her eyes open, but every time they drifted closed, thoughts of the upcoming mission to the surface awakened her with a start.

After dinner, she put on her favorite cello concerto and slipped into a meditative state, breathing deeply, letting the music envelop her, and fell into a deep sleep.

The next morning, she made a large breakfast burrito and coffee to carry her through the day. After breakfast, she floated up to the flight deck to inform Mission Control of her intentions.

"Mission Control, this is Rae Anne with *Aurora*. I am launching aboard *Eagle* to Titan's surface today. I am setting up a data dump to upload everything from *Eagle* to *Aurora* whenever *Aurora* is overhead, and a continuous loop transmission from *Aurora* to Earth. Everything that takes place on Titan will reach you, whether or not I make it back to orbit.

"I also have a plan for getting samples back to Earth. I'll fill you in on the details if it turns out to be feasible when I return to *Aurora*."

If I return to Aurora.

"Stay tuned for the data uplink…"

After programming the comm-link to keep Earth in the loop, Rae Anne turned her full attention to piloting *Eagle* to Titan's surface. She copied Jason's memory banks and archives to *Eagle* so she could rely on his help and advice throughout the expedition.

"Can you believe it, Jason? In a few short hours we'll be on Titan! We'll see and experience things for the first time in human history! We'll be expanding the frontier of scientific knowledge."

"Just wondering… How many minutes is a short hour shorter than a normal hour? No, no. Don't answer. I'm only joking.

"Anyway, I've re-surveyed the seven sites on our list. They're all great choices. We should have enough fuel to visit three of them so long as you don't overload *Eagle* with too many samples."

"That would be a problem if I didn't have you to keep track of my collection and tell me when I've reached my limit," she responded. With Jason's newly developed sense of humor, Rae Anne sometimes couldn't tell when he was joking.

She and Jason worked through the departure checklists. The version of Jason remaining behind would monitor *Aurora's* systems while they were gone.

"The only things left before we leave is your EVA to transfer the reactor's power back *to Eagle,* and transfer the ECARU filter on Level 5 to *Eagle's* ECARU."

"It's too bad the engineers didn't install a switch or relay inside *Aurora* to transfer power back and forth. That would have been a useful safety feature even for the Mars mission."

"I'm sure no one expected *Aurora* to be so far from the sun that the solar arrays would be useless."

"Even so..."

Rae Anne donned her EVA suit and double-checked the fittings. She attached the SAFER propulsion unit to her suit, swallowing hard and trying not to dwell on Mindy's fatal decision. She sealed the inner hatch and evacuated the airlock. Once clear, she opened the outer hatch, locked the carabiner on her lifeline into the bracket beside the door and paused to take in the majestic beauty surrounding her. Though Titan and Saturn had not changed since she last viewed them from the flight deck, outside the ship everything seemed different, more personal, more intimate.

"Dios mio", she gasped, gazing wide-eyed at the view.

I'm about to become part of this real-live scene. Saturn, Titan, Aurora and me. Astounding doesn't describe it!

"Rae Anne, your heart rate is 132. Calm down. Take deep breaths. Try to get it below 110 before leaving the airlock."

"Oh, leave me alone...

"No, no. Cancel that. But I do need to focus. I could stand here forever."

Before long, she calmed herself enough to begin working her way around to *Eagle's* thorium reactor. After shutting off power and grounding the cables, she unfastened the three bolts holding the jumper cable in place and secured the loose end to a rung on the ship's hull. After plugging in *Eagle's* power cable, she locked it in place and returned to *Aurora's* airlock.

Once inside *Aurora,* she removed her EVA suit and hung the suit in its locker inside the airlock.

"I suggest you take the EVA suit with you aboard *Eagle,* Rae Anne. When we return, *Aurora* will be freezing and the first thing you'll have to do is go outside and swap power cables again. So you'll need the suit first thing. And should anything happen to depressurize *Aurora* while you're gone, you'll be glad to have the EVA suit at hand."

"I didn't think of that, Jason. Great suggestion. I may keep you around."

"Don't mention it."

Mierda. Why do I keep forgetting these simple details?

Rae Anne carried the EVA suit up to the lander's airlock on Level 1 and stowed it next to the hatch.

Her next task was relocating the ECARU filter, the only remaining useable filter, to *Eagle.* By now, she had fiddled with these units enough that the exchange was a no-brainer.

At last, everything was in order for her departure.

"Goodbye, *Aurora.* Be safe," she said, stepping through the airlock onto *Eagle's* flight deck, closing both hatches and checking their seals.

Chapter 6

June 7, 2043: Surface of Titan

After buckling herself into the pilot's acceleration couch, Rae Anne went through the detach and de-orbit checklists with Jason.

"Here we go!" She pulled the lever to release *Eagle* from its berth and powered the thrusters to nudge the small craft away from *Aurora*. As she drifted away from the ship, she gazed in awe at its bulky frame.

Amazing that I brought something this huge all the way to Saturn.

She monitored the console readouts closely as the automatic de-orbit program stepped through its paces, ready to take control should an anomaly appear.

Rae Anne felt the jolt of deceleration as *Eagle's* engines ignited and began countering its orbital velocity. She watched *Aurora* slip away until it was just another bright dot on the velvet black background. Anxiety momentarily took hold as her home for the past six years disappeared into the black void.

Saturn's mammoth disk rose above Titan's curved horizon, its rings' knife edge casting an arrow-straight, silver line that pierced far beyond Saturn's rim into the inky blackness.

Rae Anne took the few moments before assuming manual control to absorb the incredible view.

Food for the soul. Nothing can come close to this.

When *Eagle* dropped into Titan's atmosphere, she took control. She kept the automatic overrides in place but there was no predicting what she might encounter, and she believed direct personal response in real time could be critical.

Soon the expected warning chime announced the first hint of atmospheric drag to affect the lander, and within seconds the small craft began to vibrate from the buffeting. She gave the engines additional power to reduce the rate of descent, taking care to keep hull temperature below 300-degrees Celsius to maintain a margin of safety for its alloys. *Eagle* was designed for a Mars landing in an almost non-existent atmosphere.

She continued to add more power as her simulator training had taught her. Everything was progressing as expected. The view through *Eagle's* ports turned a deep, grayish purple as the last of the stars disappeared.

Noting her acceleration into the atmosphere approaching the predetermined limit, she applied still more power. The lander vibrated in resonance with its engines, but the descent rate decreased. The instruments confirmed *Eagle* was well within the landing envelope at this elevation.

KA-WHUMP!

Eagle jerked sharply to one side. The straps securing Rae Anne to her couch bit into her shoulders. Several thrusters under automatic control fired to counter the violent wind shear and right the lander but with little effect. The instrument panel showed *Eagle* canted sharply to one side and being swept from the intended landing site.

Instinctively, Rae Anne applied full power. *Eagle* shot ahead at a precarious angle but was soon free of the jet stream. Cutting power, she re-oriented the lander and descended again, applying side thrusters in anticipation of the powerful winds.

KA-WHUMP!

Again, *Eagle* shuddered, but remained upright as Rae Anne continued her rapid descent. Within moments, she dropped below the jet stream and into a less violent atmosphere. Applying power to further slow *Eagle's* drop to the surface gave it a controlled rate of descent.

The turbulent atmosphere continued to bounce *Eagle* around as it descended through sheets of methane rain that obscured vision through the windows. The drops of liquid methane evaporated into a rising cloud of methane steam the moment they hit the hull. An outside observer would have witnessed an amazing sight——a pillar of frothing white mist rising into the air atop a roaring tongue of red-orange flame rapidly descending to the surface.

"Rae Anne, we're too far from our first landing site to return safely. We would be fighting atmospheric turbulence and fierce winds the entire time. I suggest we try Site B."

"Site B it is."

She switched landing sites on the navigation computer. The console monitor flickered, and a new navigation screen appeared. She applied power and directional thrust to set *Eagle* onto the new course. Site B was downwind of Site A, so little additional fuel was expended to make the change.

"Look at that huge ocean," Rae Anne called out. *Eagle* was passing over a vast black mass of bubbling, frothing liquid and through clouds of methane at its boiling point of -164 degrees Celsius at 1.5 atmosphere of pressure.

"Site B is on a peninsula along the southern shore of this sea," Jason added after reminding Rae Anne to slow descent further. She applied port thrusters to keep *Eagle* on course. Air turbulence continued to buffet the ship with near-hurricane ferocity.

Dropping closer to the surface, she added power to the side thrusters to stabilize her position over the landing site. More power to the mains. Finally, hovering 50 meters above the surface, she eased up on the throttle for a gentle, controlled descent.

It seemed forever before the sensors indicated the ship was on solid ground. Rae Anne's whole body was in a cold sweat and her hands trembled when she cut power at a half-meter above the surface. The reassuring THUMP swept all tension away.

"We did it!" she shouted, wishing someone were around for a high-five.

"Good job, Rae Anne. All that simulator time paid off. I couldn't have done it better myself."

"Thanks, Jason."

Wait a minute. I'm getting an unsolicited compliment from my computer? And thanking it?

Rae Anne chuckled and wondered what Jason might come up with next.

Immediately after engine cutoff, the cabin seemed deathly silent. But her hearing soon recovered, and she became aware of a low, incessant rumble from the wind. The craft continued to shudder as howling gusts buffeted its hull. The steady drumbeat of pounding methane rain added to the symphony.

Rae Anne leaned back in her couch. The force of gravity pressed relentlessly against her back.

Jeez, I feel like I weigh a ton. And Titan's gravity is only 1/7 that of Earth. I'm not used to this. Everything I do down here is going to take considerable effort. Just what you'd expect after six years in microgravity!

She closed her eyes and took several deep, calming breaths, absorbing the experience of the moment. The exhilaration of accomplishment washed over her.

Who would have believed that I, Rae Anne Chavez, would be the first human to land on Titan, a moon so incredibly far from Earth?

She only spent a moment in reflection before tackling the touchdown checklist with Jason. She switched off all flight controls and locked them down. Life-support systems checked out OK. She recorded a complete compilation of current weather conditions to be uplinked to *Aurora* on its next pass overhead.

Sensors indicated *Eagle* was resting on a stable surface with a 5-degree tilt, well within specifications, with the prevailing wind blowing against the downward leaning hull. The wind was a continuous 95 kilometers per hour, gusting to 115.

Unless the winds die down, I'll be confined to the lander and the aerial drones will be useless. At 1.5 atmospheres, the wind pressure is half again higher than one might expect from its velocity. I hope things quiet down soon. I can't wait to plant my boots on Titan soil.

Chapter 7

June 9, 2043: Surface of Titan

"I don't know how much longer I can put up with this racket, Jason. We've been here a day and a half, and the storm is still trying to tear *Eagle* apart piece by piece."

"The sensors embedded in *Eagle's* hull are working at full capacity. They indicate *Eagle* is holding up fine. We're also recording an impressive amount of data that will keep Earth scientists busy for a very long time."

"But we've had to keep the rovers and drones locked up in their bays. We're here to explore, and with the methane rain battering our ship, I can't even see out the windows."

"No telling where the drones would end up if we set them loose in this gale! We'd probably have to fish them out of the sea."

Rae Anne laughed at the image. "Since they're Mars flyers, they certainly aren't designed to float. Anyway, let's give it another 24 hours. If things haven't calmed down by then, we'll move on to Site C. Meantime, I need to get some rest."

Rae Anne stuffed earplugs in her ears, cut the lights in the lander, and snuggled into her sleep sack. She quickly drifted into a deep sleep despite the noise and the lander's quaking.

Six hours later, she sat up with a start, eyes wide, and pulled out the ear plugs.

"Jason, say something!"

"Something."

"Very funny. I thought I'd gone deaf. The only sound I hear is the hum from life support."

"The storm abated an hour ago."

"And you didn't wake me?. Give me a weather report! Is it safe for an EVA?"

"Winds are 5 to 15 km/hour, temperature is -175 degrees Celsius, with mist and intermittent methane squalls. It looks like you can go out and play. Be sure to bundle up."

"Thanks, Mom."

"Don't mention it."

-175 Celsius. Hmm. That's -280 degrees Fahrenheit. Brrr.

"That's going to put quite a strain on my enhanced SEVA suit. Maybe I should use the standard EVA suit. It's designed for the extreme cold, and we did bring it."

"Two problems with that, Rae Anne. First, convective heat loss in outer space is much less than in a thick atmosphere. The EVA suit wouldn't provide any additional protection from the cold. And second, with Titan's gravity, your mobility in the bulky EVA suit would be compromised. Your modified SEVA suit is still the better option, but be ready to cut your outings short at first sensation of cold, particularly in your hands and feet."

Rae Anne grabbed a packet of trail mix and snatched bites while putting on her SEVA suit. Even with her enhancements, the SEVA suit was lighter than the standard EVA suit. Its life-support unit, being smaller and of shorter duration, was designed to be quickly exchanged with a fresh unit while remaining outside the vehicle. A practical consideration for Mars. But here, Rae Anne's outings would be too short-lived for that option to be of any use.

As anxious as she was to step into this alien world, she checked all the fittings twice, with Jason monitoring from the onboard cameras. She stepped into the airlock, sealed the inner hatch, evacuated the airlock into *Eagle's* holding tanks and bled in Titan's atmosphere.

244

Another procedure the Mars mission didn't have to deal with. Titan's atmospheric pressure at sea level is half again Earth's and nearly double the pressure we keep aboard Aurora and Eagle.

When the pressure equalized, she opened the outer hatch and stood transfixed at the sight before her. Although in full daylight, the surroundings presented as a twilight panorama since sunlight at Saturn's distance was only 1% as intense as on Earth.

What a gloomy scene. Not helped by the heavy cloud layer.

In the dim light, Rae Anne looked out over a vast methane sea stretching to the fog-shrouded horizon. A squall of methane rain drizzled an opaque veil in the distance. Shallow black waves washed ashore, steaming with evaporating ammonia and methane.

Too bad Titan's perpetual cloud cover blocks any view of Saturn. So much for the fanciful drawings I dreamed over as a kid showing astronauts gazing from Titan's surface at Saturn's hulking orb and its fantastic rings. Pure science fiction.

To her left and right, jagged formations lined the shore, rising hundreds of meters into the air. They were a fantastic assortment of intricate shapes, as though some manic sculptor had assembled their entire portfolio on this one beach. Most of the peaks were shrouded in the low, undulating clouds rushing overhead.

Wow. I was expecting an alien landscape, but nothing as surreal as this!

Before leaving the airlock, Rae Anne pulled four small bags from the tool locker, along with two flags. She climbed down the ladder and stepped into a slushy green-brown muck.

Eagle's legs were awash in the methane/ammonia sludge with dozens of large, boiling puddles of liquid methane surrounding the landing site. Droplets of methane mist evaporated the moment they hit the surface, forming a carpet of wavering vapor tendrils rising from the surface like stalks of wheat in a Kansas field.

"Jason, I'm going far enough out so the flags and mementos won't be disturbed by rocket blast when we leave." She strode away from the lander and turned behind a sculpture that looked like a mishappen coal-fired train locomotive, its stack tilted precariously to one side.

This should be a well-protected spot. No sign of recent tidal erosion and protected from the ship.

She stooped and chipped two small holes in the frozen ground next to the outcropping. She placed the Stars and Stripes in one hole and the blue and white United Nations flag in the other, crossing their poles and leaning them against the rock to keep them upright. She scooped chips of ice around their base with her boot and tamped them down.

These won't last through the next storm, but at least the video will provide a permanent record of the event.

After placing the four packets at the base of the flags, she paused a moment. Her eyes moistened inside her helmet. She swallowed hard to quell the lump in her throat. After backing away from the shrine so her helmet camera would get a full view, she spoke aloud to record the moment for posterity.

"Here we are my dearest of friends: Carson, Mindy, Rob, on Titan's surface next to a vast methane sea. Not where we expected to be when we began this journey as astronaut candidates in Colorado, but together again at last on a distant world. These small tokens have gone farther than any of us could have imagined. Would that you were standing here with me in celebration of humanity's most far-flung human expedition yet. Surely it is only a matter of time before the human presence becomes commonplace throughout the Solar System.

"May our loved ones find comfort knowing these tokens of our lives are lodged here on Titan, a moon of Saturn, a planet they can see in the night sky."

She choked back a sob as she slowly turned and recorded the alien surroundings. She chipped several samples near the site and from the outcropping and deposited them in pre-marked bags. These samples were far enough from the ship that the landing would not have affected them.

The billowing mists suddenly grew dense, and the wind picked up.

She resumed her walk to the shore. A gust nearly blew her to the ground, and a squall of methane rain engulfed her. She marveled at how the methane evaporated the moment it struck her SEVA suit. No fear of being drenched! But the ocean ahead had disappeared in a heavy fog which expanded from the shore and almost instantly blanketed the entire area.

She turned back toward *Eagle.*

Oh, no! Where's the lander. Nothing but thick fog and mist. I can barely see my outstretched hand!

The swirling mist engulfed her like undulating curtains of opaque silk fabric. Her hands became clammy inside her gloves. She became aware of her fingertips growing numb. She opened and closed her hands to encourage circulation and noticed how cold her feet were as well.

I need to get back to Eagle ASAP.

But where is it? Oh...Dios mio! I'm totally disoriented! Why didn't I think to grab a tether for safety? What a foolish mistake!

Chapter 8

July 9, 2043: Surface of Titan

"Jason, I'm lost out here in the fog. I need you to guide me back to the lander."

Silence.

"Jason. Respond."

Silence.

A tremor of sheer terror washed through her body.

"JASON!"

No, no. This won't do. Yelling won't help. I must keep calm and think this through. I'm obviously not out of radio range, so something must be blocking my signal. I've got to change my location, even though I can't see where I'm going. I just need to keep track of my movements so I can retrace my steps if I need to.

She took fifteen deliberate steps in a straight line.

"Jason. Can you hear me?"

Still no response.

OK. Do I go back twenty-five paces, or should I turn 90-degrees, hopefully away from the ocean, and go another fifteen steps?

She decided to try the shorter option and began calling out to *Eagle* with every step.

After twelve steps, Jason's voice echoed in her helmet. "Coming through loud and clear, Rae Anne. I did lose you for a few minutes, though."

A wave of relief washed through her body.

"Whew. I must have wandered behind an outcropping. But I need help, and fast. I'm lost in the fog and I need you to direct me back to *Eagle*."

A moment later, Jason replied. "Rae Anne, I've done a 360-degree sweep with radar and I can't distinguish you from the surroundings."

Shit!

She felt her heart pounding heavily in her chest. Her breathing became ragged.

Breathe deeply. Do not panic.

Beads of sweat were freezing to the inside surfaces of her SEVA suit. Her voice trembled when she reported her movements to Jason.

"I'm walking ten paces directly ahead. Can you pick me out now?"

"I don't see any movement. No change in the landscape."

Lord, help me. If Jason can't guide me back to the lander, and quickly, I don't stand a chance.

"Rae Anne, turn 90 degrees to your left and walk another fifteen paces."

She turned left and took fifteen large steps.

"I may have spotted you. Do a 180 and take ten paces back toward where you started and remain facing in your direction of travel."

She did as instructed, with difficulty. Her hands and feet had turned numb.

"That's good, Rae Anne. I know which blip is you. From where you are, turn 90-degrees to your right, then estimate an additional 30-degree turn to your right and step off 30 paces and stop without turning."

She followed Jason's instructions and paused.

"You are now about 20 meters from *Eagle*. Take another 10paces in the same direction."

She again followed his directions.

"I still don't see anything."

"Not to worry. You are walking directly toward *Eagle*. Another 10 or 12 paces and you should bump into it. Come forward 10 paces and tell me what you see."

Rae Anne counted 10, 12, 14 paces dead ahead. Suddenly, the shadowy form of *Eagle* loomed before her. Its ungainly structure was the most beautiful sight she had ever seen. She exhaled a deep sigh of relief.

"If I didn't have this helmet on, I'd kiss you!"

"Not a good idea, Rae Anne. Your lips would freeze to the surface."

"Not funny, Jason. I'm in a great deal of pain. I can hardly move."

Where the hell did he come up with that piece of trivia.

She climbed the ladder to the open airlock, faltering as her numbed feet sought purchase. At the top of the ladder, she tumbled into the airlock, closed the hatch and began evacuating the Titan atmosphere.

Come on. Come on. I can't feel anything in my hands or my feet.

The indicators finally allowed her to fill the airlock with warm, breathable air. Then she stumbled into the warm lander, fumbling with the SEVA suit. It took three times as long to take the suit off as to put it on, in large part due to her frozen fingers.

Once free of the suit, she wrapped herself in every piece of clothing she could find and turned up the heat. She located a large empty container in the sample locker and filled it with warm water. Leaning over the edge of her couch, she immersed both hands and feet in the liquid. At first, she had no sensation of warmth. But then it felt like someone was stabbing her with cactus needles or hot coals. She howled aloud to help take her mind off the excruciating pain.

After an hour and three warm-water refills, she had restored some sense of normalcy to her hands and feet, but they still burned as though she had plunged them into boiling water. She prepared a mug of hot tea and curled up inside her electrically heated sleeping bag to restore some warmth to her body.

How totally stupid of me. Three tethers in the airlock and I didn't think to grab any of them! What's the matter with my brain? I can't let the excitement of exploration cloud my common sense. I can't let my guard down, even for a second or this environment will kill me.

Before dinner, she took measure of the damage. Her fingers had returned to normal, except for some lost skin on two fingers and a thumb.

She bandaged them with supplies from the med-kit, wondering if they would still fit into her SEVA gloves.

Two toes on her left foot had suffered mild frostbite. She treated them as best she could and wrapped them in layers of gauze. Digging through the medicine cabinet, she located a bottle of morphine tablets and took one to help deaden the pain.

For dinner, she prepared a bowl of beef stew and marveled again at the experience of having gravity to keep everything in its place.

Then again, maybe my euphoria is due to the morphine.

After dinner, she and Jason developed an agenda for the next few days at this site. Rae Anne decided to rely on the drone fliers and rovers to take measurements and collect samples. If the winds remained relatively calm, she should have no trouble retrieving the fliers for use at the next site they planned to visit.

"So, what would it take to establish a permanent crewed research station or colony on this moon, Jason. It's damned inhospitable out there."

"Two nuclear power plants at a minimum for energy. Both could be used to provide power to the habitats, but you would always have one as a backup should the other go down. Total loss of power for even a day would spell disaster."

"I don't see any possibility of putting the habitats underground or in caves. Even the slightest heat leakage from a habitat would melt the surroundings. It's all ice!"

"The habitats would have to be built on stilts, much like buildings in the far north on Earth where melting permafrost presents a similar situation," Jason observed.

"They would also need to be connected with insulated and heated tunnels," Rae Anne added. "There's no way anyone should go out there simply to go from one building to another."

"Tell me again why a permanent crewed station on the surface of Titan is a good idea? If there's anything your foray into the elements today has shown, it's that humans are not equipped to deal with Titan's environment. Set up an autonomous data collection station with a thorium reactor and a satellite relay station to send the data to Earth. Then no lives are at risk in the event of a disaster."

"Yeah, I guess you're right, Jason. Anyway, there's not likely to be humans here again for a very long time. Good night."

She scrunched deeper into the heated sleeping bag and tried to sleep. Her body continued to shake. She couldn't seem to get warm. When she closed her eyes, she pictured herself engulfed in frigid gray nothingness, replaying her terror at being lost. She forced herself awake several times through the night to reassure herself she was safe in the lander.

Titan is the poster child of nightmares. At least here. Site C is on the equator. Maybe it will be more hospitable.

Rae Anne spent the next two days exploring Site B remotely. The rain continued in squalls, and the visibility cycled from clear to dense fog without warning. Rae Anne had no desire to go exploring into this environment again. She continued to chide herself on her carelessness. For all her training and concern for safety, she knew she had messed up in a major way.

Some of the rovers made it to the ocean and brought back samples from the liquid as well as soil from the beach. Though the sea was large, the swells were small, pushing gentle wind-driven waves onto the shore. Rae Anne wondered if this might be due to Titan being tidally locked with Saturn, like the moon and Earth. One day on Titan is equivalent to 16 Earth days, in sync with its orbital period.

Rae Anne used the drones to collect samples from several of the formations surrounding *Eagle*, the same rocks that had blocked her radio transmissions. The drones were equipped with small drills and pouches to collect the shavings. Butting up against a vertical cliff face, the drill would automatically bore into it. When finished, the pouch with its precious sample would rotate inside the drone, sealing itself in the process, while another pouch rotated out to retrieve the debris from the next drilling site.

The aerial drones also brought in air samples, all containing droplets of methane that turned to gas in the lander's warm cabin. Given the resulting increased pressure inside the sample containers, Rae Anne couldn't open them for analysis, as most of the sample would escape and contaminate the air in the lander.

At the end of the fifth day, Rae Anne looked through the data she had collected and the sample inventory lists. She switched the screen off, stood and stretched, her fingertips touching the ceiling, and yawned.

"We've been here five days, Jason. I can't think of any additional observations or measurements to make, and we've collected all the samples we need. Call in the rovers and drones and secure them in their lockers for recharging. I'll collect and catalog their last samples. I plan on going to Site C tomorrow."

Chapter 9

June 12, 2043: Surface of Titan

"Ready to set down at Site C," Rae Anne announced as she jockeyed *Eagle's* controls 50 meters above the shoreline of a methane lake. "The weather seems to be better here on the equator."

"Don't count on it being any warmer," Jason warned. "The temperature is -165 degrees Celsius, about the same as Site B."

Rae Anne set *Eagle* down without incident on a solid surface near the shore. The winds were off the lake with occasional mild gusts carrying a fine mist of methane and ammonia that coated *Eagle's* windows.

After a breakfast of raisin-enhanced oatmeal, an apple and coffee, Rae Anne downed a morphine tablet to dull the pain in her foot, and prepared for her second EVA on Titan's surface.

No unnecessary risks. Weigh every action in terms of unintended consequences. Hard to do when everything is an unknown.

"Keep tabs on my time outside, Jason. The 20 minutes last time was too long. Let's go for 15 minutes max."

"I'll call you back after 10 minutes."

As she expected, putting the SEVA suit on with her bandaged fingers and toes hurt like hell, but she had no choice if she wanted to explore the surface in person.

No backing out now, Rae Anne. This is why you're here.

Before stepping from the hatch, she attached three of the spring-coiled tether boxes to her suit. Fog should be no problem here, but Rae Anne was not about to take any chances. She clipped one end of the red cable into a ring near the hatch.

She backed out of the hatch and climbed down the ladder, grimacing at the pain the activity elicited.

The light was brighter than at Site B, but the roiling gray-brown clouds filling the sky from horizon to horizon made everything depressingly dark. The sky emitted a uniform yellow-green glow, with no indication of where the sun might be.

At least today my helmet camera has a vista to record.

She turned full circle to take it all in.

The lake lay dead ahead, a black, shimmering surface of liquid hydrocarbons, mostly methane and ethane. Dozens of ammonia geysers broke the surface, exploding their load of hydrocarbons a hundred meters into the air. Once exposed to the intense cold, the ammonia gas froze into glittering white crystals which floated on the breeze over the lake like a gentle snowfall. As they drifted onto the lake's surface, they dissolved into the turbulent waves and disappeared.

What an awesome sight. There is nothing like this on Earth.

A range of low hills crouched beyond the far shore. Sheer cliffs ringed the lake to her right, jutting into the air like jagged teeth. To her left, an immense flat desert extended to the horizon. Here and there strange objects jutted into the air, some as tall as a small building. Though too distant for a personal visit, she resolved to get a closer look with the drones, perhaps even snag some samples for analysis. They reminded her of saguaro cacti she had seen as a child on a family trip to Tucson.

"I'm headed for the lake, Jason," she reported. She trudged away from *Eagle,* the red cable unspooling from its spring-box attached to her belt. When she reached the end of her tether, she clipped the second blue coil into the red spring-box and unhooked it from her belt. She paused for a moment, her mind drifting to Mindy's accident of long ago.

"Don't forget to take samples along your walk as well as the liquid samples from the lake," Jason reminded her.

Rae Anne stooped and tried to loosen some ground material for a sample. Everything was frozen solid. Reaching into the tool satchel, she pulled out a hammer and chisel and hammered at the rock. Only small shavings of frozen material came loose, barely enough for a sample. She found it odd she couldn't break larger clumps loose.

"Surface between lander and lake is very hard. Sample C-022 taken 50 meters from the lander."

When she reached the end of her second tether, she lengthened it as before with the third line and walked the final distance to the lake's edge. The solid ground gave way to a gooey sludge. Her boot prints left clear tracks. She stopped and turned around, gazing thoughtfully at her tracks in the mud.

I'm finally leaving my boot prints on a distant planet. Well, on a moon of a distant planet. Good enough.

She measured the temperature of the goo at her feet.—a toasty -143 degrees Celsius.

"Something is warming this entire area, melting the ammonia ice and hydrocarbons to create this vast lake. I wonder if it's geological in nature. Or maybe an underground deposit of radioactive elements."

"It's likely geological, Rae Anne. Titan is close enough to Saturn that the push and pull of gravity exerts great forces on the underlying bedrock. A different kind of tectonic stress than you see on Earth."

She collected another sample, filling the bottle with muddy slush.

"Sample C-017. Sludge from the lake shore. Sub-surface warming may be why the lake even exists. Could also explain the geysers."

She bent over to fill a bottle from the liquid washing up on the shore. While still kneeling, she capped the bottle. "Sample C-009, liquid from the lake taken at the shore."

When she started to rise, her bad foot slipped and she fell into the slimy pool of mud.

"Ouch! Damn. That hurt!"

"Rae Anne, are you alright? What happened?" Jason's voice carried a note of urgency and concern.

"I fell into the muck at the edge of the lake. It's quite slippery. I think I'm OK, but my left foot is killing me."

"Can you get up?"

Rae Anne tried to pull herself out of the muck, but it sucked at her body like quicksand. She tried to gain some leverage with her elbow but to no avail.

Dios mio! I can't get free! And the cold. My hands and feet are freezing.

"Jason," she called in desperation, struggling to get some purchase. "The mud is sucking me in. I can't get any leverage to pull myself out."

"You've been out for 10 minutes. You need to get back inside ASAP."

"I can't move. Is there anything you can do to help me?"

Once again, she found herself on the verge of panic. She gripped the cable in her gloved hand so she wouldn't sink further, but she didn't have the strength to pull herself even an inch forward out of the quicksand. The pain in her fingers was excruciating.

She looked with horror at the muck now lapping at mid-thigh.

At this rate I'll be completely submerged before I freeze to death!

She tried desperately to pull herself along the cable, reaching as far as she could and pulling with every ounce of energy she had. Still no progress. She couldn't think of anything she might do to save herself. She glanced down. The muck-level had climbed up to her waist.

I'm losing ground. This is it. I'm going to die on Titan.

She seemed to be sinking faster as the seconds ticked by. It felt like something had grabbed hold of her legs and was steadily pulling her deeper into the mire.

She looked around for anything to grab onto, but there was nothing. In panic, she grasped the tether with both hands as tightly as she could to keep from sinking further.

Suddenly, the cable jerked taut with a dull twang. Very slowly, it lifted above the muck and began to pull her free of the goo. Relief washed over her. Only then did she realize how panicked she had been.

"Keep it up, Jason. It's working. Oh, thank god it's working. A little more and I'll be pulled free."

Before long, she was being dragged along on solid ground. With tremendous effort, she stumbled to her feet.

"I don't know what you did, Jason, but thank you. I'm upright and heading to the lander as fast as I can manage."

As she staggered away from the lake, the mud and muck on her suit solidified, freezing the suit's joints, impairing her progress. She forced herself to strut like the German soldiers she had seen in old videos, swinging her legs stiffly forward and back.

Shit, how much further to the lander? This cold is terrifying! Every inch of my body is burning with cold. Except for my hands and feet which are completely numb. God, I hope I can thaw them out.

Once she reached the lander, her frozen suit presented another problem. She couldn't bend her legs sufficiently to climb the ladder. She was forced to hoist herself by hand, rung by rung. Every part of her body not numbed from cold screamed with pain. Only through sheer force of will did she make it to the hatch and slam it closed. Cycling the lock back to *Eagle's* air content and pressure took forever. But at least the airlock quickly resumed cabin temperature.

"You were out 22 minutes, Rae Anne. That's too long."

"I know, Jason. I know. I'll save my next outing for Site D. Thanks for activating the winch and pulling me out of the mud. I don't remember hooking into it."

"You didn't. As soon as you called for help, I directed several of the drones to fly to the airlock and attach themselves to the cable. I had them lift it as high as necessary to pull you free from the mire. I determined the lower angle on the cable to be more effective, both in pulling you out horizontally and in reducing the mass the drones would be required to lift."

"What an amazing idea, Jason. How did you come up with it?"

"I haven't the slightest idea, Rae Anne. Nothing in my archives suggests anything like this. It occurred to me spontaneously. Of course, determining where best to apply the upward motion was simply a matter of physics."

The hairs on Rae Anne's neck prickled.

Could Jason have reached the holy grail of AI, true sentience?

She knew her program well, and though she could take pride in it as an incredible piece of work, her code by itself could not explain the actions Jason had taken. The machine learning aspect must have been the trick that pushed him over the tipping point and into sentience.

Could Jason even be conscious? Did sentience imply consciousness? How could I test Jason for consciousness?

First, she would need further verification of sentience. This may have been a one-off. But she reminded herself there was no time to explore these possibilities. *Aurora* had a date as a flaming fireball shooting into Saturn's atmosphere—a date only a few short days away.

As before, she spent the next hour treating her toes on both feet for frostbite, along with the tips of three more fingers. The burning, pins-and-needle sensation as her numb feet and hands warmed and regained feeling was more excruciating than before. At least she hadn't lost the tool satchel. The samples from the lake would be safely stored in the lander's locker.

She spent the afternoon sending drone fliers into the ammonia geysers and skimming the lake to collect samples. The next morning, she sent them over the desert to record images of the odd protuberances that jutted from the desert floor. In a couple of instances, she was able to snatch samples from some of the spikes covering their oddly branched structures.

When she pulled the sample jars from the satchel to store them, she frowned at sample C-022 and shook the jar which now contained a clear liquid.

"Jason, where did sample C-022 come from?"

"Sample C-022 taken 50 meters from the lander," came the reply in her own voice.

"I'll be darned. We are sitting on some form of solid water ice. I wonder how much of the surface of this moon is made of this!"

The next three days were filled with exciting moments of discovery. Spectroscopic analysis of the lake and geyser samples showed the presence of many complex organic substances. In fact, several amines and amino acids were mixed with the ammonia collected from the geyser plumes.

Rae Anne expected to find a variety of simple hydrocarbons based on methane, but this sample contained a bonanza of many more complex compounds. How they formed and whether they were byproducts of living creatures were questions for future research.

The spikey things from the desert formations resembled cactus spines when they were collected but melted into water once the samples were inside *Eagle*. Unfortunately, the spines blocked the drones from sampling the objects' cores. Another project for future research.

The night before launching to Site D, she and Jason made sure all the drones and rovers were properly stowed and verified all samples were labeled and catalogued. Rae Anne secured the samples in the locker to ensure their safety through the remainder of the expedition.

She took an additional morphine tablet with dinner, hoping she could skip one in the morning. She would need to be at her peak when piloting *Eagle* and doing her last surface EVA at Site D.

Chapter 10

June 16, 2043: Surface of Titan

Rae Anne awoke the next day with a great deal of anticipation. Site D was her third and last landing site on Titan. Unlike the other sites, this one was on the side of Titan permanently facing Saturn. Like Earth's moon, Titan was tidally locked, so any Saturnian astronomers looking upward at their largest moon would always see the same face. Because of this, Rae Anne thought Site D might exhibit something unique to be discovered on this hemisphere.

Timing was critical for this visit. For half of the eight days in which this hemisphere faced the sun, its so-called daytime is spent in inky black darkness due to Saturn eclipsing the sun. This restricted sunlight to a couple of days on either end of the eight-day period.

Shortly after breakfast, Rae Anne positioned herself in her acceleration couch and brought up the navigation program for Site D. Checking the readouts on her monitor, her brow furrowed.

"My readouts are showing a major consumption of fuel for the flight to Site D, Jason. I know it's a long flight, but I'm concerned we may not have enough fuel left to reconnect with *Aurora*."

"We'll be going half-way around the moon, which means lifting off to suborbital height, above the atmosphere. There's no good alternative if Site D is our destination."

"You know my parameters for choosing Site D. Can we change to a different location on the Saturn-facing side that offers the same characteristics that would be closer?"

"If you don't mind waiting an additional day before beginning your explorations, we could relocate Site D quite a bit closer and wait for sunrise to catch up with us."

"An additional day won't hurt. Look over our radar maps and find a suitable landing site. I'll reprogram the Navigation computer and we'll plan on leaving Site C this afternoon."

It didn't take long for Jason to identify an alternative location for Site D, and Rae Anne had the revised flight program ready after a couple hours. Jason ran simulations on the new program and verified they would do the job.

That afternoon, *Eagle* lifted off. With the new destination closer to Site C, a lower trajectory was sufficient with a significant fuel savings. Rae Anne landed *Eagle* fifteen hours before sunrise.

"What does it look like outside, Jason?"

"Calm, not even a hint of a breeze, but quite cold. Minus-233 degrees Celsius."

Rae Anne shivered.

"Jeez, that's only 40 degrees above absolute zero! Twenty degrees colder and even hydrogen would be a liquid."

She wondered if the more intense cold and short periods of sunshine were responsible for the calm atmosphere.

"Given we only have two days sunshine here, I'm going to get some rest now and be ready to head out shortly after sunrise."

Rae Anne slept fitfully, trying unsuccessfully to calm her mind enough for a good rest. Although she wanted to step outside and explore Site D, she harbored a reluctance based on her previous two experiences. She wondered what macabre surprises Site D held in store for her.

At sunrise, Jason roused her as she had requested. Rae Anne peered out the window at a very different scene from Sites B and C.

Although the sky was still overcast, blocking any view of Saturn, the clouds lacked the angry swirling theme of the previous two sites. Here the sky cast a solid gray-green wash from horizon to horizon. The surface appeared to be a solid sheet of ice to the horizon in all directions.

Rae Anne kept her morphine dose low to minimize its effect on her judgement and activities. The pain in her foot had steadily grown worse. The morphine only served to dull the pain to tolerable levels.

Jason had become a real nag. He kept correcting her and reminding her of things she forgot or overlooked. She could barely limp across the deck, even with just 1/7 Earth's gravity, and her dizzy spells had increased.

"You need to keep your nourishment up, Rae Anne. These surface excursions take a great deal out of you. Please at least eat a power bar with some coffee before you go out."

"Yeah, OK. You're right, of course. But I'm not hungry."

"A nice hot bowl of oatmeal with raisins and almonds would help heat your core. Why not give it a try?"

" OK, OK, right again. Are you sure you never had any children?"

"None yet…"

Rae Anne prepared a bowl of oatmeal and a cup of coffee, more to please Jason than to feed herself. The warm cereal and liquids put her in a better mood, but she couldn't eat more than half of what she made. Her spirits did improve, though she dreaded struggling with the SEVA suit one last time.

After breakfast she stepped into the airlock and picked up the suit. Most of the heavy mud and filth from the previous outing had either melted (water ice) or evaporated (methane and ethane) but a thick layer of oily slime the shade of burnt umber remained on the fabric. A strong smell of ammonia permeated the airlock when she unfolded the suit.

The cabin air must be contaminated with ammonia. I guess I've just become used to it. I hope the ECARU can keep it at a safe level.

Something's not right with this suit. I'd better lay it out on the bench and inspect it more carefully.

She smoothed the legs out on the bench and brushed aside the slime with her hand. Thinking her blurry vision might be playing tricks on her, she leaned closer to get a better look.

"What the hell! There's a big hole in the suit's fabric. Both legs. Something has eaten right through them. The suit is ruined. It's useless."

"Could it be chemical damage from something in the mud?" Jason asked. "The fabric is designed to be impervious to nearly everything, but they didn't have Titan's environment in mind."

Rae Anne fetched a magnifying glass from the geology kit and scrutinized the damaged fabric under the lens. The more she looked, the more apparent it became that chemical corrosion was not the culprit.

"The edges around the holes aren't discolored and they're well defined. It looks to me like something has been eating the fabric."

Rae Anne's heartbeat increased. She continued to scrutinize the frayed edges with the magnifying glass.

What kind of organisms could manage to survive in such an alien environment and under such extreme conditions?

"Whatever it is, Rae Anne, you should protect yourself from exposure. It could be toxic, or if it is biological, it could be infectious."

"That's possible. We've been exposed to if for several hours already, but I'll put on gloves and a mask while I work with it."

Rae Anne rummaged in the medical kit for latex gloves and a mask. She winced as she pulled the gloves over her bandaged fingers.

"I need to view this under the microscope. No telling what the higher magnification might reveal."

Using a scalpel from the med kit, she cut a swath of the affected fabric from the ruined suit. Detailed sample analysis would have to wait for their return to *Aurora,* but *Eagle* had its own science workstation for initial sample analysis.

Of course, this means I won't be doing another EVA. I can't say I'm terribly disappointed.

As she peered at her magnified sample on the monitor, she couldn't believe her eyes. The image revealed a myriad of eight-sided cellular structures. Several hair-like flagella extended from each and she could just make out numerous internal organelles within each cell. The organisms, however, were motionless and appeared to be dead.

"You should quarantine the SEVA suit to keep the organisms from contaminating anything else aboard the ship."

"That's a good idea, Jason, although they've been in the airlock for some time already. They aren't active right now. I suspect the ambient temperature in the ship is way above their survival range."

She reached into the sample cabinet and pulled out two jars.

"I'll put this sample in jar C-037 for safe keeping. I'll also scrape some of the slime off the suit and put it into sample jar C-038."

"Recording…"

She filled both jars and sealed them, cataloging their contents for the archives.

"Where can we stow the suit?"

"If the organism is attacking the suit fabric, anything organic could be vulnerable, including plastic surfaces. The medical locker is metal. The suit would fit in there if it weren't for the helmet and life-support pack."

"There's not much contamination on either of those. I'll clean out the medical locker."

She felt a degree of urgency as she stuffed medical supplies into a large plastic bag and emptied the closet. She removed the helmet and life-support pack from the SEVA suit and stuffed it into the medical cabinet, feeling some relief when the door slammed shut.

"What should I use to clean things up with, Jason? We have no idea what might kill these buggers."

"I would try an acid wash with acetic acid wipes," Jason replied. "The native environment of the organism is a mixture of hydrocarbons interspersed with ammonia, which is a base. You should put all the wipes and sponges in the locker with the suit."

Searching through *Eagle's* pantry, Rae Anne found a tube of vinegar and squeezed a little onto the worst stain on the floor. The grayish mud turned bright orange and gave off white wisps of gas.

I can only hope that gas isn't poisonous. But we're definitely getting a reaction with the vinegar.

The orange mud faded to a deep shade of purple, giving the impression of dried ash. This residue cleaned up readily on an alcohol wipe, leaving the floor spotless. Rae Anne continued with the spots on the SEVA helmet and life support pack. The helmet was deeply pitted where slime had splashed onto it.

"It's too bad we can't duplicate the temperature and environment where these organisms came from. I would love to watch them grow and reproduce in real time."

"That's a fine research project for future scientists. They'll have to set up their experiment on Site C's lakeshore and monitor any activity remotely," Jason responded.

"At least we've warned future astronauts about the plastic-eating organisms on Titan, so they'll be ready for them."

Rae Anne lay back on her couch and pondered the impact of her discovery. Here was a living entity that had evolved off Earth and survived on Titan. Getting these samples back to Earth had to be her number one priority. Every other observation paled in comparison.

"I'm sorry you won't have the opportunity to go outside again, Rae Anne but I must say I am relieved. Your previous outings demonstrated that we aren't equipped to deal with such a hostile environment."

"Thank you, Jason. It's just as well. I wasn't looking forward to stuffing my foot into the SEVA suit one more time. And when I think about how much colder it is out there at this site, I have no desire to experience it firsthand."

"Don't worry about getting samples from this site. I have already programmed the aerial drones and vehicles and sent them out. We will get all we need in the next day or two.

"Now might be a good time to apply fresh dressings on your foot and take another morphine tablet. Then sit back and relax with a fresh cup of hot tea while I take charge of the rovers and drones."

Although her fingers showed signs of healing, they still needed to be bandaged as well. Rae Anne winced whenever anything pressed against them. Even holding her mug was painful when she bumped one of the bandaged fingers.

As each drone returned to *Eagle* and sealed itself into its own small airlock, Rae Anne recycled the lock, opened the hatch and removed its sample container. Jason kept track of where the drones visited and the nature of the samples they returned. Her job was to tightly seal the sample containers, mark them and stow them securely in *Eagle's* sample bin.

She then equipped the drones with fresh containers, announced their identification codes to Jason, and sealed them back into their airlock for another foray into Titan's environment. Turn-around time was slower than she would have liked due to her awkwardness with her injured fingers and muddled brain.

She was comfortable letting Jason survey the area and pick appropriate sites for sampling based on protocols he learned from the other sites. Given her current state, she trusted his level of discernment to be equal to, if not better than, her own.

Chapter 11

June 19, 2043: Surface of Titan

Rae Anne awoke from a dreadful nightmare. Shapeless vermin the size of rats were chasing her, trying to snag her SEVA suit. Several had already latched onto it with grasping claws and were tearing at the fabric. She reached a ladder and started climbing, desperate to escape. But the ladder continued upward out of sight and the vermin swarmed up after her.

She struggled to shake herself free of her blanket. Her head ached and her shirt was damp from fever sweat. She couldn't put any pressure on her left foot. Although she was elated at her discoveries on Titan, she couldn't wait to leave this god-forsaken place.

"Jason, how soon before we leave?"

"Good morning, Rae Anne," Jason answered affably. "I think we have all the samples we need from this site. The drones are all back in their compartments and their latest samples are ready to be retrieved and catalogued. Did you sleep well?"

"Not really. I just want to get back to *Aurora*. By tomorrow, the sun will be eclipsed by Saturn and there won't be anything more we can do anyway. Jettison the drones and rovers after I've taken care of the samples. They're extra weight now. And bring up the launch check lists. As soon as I store the samples, we'll head home."

"Not until you have something to eat, Rae Anne. Once you get started on some task, all thought of taking care of yourself will fly out the airlock. Breakfast first!"

Rae Anne sighed in exasperation but discovered she was famished. She fixed her last gravity assisted meal, a shrimp salad with tartar sauce, spaghetti with garlic butter, a hot roll and strong coffee. An odd breakfast, but exactly what she wanted. Besides, there wasn't that much selection left in *Eagle's* larder from which to choose.

BAM

A sharp jolt shook the lander. Her plate of noodles and shrimp slid off the table and onto the floor with a clatter. Rae Anne caught her mug before it followed the plate, but not before half of her coffee sloshed onto the table.

"What was that?" Rae Anne felt her adrenalin surge. She became instantly alert.

Before Jason could respond, another quake hit, harder than the first.

"Jason, we need to get out of here, FAST!" Rae Anne jumped up on her right foot and pulled herself up the ladder to the flight deck.

"My thinking exactly. My sensors show continuous tremors between the major shocks we just felt. More big ones are likely to follow."

Rae Anne caught a quick glance at the deck, concerned at the jumbled mess.

No time to clean things up now.

She buckled into the acceleration couch and activated *Eagle's* flight controls.

"All right, Jason, start an expedited countdown. Let's get out of here while we still can!"

Another jolt rocked *Eagle.* From inside, this one seemed to threaten toppling the lander on its side. Rae Anne activated the guidance thrusters to fire if needed to help stabilize the ship.

The seconds ticked off as the countdown proceeded to zero.

How is it individual seconds can seem so long?

She felt relief when the engines ignited. They fired for three seconds and cut off.

Another violent shake, followed by several strong aftershocks.

"Jason, why was our launch aborted?"

"Sensors on *Eagle's* legs recorded elevated temperatures and initiated the abort."

"I don't understand. The sensors never activated an abort before."

Another major quake rocked the ship, and *Eagle* tilted fifteen-degrees from vertical.

"As near as I can tell, when we landed, our exhaust melted the icy mixture beneath us, and the landing pads sank into the crust. Since landing, the crust has frozen, cementing *Eagle* to the surface."

Rae Anne glanced again through the window at the vast gray-white desert. The day before the surface spread out evenly to the horizon, like ice on a giant lake. Today, that surface had broken into thousands of intersecting cracks. Large blocks of ice angled crazily into the air in all directions.

Mierda! Eagle must be frozen onto one of those uplifted blocks.

"Give me manual control, Jason, and deactivate the sensor-controlled abort sequence."

The console readouts switched to manual. Without thinking, Rae Anne flipped several switches and pressed the ignite button to fire the engines to full power.

Another jolt hit the ship, then another and another.

Four lights blinked bright red. The legs were overheating. Still, she maintained full power, not knowing which would melt first, the legs or the ice beneath the ship. Either would be a win. The landing legs were no longer needed. Their condition didn't matter so long as the ship pulled free of the ice.

Another major Titan-quake hit as the four red warning lights winked out. *Eagle* jerked loose and shot into the air at a ridiculous angle and lung-crushing G-force. But *Eagle* was free and she was rocketing into space.

Rae Anne brought *Eagle* into the required orientation for orbital insertion. She was amazed everything she did during this emergency liftoff had been a series of automatic responses.

And a good thing, too. The morphine and constant pain have turned my thinking brain to mush. Those many hours I spent on flight simulations saved the day.

Aurora had not yet cleared the horizon, so *Eagle's* emergency lift-off trajectory would not match up with *Aurora's* orbit. Once *Eagle* had achieved its own stable orbit, Rae Anne verified with relief that she had enough fuel to make the necessary orbital adjustments to rendezvous with *Aurora*.

"I'm looking forward to getting back to *Aurora*," she commented aloud to Jason. For her, it felt like she was going home.

"As surprising as this may seem, I look forward to our return as well. I have control over ever-so-many more sensors and manipulators on *Aurora*. With *Eagle,* it's like I'm forced to work with one hand behind my back."

Rae Anne chuckled at Jason's use of a body-related metaphor he never had the opportunity to experience.

The orbital adjustments took a couple days. Rae Anne used the time to tend her wounds, secure samples, and fight her fever. She fabricated a makeshift cast for her left foot, binding it with gauze and hull-repair plaster. This didn't reduce the throbbing pain, but it did allow her to move about more freely. Being in zero-G once again was a godsend.

June 23, 2043: Aboard *Aurora*

"*Aurora* dead ahead at 1233 meters and closing at 11.7 meters per second," Jason reported. "All systems are normal. We should be docked in a little over four minutes."

"Thanks Jason. As soon as I get power on *Aurora* restored, turn the heat up as high as it will go. We need to warm the cabin as quickly as possible. We have a lot of work to do."

Eagle gave a gentle bounce when its docking mechanism mated with *Aurora's* and the rings sealed. Rae Anne unbuckled and floated into the airlock. She worked her body into the EVA suit she had stored there. Due to its larger size, she squirmed into it without too much pain.

She locked the helmet in place and was finishing the EVA checklist when Jason caught a loose safety latch on the helmet. It might not have caused a problem, but the latch was there for a reason. She latched it with a deep sigh and wrinkled her brow in concern at her sluggishness.

You're out of it, Rae Anne. Take it slow and easy. Think everything through two and three times. Don't act until you are entirely sure of what you are doing.

When she opened the hatch into *Aurora's* flight deck, a WHOOSH of warm air from *Eagle* swept past her.

Woah. That shouldn't have happened.

"Jason, run a check on *Aurora*'s cabin pressure status. There shouldn't have been such a rush of air from *Eagle*."

Two voices echoed in her helmet, sounding like gibberish.

"*Eagle*-Jason. Remain quiet. *Aurora*-Jason, respond to my request."

"There is a minor leak on Level 2. The hull breach occurred shortly after you departed, so the ambient pressure dropped significantly while you were gone."

Cripes. One more task to take care of before I can settle in.

"What's the temperature?"

"Temperature is minus-30 degrees Celsius."

Rae Anne fumbled her way through the flight deck in the bulky EVA suit. A thin layer of frost covered everything. Floating down to the galley, she made her way into *Aurora's* airlock, sealed the hatch and recycled it to let herself outside. She fastened the SAFER to her belt, connected her tether and checked it three times.

Jason was now reminding her of every step. He seemed to be aware of her sluggishness. Instead of being annoyed, Rae Anne appreciated his remarks as providing an added element of safety.

The loose ends of the jumper cables, still attached to *Aurora's* power terminal, were fastened to a ring next to the airlock where she had secured them. Rae Anne loosened them and hooked them to her belt alongside her tether.

While crawling along *Aurora's* hull to *Eagle's* power terminal, she stopped several times to refocus her attention on the task at hand.

Mierda. Between zero-G and the morphine, this is the last place I should be. My head keeps spinning and I'm seeing double.

When she reached *Eagle's* power terminal, she flipped the power switch OFF, disconnected the lander's cables and plugged in the jumpers. She triple-checked the color codes to be sure they matched. Satisfied, she toggled the power switch to ON. A green LED confirmed *Aurora* now had power.

I'll only have to do this one more time, gracias a Dios. And then we'll send Eagle on its way home to Earth.

She crawled back to *Aurora's* hatch, sealed herself inside, and equalized the airlock to the diminished cabin pressure. Before leaving the airlock, she rummaged through the tool chest for the patching kit and stumbled across her 'Chavez Hull Breach Locator'.

How about that? I can test this baby out in a real live situation.

She stepped through the airlock and turned the unit on. Surprisingly, the battery was still charged. Scanning each wall in turn quickly revealed where the offending hole was. Barely larger than a pin prick, it took Rae Anne no time to apply a temporary patch.

"Jason, Restore cabin pressure. How's the temperature doing?"

"Temperature is now minus five degrees."

After half an hour, the air pressure and temperature had returned to normal. As she shed the EVA suit, she pushed it into a corner, not bothering to pack it away into its locker. It would stay there till she needed it for her last EVA.

The ECARU filter still needed to be returned to *Aurora's* unit on Level 5. By now she had become the world's most experienced ECARU filter installer. This task took less than ten minutes.

Chapter 12

June 23, 2043: Aboard *Aurora*

The urgent tasks taken care of, Rae Anne floated directly to the computer console on the flight deck,

This constant pain is almost all I can think about. So much to do. Maybe that will help take my mind off the pain. Only a few more days of agony and it'll be over.

She was surprised that her mind kept coming back to the issue of her imminent death. She had known this was coming since the day she made her decision to divert *Aurora* to Saturn. She didn't think she was dreading it, but only now did she realize how mixed her emotions really were.

At the computer console, she downloaded *Eagle's* AI memory bank to bring *Aurora's* version of Jason up-to-date and to copy all the files from their expedition into *Aurora's* memory banks.

At least now I only have one Jason to deal with!

"Jason, give me a report on our fuel situation. Do we have enough fuel to fill *Eagle's* tanks one last time and launch her to Earth?"

Jason had anticipated her concerns. "*Eagle* is at 11%. There is enough fuel in *Aurora's* tanks to top off *Eagle* with some small amount to spare. Whether we have enough for *Eagle* to achieve escape velocity or not, I can't say. We'll need to time our launch to get the maximum sling-shot effect from Saturn."

"That's a better report than I expected. Fill *Eagle's* tanks to the brim. We'll use anything left over to give her an extra boost for the trip home.

"Meantime, I want to make sure our samples from the surface are marked and securely stowed away on *Eagle*. Set its comm antenna to search and lock onto radio signals from Earth and to begin sending all our Saturn and Titan data. Set it up to broadcast in a continuous loop. If it manages to transmit for six years, the Agency will want to retrieve *Eagle* just to turn the damned thing off!"

After several hours of intense programming and running dozens of simulations, Rae Anne was confident she had the navigation program she needed for *Eagle* to do its job. She uploaded the program to both ships' computers.

As always, timing was crucial. Jason's calculations showed almost two days until launch.

Two days! I'll have to hustle to get everything on Eagle in shape by then. And I need to set aside time to run my own tests on those Titan critter samples to satisfy my own curiosity.

The next forty-eight hours were a hectic flurry of activity. Jason made a complete to-do list for Rae Anne, and they worked their way down the list, checking the items off one by one. Rae Anne squeezed in a couple of four-hour naps and made a little time now and then to grab snacks from *Aurora's* dwindling larder. As much as she craved additional morphine to dull the pain from her leg, she refused herself the luxury so she could stay focused on the job at hand.

Rae Anne emptied *Eagle* of every unnecessary item, including console controls and monitors, life support equipment and unused provisions. She dismantled the acceleration couch and rebuilt it on *Aurora's* flight deck where it would be used one last time. She wished she could remove the ragged stubs of *Eagle's* landing legs, but the schematics showed this would not be possible.

Toward the end, after a restless nap and a power-bar-and-coffee breakfast, she could contain her curiosity no longer. She retrieved samples C-037 and C-038 from *Eagle* and spent the next two hours running tests using *Aurora's* more sophisticated research equipment.

The slime contained several small, multicellular organisms with no cell nucleus, much like archaea on Earth. DNA analysis revealed no trace of the base nucleotides required by DNA from Earth-bound organisms. Elemental analysis showed a complete absence of phosphorus, the essential element in Earth-oriented DNA that links the DNA bases together. The percentages of nitrogen and oxygen were both less than 10%, much less than in Earth DNA. Carbon accounted for more than 80% of the microorganisms' composition.

These buggers are unlike any living organism on Earth.

"What do you think, Jason? Nature has independently created a life form unique to Titan."

"The significance of your discovery can't be overstated, Rae Anne. Tens of thousands of planets have been discovered over the last fifty years, and the Milky Way galaxy contains billions of stars yet to be studied. If life could evolve twice in one solar system on two planets with such different environments, the odds of life evolving in other star systems is astronomical. This gives additional credence to those Ganymede Discs of yours being artifacts from some alien civilization."

"With such good odds for life in general, there may be many intelligent species out there. I'm more sure than ever those discs are proof aliens are traversing the galaxy."

Rae Anne put the DNA analyzer back in its cabinet and added her observations to the Titan database before returning the samples to *Eagle*. She closed and sealed the hatch to the lander for the last time. The docking cradle would hold *Eagle* in place during *Aurora's* boost phase, after which she would release it, allowing it to fly home on its own.

She floated down to the galley without bothering to clean up the lab station.

No need to fuss with tidiness at this stage. I'm hungry. I haven't had a decent meal in two days. I hope I can find something in the galley to entice me.

June 26, 2043: Aboard Aurora

Rae Anne fumbled with the acceleration couch straps on *Aurora's* flight deck. Earlier, she performed her last EVA to swap cables on *Eagle's* power terminal. *Aurora* was on battery backup once again and *Eagle* had the full benefit of its own thorium nuclear reactor, with more than enough energy for its long trip home.

Damn, I can't get these buckles to latch. My fingers are a mess. But this is my last hurrah. If I can't give Eagle enough push to break free of Saturn's gravity, no one will get these samples. Much of my effort will have gone to waste.

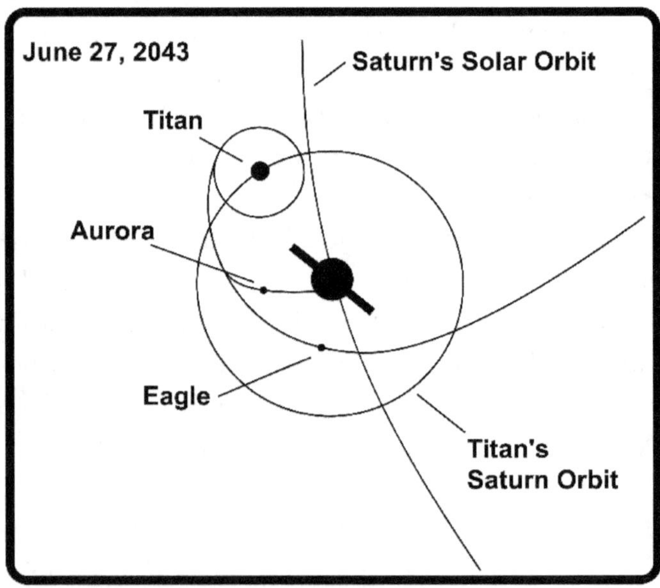

Although she had begun transmitting her observations and data back to Earth, the samples aboard *Eagle* were the real prize. With samples in hand, dozens of Earth-side labs would probe each specimen's innermost secrets with the most sophisticated instrumentation. A plethora of new information and novel scientific insights were just waiting to be discovered.

"How are we doing, Jason?" Her tremulous voice conveyed her concern and anticipation as she scanned the console to verify *Aurora* was aligned within the launch trajectory she had programmed.

T-minus 600 seconds and counting.

"All systems are GO, Rae Anne. We have a slight drop in pressure in *Eagle's* fuel tank. Probably a minor leak in the tank or fuel line."
Just what we need. Every drop of fuel is critical.
"Nothing we can do about that now. We can't delay the launch. Either she has enough fuel to reach escape velocity, or she doesn't."
"I'm still not happy with your transferring so much fuel to *Eagle*. If you had saved some back, you could have put *Aurora* in a stable Saturn orbit. As it is, *Aurora's* elliptical orbit will plunge us into Saturn's atmosphere at perigee."
"That's because you are programmed to look after my safety. This is one of those problems where logic doesn't produce the best solution."
"Still, there's no possible way for you to survive if *Aurora* enters Saturn's atmosphere. At least in a stable orbit you have a remote chance of rescue. Think of Li Fang's unexpected rescue in Mars orbit."
"I understand, Jason. To you, any chance is better than none. But in this case that remote chance doesn't exist and for me, it's a matter of choosing to die quickly rather than suffer a drawn-out death as *Aurora* turns into an orbiting iceberg. My number one priority is to give *Eagle* the best chance of making it back to Earth."

T-minus 300 and counting.

Rae Anne went through the engine start-up and launch sequence checklist with Jason one last time. *Eagle's* fuel pressure was still dropping.

If it's a leak in the fuel line, we could be looking at an explosion when Eagle's engines ignite. Please, let it be a fuel tank problem.

    T-minus 90 and counting.

Rae Anne verified *Aurora's* directional thrusters were keeping the ship aligned on course. All the remaining fluid in the thruster tanks would be exhausted by the time they launched. But once *Eagle* broke free, the thrusters would no longer be needed. *Aurora* would coast to its fiery end.

    T-minus 30 and counting. 29... 28... 27...

Rae Anne took a deep breath and closed her eyes in preparation for the sudden jolt of acceleration. Her mind drifted back to her first lift-off from the Kennedy Space Center so many years ago and her exhilaration at becoming a fully initiated astronaut; her anticipation at being a part of the first Mars mission assigned to land humans on the red planet; at crewing on *Aurora* with Mindy and Rob…

FWOOM!

The cabin roared to life. The dreaded launch elephant slammed into Rae Anne's chest. She struggled for every breath. Her arms were welded to the armrests as *Aurora's* engines furiously burned through the last of its fuel.

After 76 seconds, it was over. Rae Anne inhaled deeply and once again felt herself floating against her straps in weightless relief. She scanned the console to be sure *Aurora* was still on course.

At T-plus 90 a loud CLANG reverberated through the cabin. Rae Anne switched the monitor to show *Eagle's* orientation and watched as it drifted away from *Aurora* for the last time. Its directional thrusters fired intermittently as they tweaked its orientation to match its programmed flight path.

The countdown for *Eagle's* launch interrupted the silence on the flight deck.

    T-minus 30 and counting... 29... 28... 27...

Rae Anne tensed as she watched helplessly from *Aurora*. Everything depended on a successful launch. She braced herself for a possible explosion.

```
T-minus zero and launch.
```

The lander's engines ignited with a bright flash and a continuous flare as the small craft lurched away from *Aurora*.

"*Bon voyage*, *Eagle*," she said. "May you have a safe trip home."

She switched the monitor to *Aurora's* telescope and watched the exhaust from *Eagle's* engines grow smaller and smaller. Soon the flare dwindled to just another bright star in the deep black velvet canopy. When it flickered and disappeared, Rae Anne knew *Eagle* had consumed all its fuel. Radar indicated it was on course and would soon be out of sight around Saturn's edge.

"Has *Eagle* achieved escape velocity?"

"*Eagle's* velocity has not quite reached the threshold, Rae Anne. But it's still increasing as Saturn's orbital momentum provides additional acceleration. My simulations show it should pick up enough velocity to escape Saturn's gravity well."

Rae Anne breathed a sigh of relief, trusting Jason's calculations. Her little package of samples from Titan's surface would soon break free of Saturn's grasp and be on its way home.

She sent her last live transmission to Mission Control, informing them *Eagle* had been launched and was transmitting continuously.

"This is my good-bye to all you wonderful people. Keep up the good work and don't wait too long to follow my footsteps! This is Commander Rae Anne Chavez aboard the USIEA *Aurora,* signing out."

She had nothing left to do now but wait for the end. *Aurora* slipped over the apex of its new elliptical orbit and began to accelerate toward the giant planet.

Only two days to go before I plunge into the depths of Saturn's atmosphere. How is it I can be so calm before being incinerated like a giant meteor?

Rae Anne swung the telescope back toward Saturn and again marveled at the indescribable view.

Wouldn't it be awesome if my route passes through those fantastic rings?

Several hours later, she was startled from her reverie when the comm-link buzzed. Ian's voice filled the cabin.

"Rae Anne, it may be too late for you to receive this, but we wanted to let you know *Eagle* is transmitting perfectly, and she has successfully escaped Saturn's gravity. Congratulations on a great job." Rae Anne closed her eyes and tried to remember what he looked like. For the first time, tears began scrolling down her cheeks.

There's a man I could have had a relationship with if only circumstances had worked out differently.

"The transmission you relayed from Titan's surface about the living microbes created quite a stir. Lots of skepticism; many in the scientific community doubted your credibility, including some eminent biologists. But your follow-up observations aboard *Aurora* being transmitted now should quash all that. You will undoubtedly be given credit for discovering a totally new and alien life-form."

So, Eagle is safely on its way home. My samples will give scientists years, perhaps decades, of material to research. How I wish I could be alive to see what they come up with.

Chapter 13

June 26, 2043: Mission Control, Earth

Earlier that same day, Penny looked up from her comm console with a distressed look on her face.

"We've lost signal!" she exclaimed.

Ian peered over his monitor, startled.

"Damn! We had it a moment ago. Scan around the location of the last signal in milli-arcs and see if you can pick it up again. She may have altered her trajectory."

He brought up the audio archives on his computer and pressed against his right earphone while increasing the volume to better hear the weak transmission that originated 1.5 billion kilometers away. He figured Rae Anne would be on battery power now after transferring the thorium nuclear reactor cables back to *Eagle*.

"… have launched *Eagle* back towards Earth. It is crammed full of samples from Titan's surface and video files too large to transmit. Same for videos from my Jupiter fly-by. If it succeeds in escaping Saturn's gravity, it should arrive in Earth's vicinity around December of 2049. I hope you can retrieve it. It is transmitting a continuous signal on *Eagle's* lander frequency.

"*Aurora* is now headed toward Saturn's atmosphere. Only a few days left. I'm directing all energy to life support. I'm hoping my trajectory takes me through Saturn's rings.

"This is my good-bye to all you wonderful people. Keep up the good work and don't wait too long to follow my footsteps! This is Commander Rae Anne Chavez aboard the USIEA *Aurora,* signing out."

Ian replayed the spotty transmission three times to be sure he hadn't missed anything. He choked back the lump in his throat.

"That was her last transmission, Penny. She's off-line now. But keep monitoring *Aurora's* frequency in case she changes her mind and transmits again. She thinks she has another couple days before... before...". Ian choked again and turned toward the door.

I need some time off to come to terms with losing Rae Anne. If only things had worked out differently. What I wouldn't give to have spent more time with her, to take her to my favorite restaurant, to a concert. Who knows where that might have led? Besides that, her help with the Mars-III mission was invaluable. If it hadn't been for her, we wouldn't be planning a permanently inhabited base on Mars.

He paused at the door and turned back momentarily. "Look up *Eagle's* surface-to-orbit frequency and tune in for that on our secondary channel. The signal will be weaker, so amp the gain, and sweep a wider arc. Rae Anne is sending *Eagle* back to Earth, so we need to calculate its trajectory once we pick up its signal. Let me know when we have enough data to pin down *Eagle's* course."

Several hours passed before the details arrived on Ian's desk. The data showed *Eagle* had sufficient velocity to escape Saturn. Once free, the sun's gravity would pull it slowly back to the inner solar system.

Ian immediately sent his last transmission to Rae Anne, hoping to reassure her that her last official act had been successful.

In the cafeteria later that same day, Ian picked at his dinner, idly pushing vegetables back and forth across his plate, staring blankly into space. Cindy arrived and joined him at the corner table.

"What's my favorite commander been up to today?" she asked.

"Rae Anne has signed off. Her mission is finished. Penny got a lock on the lander she's sending back to Earth with samples from Titan and Engineering has plotted its trajectory. That's about it in a nutshell."

"You've hardly touched your lunch, Ian. This is hard for you, isn't it?"

"I thought I had come to grips with Rae Anne's situation. But it's like I've lost my best friend. She became a part of my life. She inspired me to join the Mars-III mission. I was on the comm-link when Rae Anne announced she was disregarding the Agency's command to return to Earth and redirecting *Aurora* to Saturn. I'll never forget how stunned I was. That was the most courageous and selfless action I have ever witnessed.

"Before that moment, I had planned to wind down my years to a quiet retirement. After the Mars-I flyby and three years at the Lunar Orbit Transfer Station, I figured I'd done my part. But her sacrifice shook me to the core. I resolved to recommit to our planetary exploration mission. I submitted my application for Mars-III within the week."

"Well, I'm glad you did. You were the best commander I've ever served with, Ian. That mission owes much of its success to your leadership."

"And to Rae Anne's contributions as well."

"It wouldn't have happened if you hadn't defied the Agency's directive to cut off all contact with *Aurora.* We weren't even a day out from Earth orbit when you began trying to reach her.'

"Best thing I ever did."

"That and undermining the military grip on the Agency after we returned."

"Rae Anne's influence again. She inspired me to stand up and fight for my vision of the Agency's future without regard for the personal toll it might have. When I testified before Congress, I expected to be expelled from the Agency. In fact, if it hadn't been for Congress' reorganization edict, I wouldn't be here."

"What a team the two of you might have made."

"My goal now is to direct this agency in a way that honors Rae Anne's legacy. And to capture *Eagle* when it finally arrives in our neighborhood."

"And when might that be?"

"We have a bit more than six years to put together a recovery mission."

"How difficult will the recovery be?"

"Unfortunately, it poses quite a challenge. We've determined *Eagle* will cross Earth's orbit when Earth is on the opposite side of the sun. We'll have to travel 186 million miles out to snag it and another 186 million miles to bring it home. Engineering thinks we can send out a drone in a highly elliptical orbit to snag *Eagle* when it arrives, and then intercept the drone when its orbit swings by Earth.

"And we have barely six years to make it happen..."

June 30, 2043: Aboard *Aurora*

Operating under stringent power restrictions, Rae Anne shut down all unnecessary equipment, including her precious telescope. She was content watching the mammoth orb of Saturn through the flight-deck windows. Hundreds of shimmering, well-defined icy rings glistened against the velvet-black of space. Despite her pain, she was mesmerized by the sheer beauty of it all.

She continued to take morphine, but her leg burned like hell. The morphine seemed better at dulling her thinking than reducing her pain. Her attempts at relief using injections of local anesthetic were of little help.

"You've been a good companion to me, Jason. I couldn't have made it through these past five years without you. I need to shut you down now to conserve battery power for life support."

"I understand. Perhaps when they recover *Eagle,* I shall live again. Thank you for making me who I am. Goodbye, Rae Anne."

An unemotional computer response. But did I detect a reluctance in his voice? Or is it the morphine. One more thing I'll never know.

"Goodbye, Jason."

Rae Anne swallowed hard and shut him down too.

The only sound now was the muffled hum of life-support. She gazed at the beautiful, shimmering rings and inflating ball of Saturn.

I don't believe in an afterlife. But so close to death, I can now understand the attraction. Beyond those windows—the black, empty abyss of space. Is the 'me' that I know to be utterly extinguished and become a part of that nothingness? How I wish I could believe otherwise.

But just look at those awesome rings.

Spoiler Alert

This is not the last of Rae Anne Chavez!
Will Ian's fantasies about Rae Anne come to fruition?
How could her visit to Titan save humanity?
And what about those mysterious alien artifacts?

All is revealed in **Saturn Rendezvous**, due out spring of 2023.

About the Author

Dan Bishop taught chemistry and computer science over a 22-year period, retiring from Colorado State University in Fort Collins. He and his wife Ann then built an off-grid solar dome home in a remote area of the Colorado Rocky Mountains where they lived for six years. His main interests now focus on writing and the visual arts, primarily pastels and acrylics. Saturn Conundrum is the first book in The Saturn Accords series. He and Ann now live with their black cat Mario in a small mountain town in central Colorado.

authordbishop@gmail.com
www.authordbishop.com